PENGUIN BOOKS

THE LONG VALLEY

Born in Salinas, California, in 1902, John Steinbeck grew up in a fertile agricultural valley about twenty-five miles from the Pacific Coast—and both valley and coast would serve as settings for some of his best fiction. In 1919 he went to Stanford University, where he intermittently enrolled in literature and writing courses until he left in 1925 without taking a degree. During the next five years he supported himself as a laborer and journalist in New York City, all the time working on his first novel, *Cup of Gold* (1929). After marriage and a move to Pacific Grove, he published two California fictions, *The Pastures of Heaven* (1932) and *To a God Unknown* (1933), and worked on short stories later collected in *The Long Valley* (1938). Popular success and financial security came only with *Tortilla Flat* (1935), stories about Monterey's paisanos. A ceaseless experimenter throughout his career, Steinbeck changed courses regularly. Three powerful novels of the late 1930s focused on the California laboring class: *In Dubious Battle* (1936), *Of Mice and Men* (1937), and the book considered by many his finest, *The Grapes of Wrath* (1939). Early in the 1940s, Steinbeck became a filmmaker with *The Forgotten Village* (1941). He devoted his services to the war, writing *Bombs Away* (1942) and the controversial play-novelette *The Moon is Down* (1942). *Cannery Row* (1945), *The Wayward Bus* (1947), *The Pearl* (1947), *A Russian Journal* (1948), another experimental drama, *Burning Bright* (1950), and *The Log from The Sea of Cortez* (1951) preceded publication of the monumental *East of Eden* (1952), an ambitious saga of the Salinas Valley and his own family's history. The last decades of his life were spent in New York City and Sag Harbor with his third wife, with whom he traveled widely. Later books include *Sweet Thursday* (1954), *The Short Reign of Pippin IV: A Fabrication* (1957), *Once There Was a War* (1958), *The Winter of Our Discontent* (1961), *Travels with Charley in Search of America* (1962), *America and Americans* (1966), and the posthumously published *Journal of a Novel: The* East of Eden *Letters* (1969), *Viva Zapata!* (1975), *The Acts of King Arthur and His Noble Knights* (1976), and *Working Days: The Journals of* The Grapes of Wrath (1989). He died in 1968, having won a Nobel Prize in 1962.

By John Steinbeck

FICTION

Cup of Gold
The Pastures of Heaven
To a God Unknown
Tortilla Flat
In Dubious Battle
Saint Katy the Virgin
Of Mice and Men
The Red Pony
The Long Valley
The Grapes of Wrath
The Moon Is Down
Cannery Row
The Wayward Bus
The Pearl
Burning Bright
East of Eden
Sweet Thursday
The Winter of Our Discontent
The Short Reign of Pippin IV

NONFICTION

Sea of Cortez: A Leisurely Journal of Travel and Research
(In collaboration with Edward F. Ricketts)
Bombs Away: The Story of a Bomber Team
A Russian Journal *(with pictures by Robert Capa)*
The Log from the *Sea of Cortez*
Once There Was a War
Travels with Charley in Search of America
America and Americans
Journal of a Novel: The *East of Eden* Letters

PLAYS

Of Mice and Men
The Moon Is Down

COLLECTIONS

The Portable Steinbeck
The Short Novels of John Steinbeck
Steinbeck: A Life in Letters

OTHER WORKS

The Forgotten Village (documentary)
Viva Zapata! (screenplay)

CRITICAL LIBRARY EDITION

The Grapes of Wrath
(edited by Peter Lisca)

By John [illegible]

[illegible]

[illegible] The [illegible]
The Pastures of Heaven [illegible]
[illegible]
[illegible]
[illegible]
[illegible]
[illegible]
[illegible]
[illegible]
The Long [illegible]

[illegible]

[illegible]

The Moon is Down [illegible]

[illegible]

JOHN STEINBECK

THE LONG VALLEY

PENGUIN BOOKS

PENGUIN BOOKS
Published by the Penguin Group
Penguin Books USA Inc.,
375 Hudson Street, New York, New York 10014, U.S.A.
Penguin Books Ltd, 27 Wrights Lane, London W8 5TZ, England
Penguin Books Australia Ltd, Ringwood, Victoria, Australia
Penguin Books Canada Ltd, 10 Alcorn Avenue,
Toronto, Ontario, Canada M4V 3B2
Penguin Books (N.Z.) Ltd, 182-190 Wairau Road,
Auckland 10, New Zealand

Penguin Books Ltd, Registered Offices:
Harmondsworth, Middlesex, England

First published in the United States of America by
Viking Penguin Inc. 1938
First published in Penguin Books 1986

9 11 13 15 14 12 10

LIBRARY OF CONGRESS CATALOGING IN PUBLICATION DATA
Steinbeck, John, 1902–1968.
The long valley.
1. Salinas River Valley (Calif.)—Fiction.
I. Title.
PS3537.T3234L6 1986 813'.52 86-2343
ISBN 0 14 00.8038 4

Printed in the United States of America
Set in Bodoni Book

CONTENTS

THE CHRYSANTHEMUMS

THE CHRYSANTHEMUMS

The high grey-flannel fog of winter closed off the Salinas Valley from the sky and from all the rest of the world. On every side it sat like a lid on the mountains and made of the great valley a closed pot. On the broad, level land floor the gang plows bit deep and left the black earth shining like metal where the shares had cut. On the foothill ranches across the Salinas River, the yellow stubble fields seemed to be bathed in pale cold sunshine, but there was no sunshine in the valley now in December. The thick willow scrub along the river flamed with sharp and positive yellow leaves.

It was a time of quiet and of waiting. The air was cold and tender. A light wind blew up from the southwest so that the farmers were mildly hopeful of a good rain before long; but fog and rain do not go together.

Across the river, on Henry Allen's foothill ranch there was little work to be done, for the hay was cut and stored and the orchards were plowed up to receive the rain deeply when it should come. The cattle on the higher slopes were becoming shaggy and rough-coated.

Elisa Allen, working in her flower garden, looked down across the yard and saw Henry, her husband, talking to two men in business suits. The three of them stood by the tractor shed, each man with one foot on the side of the little Fordson. They smoked cigarettes and studied the machine as they talked.

Elisa watched them for a moment and then went back to her work. She was thirty-five. Her face was lean and strong and her eyes were as clear as water. Her figure looked blocked and heavy in her gardening costume, a man's black hat pulled low down over her eyes, clodhopper shoes, a figured print dress almost completely covered by a big corduroy apron with four big pockets to hold the snips, the trowel and scratcher, the seeds and the knife she worked with. She wore heavy leather gloves to protect her hands while she worked.

She was cutting down the old year's chrysanthemum stalks with a pair of short and powerful scissors. She looked down toward the men by the tractor shed now and then. Her face was eager and mature and handsome; even her work with the scissors was over-eager, over-powerful. The chrysanthemum stems seemed too small and easy for her energy.

She brushed a cloud of hair out of her eyes with the back of her glove, and left a smudge of earth on her cheek in doing it. Behind her stood the neat white farm house with red geraniums close-banked around it as high as the windows. It was a hard-swept looking little house with hard-polished windows, and a clean mud-mat on the front steps.

Elisa cast another glance toward the tractor shed. The strangers were getting into their Ford coupe. She took off a glove and put her strong fingers down into the forest of new green chrysanthemum sprouts that were growing around the old roots. She spread the leaves and looked down among the close-growing stems. No aphids were there, no sowbugs or snails or cutworms. Her terrier fingers destroyed such pests before they could get started.

Elisa started at the sound of her husband's voice. He had come near quietly, and he leaned over the wire fence that protected her flower garden from cattle and dogs and chickens.

"At it again," he said. "You've got a strong new crop coming."

Elisa straightened her back and pulled on the gardening glove again. "Yes. They'll be strong this coming year." In her tone and on her face there was a little smugness.

"You've got a gift with things," Henry observed. "Some of those yellow chrysanthemums you had this year were ten inches across. I wish you'd work out in the orchard and raise some apples that big."

Her eyes sharpened. "Maybe I could do it, too. I've a gift with things, all right. My mother had it. She could stick anything in the ground and make it grow. She said it was having planters' hands that knew how to do it."

"Well, it sure works with flowers," he said.

"Henry, who were those men you were talking to?"

"Why, sure, that's what I came to tell you. They were from the Western Meat Company. I sold those thirty head of three-year-old steers. Got nearly my own price, too."

"Good," she said. "Good for you."

"And I thought," he continued, "I thought how it's Saturday afternoon, and we might go into Salinas for dinner at a restaurant, and then to a picture show—to celebrate, you see."

"Good," she repeated. "Oh, yes. That will be good."

Henry put on his joking tone. "There's fights tonight. How'd you like to go to the fights?"

"Oh, no," she said breathlessly. "No, I wouldn't like fights."

"Just fooling, Elisa. We'll go to a movie. Let's see. It's two now. I'm going to take Scotty and bring down those steers from the hill. It'll take us maybe two hours. We'll go in town about five and have dinner at the Cominos Hotel. Like that?"

"Of course I'll like it. It's good to eat away from home."

"All right, then. I'll go get up a couple of horses."

She said, "I'll have plenty of time to transplant some of these sets, I guess."

She heard her husband calling Scotty down by the barn. And a little later she saw the two men ride up the pale yellow hillside in search of the steers.

There was a little square sandy bed kept for rooting the chrysanthemums. With her trowel she turned the soil over and over, and smoothed it and patted it firm. Then she dug ten parallel trenches to receive the sets. Back at the chrysanthemum bed she pulled out the little crisp shoots, trimmed off the leaves of each one with her scissors and laid it on a small orderly pile.

A squeak of wheels and plod of hoofs came from the road. Elisa looked up. The country road ran along the dense bank of willows and cottonwoods that bordered the river, and up this road came a curious vehicle, curiously drawn. It was an old spring-wagon, with a round canvas top on it like the cover of a prairie schooner. It was drawn by an old bay horse and a little grey-and-white burro. A big stubble-bearded man sat between the cover flaps and drove the crawling team. Underneath the wagon, between the hind wheels, a lean and rangy mongrel dog walked sedately. Words were painted on the canvas, in clumsy, crooked letters. "Pots, pans, knives, sisors, lawn mores, Fixed." Two rows of articles, and the triumphantly definitive "Fixed" below. The black paint had run down in little sharp points beneath each letter.

Elisa, squatting on the ground, watched to see the crazy, loose-jointed wagon pass by. But it didn't pass. It turned into the farm road in front of her house, crooked old wheels skirling and squeaking. The rangy dog darted from between the wheels and ran ahead. Instantly the two ranch shepherds flew out at him. Then all three stopped, and with stiff and quivering tails, with taut straight legs, with ambassadorial dignity, they slowly circled, sniffing daintily. The caravan pulled up to Elisa's wire fence and stopped. Now the newcomer dog, feeling out-numbered, lowered his tail and retired under the wagon with raised hackles and bared teeth.

The man on the wagon seat called out, "That's a bad dog in a fight when he gets started."

Elisa laughed. "I see he is. How soon does he generally get started?"

The man caught up her laughter and echoed it heartily. "Sometimes not for weeks and weeks," he said. He climbed stiffly down, over the wheel. The horse and the donkey drooped like unwatered flowers

Elisa saw that he was a very big man. Although his hair and beard were greying, he did not look old. His worn black suit was wrinkled and spotted with grease. The laughter had disappeared from his face and eyes the moment his laughing voice ceased. His eyes were dark, and they were full of the brooding that gets in the eyes of teamsters and of sailors. The calloused hands he rested on the wire fence were cracked, and every crack was a black line. He took off his battered hat.

"I'm off my general road, ma'am," he said. "Does this dirt road cut over across the river to the Los Angeles highway?"

Elisa stood up and shoved the thick scissors in her apron pocket. "Well, yes, it does, but it winds around and then fords the river. I don't think your team could pull through the sand."

He replied with some asperity, "It might surprise you what them beasts can pull through."

"When they get started?" she asked.

He smiled for a second. "Yes. When they get started."

"Well," said Elisa, "I think you'll save time if you go back to the Salinas road and pick up the highway there."

He drew a big finger down the chicken wire and made it sing. "I ain't in any hurry, ma'am. I go from Seattle to San Diego and back every year. Takes all my time. About six months each way. I aim to follow nice weather."

Elisa took off her gloves and stuffed them in the apron pocket with the scissors. She touched the under edge of her man's hat, searching for fugitive hairs.

"That sounds like a nice kind of a way to live," she said.

He leaned confidentially over the fence. "Maybe you noticed the writing on my wagon. I mend pots and sharpen knives and scissors. You got any of them things to do?"

"Oh, no," she said quickly. "Nothing like that." Her eyes hardened with resistance.

"Scissors is the worst thing," he explained. "Most people just ruin scissors trying to sharpen 'em, but I know how. I got a special tool. It's a little bobbit kind of thing, and patented. But it sure does the trick."

"No. My scissors are all sharp."

"All right, then. Take a pot," he continued earnestly, "a bent pot, or a pot with a hole. I can make it like new so you don't have to buy no new ones. That's a saving for you."

"No," she said shortly. "I tell you I have nothing like that for you to do."

His face fell to an exaggerated sadness. His voice took on a whining undertone. "I ain't had a thing to do today. Maybe I won't have no supper tonight. You see I'm off my regular road. I know folks on the highway clear from Seattle to San Diego. They save their things for me to sharpen up because they know I do it so good and save them money."

"I'm sorry," Elisa said irritably. "I haven't anything for you to do."

His eyes left her face and fell to searching the ground. They roamed about until they came to the chrysanthemum bed where she had been working. "What's them plants, ma'am?"

The irritation and resistance melted from Elisa's

face. "Oh, those are chrysanthemums, giant whites and yellows. I raise them every year, bigger than anybody around here."

"Kind of a long-stemmed flower? Looks like a quick puff of colored smoke?" he asked.

"That's it. What a nice way to describe them."

"They smell kind of nasty till you get used to them," he said.

"It's a good bitter smell," she retorted, "not nasty at all."

He changed his tone quickly. "I like the smell myself."

"I had ten-inch blooms this year," she said.

The man leaned farther over the fence. "Look. I know a lady down the road a piece, has got the nicest garden you ever seen. Got nearly every kind of flower but no chrysantheums. Last time I was mending a copper-bottom washtub for her (that's a hard job but I do it good), she said to me, 'If you ever run acrost some nice chrysantheums I wish you'd try to get me a few seeds.' That's what she told me."

Elisa's eyes grew alert and eager. "She couldn't have known much about chrysanthemums. You *can* raise them from seed, but it's much easier to root the little sprouts you see there."

"Oh," he said. "I s'pose I can't take none to her, then."

"Why yes you can," Elisa cried. "I can put some in damp sand, and you can carry them right along with you. They'll take root in the pot if you keep them damp. And then she can transplant them."

"She'd sure like to have some, ma'am. You say they're nice ones?"

"Beautiful," she said. "Oh, beautiful." Her eyes shone. She tore off the battered hat and shook out her dark pretty hair. "I'll put them in a flower pot, and you can take them right with you. Come into the yard."

While the man came through the picket gate Elisa ran excitedly along the geranium-bordered path to the back of the house. And she returned carrying a big red flower pot. The gloves were forgotten now. She kneeled on the ground by the starting bed and dug up the sandy soil with her fingers and scooped it into the bright new flower pot. Then she picked up the little pile of shoots she had prepared. With her strong fingers she pressed them into the sand and tamped around them with her knuckles. The man stood over her. "I'll tell you what to do," she said. "You remember so you can tell the lady."

"Yes, I'll try to remember."

"Well, look. These will take root in about a month. Then she must set them out, about a foot apart in good rich earth like this, see?" She lifted a handful of dark soil for him to look at. "They'll grow fast and tall. Now remember this: In July tell her to cut them down, about eight inches from the ground."

"Before they bloom?" he asked.

"Yes, before they bloom." Her face was tight with eagerness. "They'll grow right up again. About the last of September the buds will start."

She stopped and seemed perplexed. "It's the budding that takes the most care," she said hesitantly. "I don't know how to tell you." She looked deep into his eyes, searchingly. Her mouth opened a little, and she seemed to be listening. "I'll try to tell you," she said. "Did you ever hear of planting hands?"

"Can't say I have, ma'am."

"Well, I can only tell you what it feels like. It's when you're picking off the buds you don't want. Everything goes right down into your fingertips. You watch your fingers work. They do it themselves. You can feel how it is. They pick and pick the buds. They never make a mistake. They're with the plant. Do you see? Your fingers and the plant. You can feel that, right up your arm. They know. They never make a mistake. You can feel it. When you're like that you can't do anything wrong. Do you see that? Can you understand that?"

She was kneeling on the ground looking up at him. Her breast swelled passionately.

The man's eyes narrowed. He looked away self-consciously. "Maybe I know," he said. "Sometimes in the night in the wagon there—"

Elisa's voice grew husky. She broke in on him, "I've never lived as you do, but I know what you mean. When the night is dark—why, the stars are sharp-pointed, and there's quiet. Why, you rise up and up! Every pointed star gets driven into your body. It's like that. Hot and sharp and—lovely."

Kneeling there, her hand went out toward his legs in the greasy black trousers. Her hesitant fingers almost touched the cloth. Then her hand dropped to the ground. She crouched low like a fawning dog.

He said, "It's nice, just like you say. Only when you don't have no dinner, it ain't."

She stood up then, very straight, and her face was ashamed. She held the flower pot out to him and placed it gently in his arms. "Here. Put it in your wagon, on the seat, where you can watch it. Maybe I can find something for you to do."

At the back of the house she dug in the can pile and found two old and battered aluminum saucepans. She carried them back and gave them to him. "Here, maybe you can fix these."

His manner changed. He became professional. "Good as new I can fix them." At the back of his wagon he set a little anvil, and out of an oily tool box dug a small machine hammer. Elisa came through the gate to watch him while he pounded out the dents in the kettles. His mouth grew sure and knowing. At a difficult part of the work he sucked his under-lip.

"You sleep right in the wagon?" Elisa asked.

"Right in the wagon, ma'am. Rain or shine I'm dry as a cow in there."

"It must be nice," she said. "It must be very nice. I wish women could do such things."

"It ain't the right kind of a life for a woman."

Her upper lip raised a little, showing her teeth. "How do you know? How can you tell?" she said.

"I don't know, ma'am," he protested. "Of course I don't know. Now here's your kettles, done. You don't have to buy no new ones."

"How much?"

"Oh, fifty cents'll do. I keep my prices down and my work good. That's why I have all them satisfied customers up and down the highway."

Elisa brought him a fifty-cent piece from the house and dropped it in his hand. "You might be surprised to have a rival some time. I can sharpen scissors, too. And I can beat the dents out of little pots. I could show you what a woman might do."

He put his hammer back in the oily box and shoved the little anvil out of sight. "It would be a lonely life for a woman, ma'am, and a scarey life, too, with animals creeping under the wagon all night." He climbed over the singletree, steadying himself with a hand on the burro's white rump. He settled himself in the seat, picked up the lines. "Thank you kindly, ma'am," he said. "I'll do like you told me; I'll go back and catch the Salinas road."

"Mind," she called, "if you're long in getting there, keep the sand damp."

"Sand, ma'am? . . . Sand? Oh, sure. You mean around the chrysantheums. Sure I will." He clucked his tongue. The beasts leaned luxuriously into their collars. The mongrel dog took his place between the back wheels. The wagon turned and crawled out the entrance road and back the way it had come, along the river.

Elisa stood in front of her wire fence watching the slow progress of the caravan. Her shoulders were straight, her head thrown back, her eyes half-closed, so that the scene came vaguely into them. Her lips moved silently, forming the words "Good-bye—good-bye." Then she whispered, "That's a bright direction. There's a glowing there." The sound of her whisper startled her. She shook herself free and looked about to see whether anyone had been listening. Only the dogs had heard. They lifted their heads toward her from their sleeping in the dust, and then stretched out their chins and settled asleep again. Elisa turned and ran hurriedly into the house.

In the kitchen she reached behind the stove and felt the water tank. It was full of hot water from the noonday cooking. In the bathroom she tore off her soiled clothes and flung them into the corner. And then she scrubbed herself with a little block of pumice, legs and thighs, loins and chest and arms, until her skin was scratched and red. When she had dried herself she stood in front of a mirror in her bedroom and looked at her body. She tightened her stomach and threw out her chest. She turned and looked over her shoulder at her back.

After a while she began to dress, slowly. She put on her newest underclothing and her nicest stockings and the dress which was the symbol of her prettiness. She worked carefully on her hair, penciled her eyebrows and rouged her lips.

Before she was finished she heard the little thunder of hoofs and the shouts of Henry and his helper as they drove the red steers into the corral. She heard the gate bang shut and set herself for Henry's arrival.

His step sounded on the porch. He entered the house calling, "Elisa, where are you?"

"In my room, dressing. I'm not ready. There's hot water for your bath. Hurry up. It's getting late."

When she heard him splashing in the tub, Elisa laid his dark suit on the bed, and shirt and socks and tie beside it. She stood his polished shoes on the floor beside the bed. Then she went to the porch and sat primly and stiffly down. She looked toward the river road where the willow-line was still yellow with frosted leaves so that under the high grey fog they seemed a thin band of sunshine. This was the only color in the grey afternoon. She sat unmoving for a long time. Her eyes blinked rarely.

Henry came banging out of the door, shoving his tie

inside his vest as he came. Elisa stiffened and her face grew tight. Henry stopped short and looked at her. "Why—why, Elisa. You look so nice!"

"Nice? You think I look nice? What do you mean by 'nice'?"

Henry blundered on. "I don't know. I mean you look different, strong and happy."

"I am strong? Yes, strong. What do you mean 'strong'?"

He looked bewildered. "You're playing some kind of a game," he said helplessly. "It's a kind of a play. You look strong enough to break a calf over your knee, happy enough to eat it like a watermelon."

For a second she lost her rigidity. "Henry! Don't talk like that. You didn't know what you said." She grew complete again. "I'm strong," she boasted. "I never knew before how strong."

Henry looked down toward the tractor shed, and when he brought his eyes back to her, they were his own again. "I'll get out the car. You can put on your coat while I'm starting."

Elisa went into the house. She heard him drive to the gate and idle down his motor, and then she took a long time to put on her hat. She pulled it here and pressed it there. When Henry turned the motor off she slipped into her coat and went out.

The little roadster bounced along on the dirt road by the river, raising the birds and driving the rabbits into the brush. Two cranes flapped heavily over the willow-line and dropped into the river-bed.

Far ahead on the road Elisa saw a dark speck. She knew.

She tried not to look as they passed it, but her eyes

would not obey. She whispered to herself sadly, "He might have thrown them off the road. That wouldn't have been much trouble, not very much. But he kept the pot," she explained. "He had to keep the pot. That's why he couldn't get them off the road."

The roadster turned a bend and she saw the caravan ahead. She swung full around toward her husband so she could not see the little covered wagon and the mismatched team as the car passed them.

In a moment it was over. The thing was done. She did not look back.

She said loudly, to be heard above the motor, "It will be good, tonight, a good dinner."

"Now you've changed again," Henry complained. He took one hand from the wheel and patted her knee. "I ought to take you in to dinner oftener. It would be good for both of us. We get so heavy out on the ranch."

"Henry," she asked, "could we have wine at dinner?"

"Sure we could. Say! That will be fine."

She was silent for a while; then she said, "Henry, at those prize fights, do the men hurt each other very much?"

"Sometimes a little, not often. Why?"

"Well, I've read how they break noses, and blood runs down their chests. I've read how the fighting gloves get heavy and soggy with blood."

He looked around at her. "What's the matter, Elisa? I didn't know you read things like that." He brought the car to a stop, then turned to the right over the Salinas River bridge.

"Do any women ever go to the fights?" she asked.

"Oh, sure, some. What's the matter, Elisa? Do you

want to go? I don't think you'd like it, but I'll take you if you really want to go."

She relaxed limply in the seat. "Oh, no. No. I don't want to go. I'm sure I don't." Her face was turned away from him. "It will be enough if we can have wine. It will be plenty." She turned up her coat collar so he could not see that she was crying weakly—like an old woman.

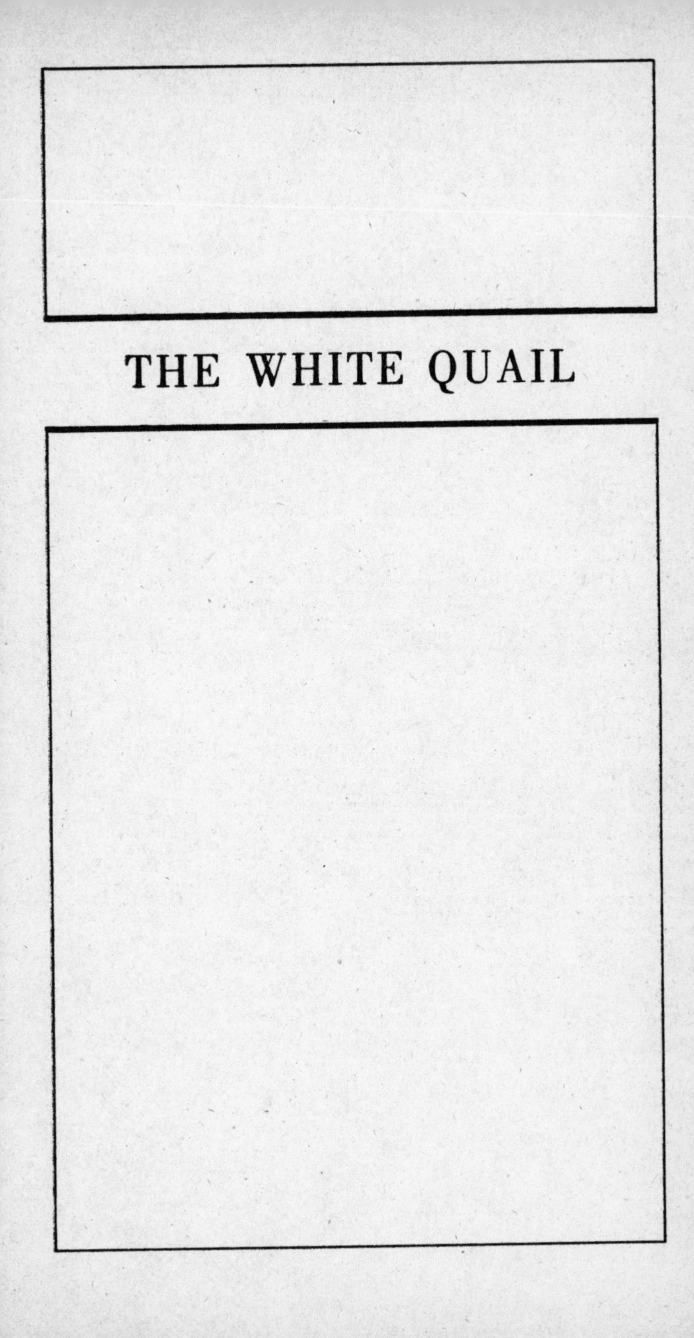

THE WHITE QUAIL

THE WHITE QUAIL

The wall opposite the fireplace in the living room was a big dormer window stretching from the cushioned window seats almost to the ceiling—small diamond panes set in lead. From the window, preferably if you were sitting on the window seat, you could look across the garden and up the hill. There was a stretch of shady lawn under the garden oaks—around each oak there was a circle of carefully tended earth in which grew cinerarias, big ones with loads of flowers so heavy they bent the stems over, and ranging in color from scarlet to ultramarine. At the edge of the lawn, a line of fuchsias grew like little symbolic trees. In front of the fuchsias lay a shallow garden pool, the coping flush with the lawn for a very good reason.

Right at the edge of the garden, the hill started up, wild with cascara bushes and poison oak, with dry grass and live oak, very wild. If you didn't go around to the front of the house you couldn't tell it was on the very edge of the town.

Mary Teller, Mrs. Harry E. Teller, that is, knew the window and the garden were Right and she had a very good reason for knowing. Hadn't she picked out the place where the house and the garden would be years ago? Hadn't she seen the house and the garden a thousand times while the place was still a dry flat against the shoulder of a hill? For that matter, hadn't she, during five years, looked at every attentive man and wondered whether he and that garden would go together? She didn't think so much, "Would this man like such a garden?" but, "Would the garden like such a man?" For the garden was herself, and after all she had to marry some one she liked.

When she met Harry Teller, the garden seemed to like him. It may have surprised him a little when, after he had proposed and was waiting sulkily for his answer, as men do, Mary broke into a description of a big dormer window and a garden with a lawn and oak trees and cinerarias and then a wild hill.

He said, "Of course," rather perfunctorily.

Mary asked, "Do you think it's silly?"

He was waiting a little sullenly. "Of course not."

And then she remembered that he had proposed to her, and she accepted him, and let him kiss her. She said, "There will be a little cement pool flush with the lawn. Do you know why? Well, there are more birds on that hill than you'd ever think, yellowhammers and wild canaries and red-wing blackbirds, and of course sparrows and linnets, and lots of quail. Of course they'll be coming down to drink there, won't they?"

She was very pretty. He wanted to kiss her over and over, and she let him. "And fuchsias," she said. "Don't forget fuchsias. They're like little tropical

Christmas trees. We'll have to have the lawn raked every day to keep the oak leaves clear."

He laughed at her. "You're a funny little bug. The lot isn't bought, and the house isn't built, and the garden isn't planted; and already you're worrying about oak leaves on the lawn. You're so pretty. You make me kind of—hungry."

That startled her a little. A little expression of annoyance crossed her face. But nevertheless she let him kiss her again, and then sent him home and went to her room, where she had a little blue writing desk and on it a copy-book to write things in. She took up a pen, of which the handle was a peacock feather, and she wrote, "Mary Teller" over and over again. Once or twice she wrote, "Mrs. Harry E. Teller."

II

The lot was bought and the house was built, and they were married. Mary drew a careful plan of the garden, and when the workmen were putting it in she didn't leave them alone for a moment. She knew to an inch where everything should be. And she drew the shape of the shallow pool for the cement workers, a kind of heart-shaped pool with no point at the bottom, with gradually sloping edges so that birds could drink easily.

Harry watched her with admiration. "Who could tell that such a pretty girl could have so much efficiency," he said.

That pleased her, too; and she was very happy, so that she said, "You can plant some of the things you like in the garden, if you want."

"No, Mary, I like too much to see your own mind coming out in the garden. You do it all your own way."

She loved him for that; but after all, it was her garden. She had invented it, and willed it, and she had worked out the colors too, so carefully. It really wouldn't have been nice if, for instance, Harry had wanted some flowers that didn't go with the garden.

At last the green lawn was up, and the cinerarias around the oak trees bloomed in sunken pots. The little fuchsia trees had been moved in so carefully that not a leaf wilted.

The window seats behind the dormer windows were piled with cushions covered with bright, fadeless fabrics, for the sun shone in that window a good part of the day.

Mary waited until it was all done, all finished exactly as her mind had seen it; and then one evening when Harry came home from the office, she led him to the window seat. "You see," she said softly. "There it is, just the way I wanted it."

"It's beautiful," said Harry, "very beautiful."

"In a way I'm sad that it's done," she said. "But mostly I'm glad. We won't ever change it, will we, Harry? If a bush dies, we'll put another one just like it in the same place."

"Curious little bug," he said.

"Well, you see I've thought about it so long that it's part of me. If anything should be changed it would be like part of me being torn out."

He put out his hand to touch her, and then withdrew it. "I love you so much," he said, and then paused. "But I'm afraid of you, too."

She smiled quietly. "You? Afraid of me? What's there about me you can be afraid of?"

"Well, you're kind of untouchable. There's an inscrutability about you. Probably you don't even know it yourself. You're kind of like your own garden—fixed, and just so. I'm afraid to move around. I might disturb some of your plants."

Mary was pleased. "Dear," she said. "You let me do it. You made it my garden. Yes, you are dear." And she let him kiss her.

III

He was proud of her when people came in to dinner. She was so pretty, so cool and perfect. Her bowls of flowers were exquisite, and she talked about the garden modestly, hesitantly, almost as though she were talking about herself. Sometimes she took her guests into the garden. She pointed to a fuchsia tree. "I didn't know whether he would succeed," she said, just as though the plant were a person. "He ate a lot of plant food before he decided to come around." She smiled quietly to herself.

She was delightful when she worked in the garden. She wore a bright print dress, quite long in the skirt, and sleeveless. Somewhere she had found an old-fashioned sunbonnet. She wore good sturdy gloves to protect her hands. Harry liked to watch her going about with a bag and a big spoon, putting plant food about the roots of her flowers. He liked it, too, when they went out at night to kill slugs and snails. Mary held the flashlight while Harry did the actual killing, crushing the slugs and snails into oozy, bubbling masses. He knew it must be a disgusting business to her, but the light never wavered. "Brave girl," he thought. "She has a sturdiness in back of that fragile beauty." She made the hunts exciting too. "There's a big one, creeping and creeping," she would say. "He's after that big bloom. Kill him! Kill him quickly!" They came into the house after the hunts laughing happily.

Mary was worried about the birds. "They don't come down to drink," she complained. "Not many of them. I wonder what's keeping them away."

"Maybe they aren't used to it yet. They'll come later. Maybe there's a cat around."

Her face flushed and she breathed deeply. Her pretty lips tightened away from her teeth. "If there's a cat, I'll put out poisoned fish," she cried. "I won't have a cat after my birds!"

Harry had to soothe her. "I'll tell you what I'll do. I'll buy an air gun. Then if a cat comes, we can shoot it, and it won't kill the cat, but it'll hurt, and the cat won't come back."

"Yes," she said more calmly. "That might be better."

The living room was very pleasant at night. The fire burned up in a sheet of flame. If there was a moon, Mary turned off the lights and then they sat looking through the window at the cool blue garden and the dark oak trees.

It was utterly calm and eternal out there. And then the garden ended and the dark thickets of the hill began.

"That's the enemy," Mary said one time. "That's the world that wants to get in, all rough and tangled and unkempt. But it can't get in because the fuchsias won't let it. That's what the fuchsias are there for, and they know it. The birds can get in. They live out in the wild, but they come to my garden for peace and for water." She laughed softly. "There's something profound in all that, Harry. I don't know quite what it is. The quail are beginning to come down now. At least a dozen were at the pool this evening."

He said, "I wish I could see the inside of your mind. It seems to flutter around, but it's a cool, collected mind. It's so—sure of itself."

Mary went to sit on his lap for a moment. "Not so awfully sure. You don't know, and I'm glad you don't."

IV

One night when Harry was reading his paper under the lamp, Mary jumped up. "I left my garden scissors outside," she said. "The dew will rust them."

Harry looked over his paper. "Can't I get them for you?"

"No, I'll go. You couldn't find them." She went out into the garden and found the shears, and then she looked in the window, into the living room. Harry was still reading his paper. The room was clear, like a picture, like the set of a play that was about to start. A curtain of fire waved up in the fireplace. Mary stood still and looked. There was the big, deep chair she had been sitting in a minute ago. What would she be doing if she hadn't come outside? Suppose only essence, only mind and sight had come, leaving Mary in the chair? She could almost see herself sitting there. Her round arms and long fingers were resting on the chair. Her delicate, sensitive face was in profile, looking reflectively into the firelight. "What is she thinking about?" Mary whispered. "I wonder what's going on in her mind. Will she get up? No, she's just sitting there. The neck of that dress is too wide, see how it slips sideways over the shoulder. But that's rather pretty. It looks careless, but neat and pretty. Now—she's smiling. She must be thinking something nice."

Suddenly Mary came to herself and realized what she had been doing. She was delighted. "There were two me's," she thought. "It was like having two lives, being able to see myself. That's wonderful. I wonder whether I can see it whenever I want to. I saw just what other people see when they look at me. I must tell Harry about that." But then a new picture formed; she saw herself explaining, trying to describe what had happened. She saw him looking over his paper with an intent, puzzled, almost pained look in his eyes. He tried so hard to understand when she told him things. He wanted to understand, and he never quite succeeded. If she told him about this vision tonight, he would ask questions. He would turn the thing over and over, trying to understand it, until finally he ruined it. He didn't want to spoil the things she told him, but he just couldn't help it. He needed too much light on things that light shriveled. No, she wouldn't tell him. She would want to come out and do it again, and she couldn't if he spoiled it for her.

Through the window she saw Harry put his paper down on his knee and look up at the door. She hurried in, showing him the shears to prove what she had gone for. "See, the rust was forming already. They'd've been all brown and nasty by morning."

He nodded and smiled at her. "It says in the paper

we're going to have more trouble with that new loan bill. They put a lot of difficulties in our way. Somebody has to loan money when people want to borrow."

"I don't understand loans," she said. "Somebody told me your company had title to nearly every automobile in town."

He laughed. "Well, not all, but a good many of them, anyway. When times are a little bit hard, we make money."

"It sounds terrible," she observed. "It sounds like taking unfair advantage."

He folded the paper and put it on the table beside his chair. "No, I don't think it's unfair," he said. "The people must have the money, and we supply it. The law regulates the interest rate. We haven't anything to do with that."

She stretched her pretty arms and fingers on the chair, as she had seen them through the window. "I suppose it really isn't unfair," she said. "It just sounds as though you took advantage of people when they were down."

Harry looked seriously into the fire for a long time. Mary could see him, and she knew he was worrying about what she said. Well, it would do him no harm to see what business really was like. Things seemed righter when you did them than when you thought about them. A little mental housecleaning mightn't be a bad thing for Harry.

After a little, he looked over at her. "Dear, you don't think it's unfair practice, do you?"

"Why, I don't know anything about loans. How can I tell what is fair?"

Harry insisted, "But do you *feel* it's unfair? Are you

ashamed of my business? I wouldn't like it if you were."

Suddenly Mary felt very glad and pleased. "I'm not ashamed, silly. Every one has a right to make a living. You do what you do well."

"You're sure, now?"

"Of course I'm sure, silly."

After she was in bed in her own little bedroom she heard a faint click and saw the door knob turn, and then turn slowly back. The door was locked. It was a signal; there were things Mary didn't like to talk about. The lock was an answer to a question, a clean, quick, decisive answer. It was peculiar about Harry, though. He always tried the door silently. It seemed as though he didn't want her to know he had tried it. But she always did know. He was sweet and gentle. It seemed to make him ashamed when he turned the knob and found the door locked.

Mary pulled the light chain, and when her eyes had become accustomed to the dark, she looked out the window at her garden in the half moonlight. Harry was sweet, and understanding, too. That time about the dog. He had come running into the house, really running. His face was so red and excited that Mary had a nasty shock. She thought there had been an accident. Later in the evening she had a headache from the shock. Harry had shouted, "Joe Adams—his Irish Terrier bitch had puppies. He's going to give me one! Thoroughbred stock, red as strawberries!" He had really wanted one of the pups. It hurt Mary that he couldn't have one. But she was proud of his quick understanding of the situation. When she explained how a dog would—do things on the plants of her garden, or even dig in her flower beds, how, worst of all, a dog would keep the birds away from the pool, Harry understood. He might have trouble with complicated things, like that vision from the garden, but he understood about the dog. Later in the evening, when her head ached, he soothed her and patted Florida Water on her head. That was the curse of imagination. Mary had seen, actually seen the dog in her garden, and the dug holes, and ruined plants. It was almost as bad as though it actually happened. Harry was ashamed, but really he couldn't help it if she had such an imagination. Mary couldn't blame him, how could he have known?

V

Late in the afternoon, when the sun had gone behind the hill, there was a time Mary called the really-garden-time. Then the high school girl was in from school and had taken charge of the kitchen. It was almost a sacred time. Mary walked out into the garden and across the lawn to a folding chair half behind one of the lawn oaks. She could watch the birds drinking in the pool from there. She could really *feel* the garden. When Harry came home from the office, he stayed in the house and read his paper until she came in from the garden, star-eyed. It made her unhappy to be disturbed.

The summer was just breaking. Mary looked into the kitchen and saw that everything was all right there. She went through the living room and lighted the laid fire, and then she was ready for the garden. The sun had just dropped behind the hill, and the blue gauze of the evening had settled among the oaks.

Mary thought, "It's like millions of not quite invisible fairies coming into my garden. You can't see one of them, but the millions change the color of the air." She smiled to herself at the nice thought. The clipped lawn was damp and fresh with watering. The brilliant cinerarias threw little haloes of color into the air. The fuchsia trees were loaded with blooms. The buds, like little red Christmas tree ornaments, and the open blooms like ballet-skirted ladies. They were so *right*, the fuchsias, so absolutely right. And they discouraged the enemy on the other side, the brush and scrubby, untrimmed trees.

Mary walked across the lawn in the evening to her chair, and sat down. She could hear the birds gathering to come down to the pool. "Making up parties," she thought, "coming to my garden in the evening. How they must love it! How I would like to come to my garden for the first time. If I could be two people— 'Good evening, come into the garden, Mary.' 'Oh, isn't it lovely.' 'Yes, I like it, especially at this time. Quiet, now, Mary. Don't frighten the birds.' " She sat as still as a mouse. Her lips were parted with expectancy. In the brush the quail twittered sharply. A yellowhammer dropped to the edge of the pool. Two little flycatchers flickered out over the water and stood still in the air, beating their wings. And then the quail ran out, with funny little steps. They stopped and cocked their heads, to see whether it was safe. Their leader, a big fellow with a crest like a black question mark, sounded the bugle-like "All clear" call, and the band came down to drink.

And then it happened, the wonderful thing. Out of the brush ran a white quail. Mary froze. Yes, it was a quail, no doubt of it, and white as snow. Oh, this was wonderful! A shiver of pleasure, a bursting of pleasure swelled in Mary's breast. She held her breath. The dainty little white hen quail went to the other side of the pool, away from the ordinary quail. She paused and looked around, and then dipped her beak in the water.

"Why," Mary cried to herself, "she's like me!" A powerful ecstasy quivered in her body. "She's like the essence of me, an essence boiled down to utter purity. She must be the queen of the quail. She makes every lovely thing that ever happened to me one thing."

The white quail dipped her beak again and threw back her head to swallow.

The memories welled in Mary and filled her chest. Something sad, always something sad. The packages that came; untying the string was the ecstasy. The thing in the package was never quite——

The marvelous candy from Italy. "Don't eat it, dear. It's prettier than it's good." Mary never ate it, but looking at it was an ecstasy like this.

"What a pretty girl Mary is. She's like a gentian, so quiet." The hearing was an ecstasy like this.

"Mary dear, be very brave now. Your father has—passed away." The first moment of loss was an ecstasy like this.

The white quail stretched a wing backward and smoothed down the feathers with her beak. "This is the me that was everything beautiful. This is the center of me, my heart."

VI

The blue air became purple in the garden. The fuchsia buds blazed like little candles. And then a gray shadow moved out of the brush. Mary's mouth dropped open. She sat paralyzed with fear. A gray cat crept like death out of the brush, crept toward the pool and the drinking birds. Mary stared in horror. Her hand rose up to her tight throat. Then she broke the paralysis. She screamed terribly. The quail flew away on muttering wings. The cat bounded back into the brush. Still Mary screamed and screamed. Harry ran out of the house crying, "Mary! What is it, Mary?"

She shuddered when he touched her. She began to cry hysterically. He took her up in his arms and carried her into the house, and into her own room. She lay quivering on the bed. "What was it, dear? What frightened you?"

"It was a cat," she moaned. "It was creeping up on the birds." She sat up; her eyes blazed. "Harry, you must put out poison. Tonight you simply must put out some poison for that cat."

"Lie back, dear. You've had a shock."

"Promise me you'll put out poison." She looked closely at him and saw a rebellious light come into his eyes. "Promise."

"Dear," he apologized, "some dog might get it. Animals suffer terribly when they get poison."

"I don't care," she cried. "I don't want any animals in my garden, any kind."

"No," he said. "I won't do that. No, I can't do that. But I'll get up early in the morning. I'll take the new air gun and I'll shoot that cat so he'll never come back. The air gun shoots hard. It'll make a hurt the cat won't forget."

It was the first thing he had ever refused. She didn't know how to combat it; but her head ached, terribly. When it ached its worst he tried to make it up to her for refusing the poison. He kept a little pad soaked with Florida Water, and he patted it on her forehead. She wondered whether she should tell him about the white quail. He wouldn't believe it. But maybe if he knew how important it was, he might poison the cat. She waited until her nerves were calm before she told him. "Dear, there was a white quail in the garden."

"A white quail? Are you sure it wasn't a pigeon?"

There it was. Right from the first he spoiled it. "I know quail," she cried. "It was quite close to me. A white hen quail."

"That would be a thing to see," he said. "I never heard of one."

"But I tell you I saw it."

He dabbed at her forehead. "Well, I suppose it was an albino. No pigment in the feathers, something like that."

She was growing hysterical again. "You don't understand. That white quail was *me*, the secret me that no one can ever get at, the me that's way inside." Harry's face was contorted with the struggle to understand. "Can't you see, dear? The cat was after me. It was going to kill me. That's why I want to poison it." She studied his face. No, he didn't understand, he couldn't. Why had she told him? If she hadn't been so upset she never would have told him.

"I'll set my alarm clock," he assured her. "Tomorrow morning I'll give that cat something to remember."

At ten o'clock he left her alone. And when he had gone Mary got up and locked the door.

His alarm-clock bell awakened Mary in the morning. It was still dark in her room, but she could see the gray light of morning through the window. She heard Harry dressing quietly. He tiptoed past her door and went outside, closing the door silently for fear of awakening her. He carried the new shining air gun in his hand. The fresh gray morning air made him throw back his shoulders and step lightly over the damp lawn. He walked to the corner of the garden and lay down on his stomach in the wet grass.

The garden grew lighter. Already the quail were twittering metallically. The little brown band came to the edge of the brush and cocked their heads. Then the big leader called, "All's well," and his charges ran with quick steps to the pool. A moment later the white quail followed them. She went to the other side of the pool and dipped her beak and threw back her head. Harry raised the gun. The white quail tipped her head and looked toward him. The air gun spat with a vicious whisper. The quail flew off into the brush. But the white quail fell over and shuddered a moment, and lay still on the lawn.

Harry walked slowly over to her and picked her up. "I didn't mean to kill it," he said to himself. "I just wanted to scare it away." He looked at the white bird in his hand. Right in the head, right under the eye the BB shot had gone. Harry stepped to the line of fuchsias and threw the quail up into the brush. The next moment he put down the gun and crashed up through the undergrowth. He found the white quail, carried her far up the hill and buried her under a pile of leaves.

Mary heard him pass her door. "Harry, did you shoot the cat?"

"It won't ever come back," he said through the door.

"Well, I hope you killed it, but I don't want to hear the details."

Harry walked on into the living room and sat down in a big chair. The room was still dusky, but through the big dormer window the garden glowed and the tops of the lawn oaks were afire with sunshine.

"What a skunk I am," Harry said to himself. "What a dirty skunk, to kill a thing she loved so much." He dropped his head and looked at the floor. "I'm lonely," he said. "Oh, Lord, I'm so lonely!"

FLIGHT

FLIGHT

About fifteen miles below Monterey, on the wild coast, the Torres family had their farm, a few sloping acres above a cliff that dropped to the brown reefs and to the hissing white waters of the ocean. Behind the farm the stone mountains stood up against the sky. The farm buildings huddled like little clinging aphids on the mountain skirts, crouched low to the ground as though the wind might blow them into the sea. The little shack, the rattling, rotting barn were grey-bitten with sea salt, beaten by the damp wind until they had taken on the color of the granite hills. Two horses, a red cow and a red calf, half a dozen pigs and a flock of lean, multicolored chickens stocked the place. A little corn was raised on the sterile slope, and it grew short and thick under the wind, and all the cobs formed on the landward sides of the stalks.

Mama Torres, a lean, dry woman with ancient eyes, had ruled the farm for ten years, ever since her husband tripped over a stone in the field one day and fell full length on a rattlesnake. When one is bitten on the chest there is not much that can be done.

Mama Torres had three children, two undersized black ones of twelve and fourteen, Emilio and Rosy, whom Mama kept fishing on the rocks below the farm when the sea was kind and when the truant officer was in some distant part of Monterey County. And there was Pepé, the tall smiling son of nineteen, a gentle, affectionate boy, but very lazy. Pepé had a tall head, pointed at the top, and from its peak, coarse black hair grew down like a thatch all around. Over his smiling little eyes Mama cut a straight bang so he could see. Pepé had sharp Indian cheek bones and an eagle nose, but his mouth was as sweet and shapely as a girl's mouth, and his chin was fragile and chiseled. He was loose and gangling, all legs and feet and wrists, and he was very lazy. Mama thought him fine and brave, but she never told him so. She said, "Some lazy cow must have got into thy father's family, else how could I have a son like thee." And she said, "When I carried thee, a sneaking lazy coyote came out of the brush and looked at me one day. That must have made thee so."

Pepé smiled sheepishly and stabbed at the ground with his knife to keep the blade sharp and free from rust. It was his inheritance, that knife, his father's knife. The long heavy blade folded back into the black handle. There was a button on the handle. When Pepé pressed the button, the blade leaped out ready for use. The knife was with Pepé always, for it had been his father's knife.

One sunny morning when the sea below the cliff was glinting and blue and the white surf creamed on the reef, when even the stone mountains looked kindly, Mama Torres called out the door of the shack, "Pepé, I have a labor for thee."

There was no answer. Mama listened. From behind the barn she heard a burst of laughter. She lifted her full long skirt and walked in the direction of the noise.

Pepé was sitting on the ground with his back against a box. His white teeth glistened. On either side of him stood the two black ones, tense and expectant. Fifteen feet away a redwood post was set in the ground. Pepé's right hand lay limply in his lap, and in the palm the big black knife rested. The blade was closed back into the handle. Pepé looked smiling at the sky.

Suddenly Emilio cried, "Ya!"

Pepé's wrist flicked like the head of a snake. The blade seemed to fly open in mid-air, and with a thump the point dug into the redwood post, and the black handle quivered. The three burst into excited laughter. Rosy ran to the post and pulled out the knife and brought it back to Pepé. He closed the blade and settled the knife carefully in his listless palm again. He grinned self-consciously at the sky.

"Ya!"

The heavy knife lanced out and sunk into the post again. Mama moved forward like a ship and scattered the play.

"All day you do foolish things with the knife, like a toy-baby," she stormed. "Get up on thy huge feet that eat up shoes. Get up!" She took him by one loose shoulder and hoisted at him. Pepé grinned sheepishly and came half-heartedly to his feet. "Look!" Mama cried. "Big lazy, you must catch the horse and put on him thy father's saddle. You must ride to Monterey.

The medicine bottle is empty. There is no salt. Go thou now, Peanut! Catch the horse."

A revolution took place in the relaxed figure of Pepé. "To Monterey, me? Alone? *Sí*, Mama."

She scowled at him. "Do not think, big sheep, that you will buy candy. No, I will give you only enough for the medicine and the salt."

Pepé smiled. "Mama, you will put the hatband on the hat?"

She relented then. "Yes, Pepé. You may wear the hatband."

His voice grew insinuating. "And the green handkerchief, Mama?"

"Yes, if you go quickly and return with no trouble, the silk green handkerchief will go. If you make sure to take off the handkerchief when you eat so no spot may fall on it. . . ."

"*Sí*, Mama. I will be careful. I am a man."

"Thou? A man? Thou art a peanut."

He went into the rickety barn and brought out a rope, and he walked agilely enough up the hill to catch the horse.

When he was ready and mounted before the door, mounted on his father's saddle that was so old that the oaken frame showed through torn leather in many places, then Mama brought out the round black hat with the tooled leather band, and she reached up and knotted the green silk handkerchief about his neck. Pepé's blue denim coat was much darker than his jeans, for it had been washed much less often.

Mama handed up the big medicine bottle and the silver coins. "That for the medicine," she said, "and that for the salt. That for a candle to burn for the papa.

That for *dulces* for the little ones. Our friend Mrs. Rodriguez will give you dinner and maybe a bed for the night. When you go to the church say only ten Paternosters and only twenty-five Ave Marias. Oh! I know, big coyote. You would sit there flapping your mouth over Aves all day while you looked at the candles and the holy pictures. That is not good devotion to stare at the pretty things."

The black hat, covering the high pointed head and black thatched hair of Pepé, gave him dignity and age. He sat the rangy horse well. Mama thought how handsome he was, dark and lean and tall. "I would not send thee now alone, thou little one, except for the medicine," she said softly. "It is not good to have no medicine, for who knows when the toothache will come, or the sadness of the stomach. These things are."

"Adios, Mama," Pepé cried. "I will come back soon. You may send me often alone. I am a man."

"Thou art a foolish chicken."

He straightened his shoulders, flipped the reins against the horse's shoulder and rode away. He turned once and saw that they still watched him, Emilio and Rosy and Mama. Pepé grinned with pride and gladness and lifted the tough buckskin horse to a trot.

When he had dropped out of sight over a little dip in the road, Mama turned to the black ones, but she spoke to herself. "He is nearly a man now," she said. "It will be a nice thing to have a man in the house again." Her eyes sharpened on the children. "Go to the rocks now. The tide is going out. There will be abalones to be found." She put the iron hooks into their hands and saw them down the steep trail to the reefs. She brought the smooth stone *metate* to the doorway and sat grinding her corn to flour and looking occasionally at the road over which Pepé had gone. The noonday came and then the afternoon, when the little ones beat the abalones on a rock to make them tender and Mama patted the tortillas to make them thin. They ate their dinner as the red sun was plunging down toward the ocean. They sat on the doorsteps and watched the big white moon come over the mountaintops.

Mama said, "He is now at the house of our friend Mrs. Rodriguez. She will give him nice things to eat and maybe a present."

Emilio said, "Some day I too will ride to Monterey for medicine. Did Pepé come to be a man today?"

Mama said wisely, "A boy gets to be a man when a man is needed. Remember this thing. I have known boys forty years old because there was no need for a man."

Soon afterwards they retired, Mama in her big oak bed on one side of the room, Emilio and Rosy in their boxes full of straw and sheepskins on the other side of the room.

The moon went over the sky and the surf roared on the rocks. The roosters crowed the first call. The surf subsided to a whispering surge against the reef. The moon dropped toward the sea. The roosters crowed again.

The moon was near to the water when Pepé rode on a winded horse to his home flat. His dog bounced out and circled the horse yelping with pleasure. Pepé slid off the saddle to the ground. The weathered little shack was silver in the moonlight and the square shadow of it was black to the north and east. Against the east the piling mountains were misty with light; their tops melted into the sky.

Pepé walked wearily up the three steps and into the house. It was dark inside. There was a rustle in the corner.

Mama cried out from her bed. "Who comes? Pepé, is it thou?"

"*Sí*, Mama."

"Did you get the medicine?"

"*Sí*, Mama."

"Well, go to sleep, then. I thought you would be sleeping at the house of Mrs. Rodriguez." Pepé stood silently in the dark room. "Why do you stand there, Pepé? Did you drink wine?"

"*Sí*, Mama."

"Well, go to bed then and sleep out the wine."

His voice was tired and patient, but very firm. "Light the candle, Mama. I must go away into the mountains."

"What is this, Pepé? You are crazy." Mama struck a sulphur match and held the little blue burr until the flame spread up the stick. She set light to the candle on the floor beside her bed. "Now, Pepé, what is this you say?" She looked anxiously into his face.

He was changed. The fragile quality seemed to have gone from his chin. His mouth was less full than it had been, the lines of the lips were straighter, but in his eyes the greatest change had taken place. There was no laughter in them any more, nor any bashfulness. They were sharp and bright and purposeful.

He told her in a tired monotone, told her everything just as it had happened. A few people came into the kitchen of Mrs. Rodriguez. There was wine to drink. Pepé drank wine. The little quarrel—the man started toward Pepé and then the knife—it went almost by itself. It flew, it darted before Pepé knew it. As he talked, Mama's face grew stern, and it seemed to grow more lean. Pepé finished. "I am a man now, Mama. The man said names to me I could not allow."

Mama nodded. "Yes, thou art a man, my poor little Pepé. Thou art a man. I have seen it coming on thee. I have watched you throwing the knife into the post, and I have been afraid." For a moment her face had softened, but now it grew stern again. "Come! We must get you ready. Go. Awaken Emilio and Rosy. Go quickly."

Pepé stepped over to the corner where his brother and sister slept among the sheepskins. He leaned down and shook them gently. "Come, Rosy! Come, Emilio! The mama says you must arise."

The little black ones sat up and rubbed their eyes in the candlelight. Mama was out of bed now, her long black shirt over her nightgown. "Emilio," she cried. "Go up and catch the other horse for Pepé. Quickly, now! Quickly." Emilio put his legs in his overalls and stumbled sleepily out the door.

"You heard no one behind you on the road?" Mama demanded.

"No, Mama. I listened carefully. No one was on the road."

Mama darted like a bird about the room. From a nail on the wall she took a canvas water bag and threw it on the floor. She stripped a blanket from her bed and rolled it into a tight tube and tied the ends with string. From a box beside the stove she lifted a flour sack half full of black stringy jerky. "Your father's black coat, Pepé. Here, put it on."

Pepé stood in the middle of the floor watching her activity. She reached behind the door and brought out the rifle, a long 38-56, worn shiny the whole length of the barrel. Pepé took it from her and held it in the crook of his elbow. Mama brought a little leather bag and counted the cartridges into his hand. "Only ten left," she warned. "You must not waste them."

Emilio put his head in the door. "*'Qui 'st 'l caballo*, Mama."

"Put on the saddle from the other horse. Tie on the blanket. Here, tie the jerky to the saddle horn."

Still Pepé stood silently watching his mother's frantic activity. His chin looked hard, and his sweet mouth was drawn and thin. His little eyes followed Mama about the room almost suspiciously.

Rosy asked softly, "Where goes Pepé?"

Mama's eyes were fierce. "Pepé goes on a journey. Pepé is a man now. He has a man's thing to do."

Pepé straightened his shoulders. His mouth changed until he looked very much like Mama.

At last the preparation was finished. The loaded horse stood outside the door. The water bag dripped a line of moisture down the bay shoulder.

The moonlight was being thinned by the dawn and the big white moon was near down to the sea. The family stood by the shack. Mama confronted Pepé. "Look, my son! Do not stop until it is dark again. Do not sleep even though you are tired. Take care of the horse in order that he may not stop of weariness. Remember to be careful with the bullets—there are only ten. Do not fill thy stomach with jerky or it will make thee sick. Eat a little jerky and fill thy stomach with grass. When thou comest to the high mountains, if thou seest any of the dark watching men, go not near to them nor try to speak to them. And forget not thy prayers." She put her lean hands on Pepé's shoulders, stood on her toes and kissed him formally on both cheeks, and Pepé kissed her on both cheeks. Then he went to Emilio and Rosy and kissed both of their cheeks.

Pepé turned back to Mama. He seemed to look for a little softness, a little weakness in her. His eyes were searching, but Mama's face remained fierce. "Go now," she said. "Do not wait to be caught like a chicken."

Pepé pulled himself into the saddle. "I am a man," he said.

It was the first dawn when he rode up the hill toward the little canyon which let a trail into the mountains. Moonlight and daylight fought with each other, and the two warring qualities made it difficult to see. Before Pepé had gone a hundred yards, the outlines of his figure were misty; and long before he entered the canyon, he had become a grey, indefinite shadow.

Mama stood stiffly in front of her doorstep, and on either side of her stood Emilio and Rosy. They cast furtive glances at Mama now and then.

When the grey shape of Pepé melted into the hillside and disappeared, Mama relaxed. She began the high, whining keen of the death wail. "Our beautiful—our brave," she cried. "Our protector, our son is gone." Emilio and Rosy moaned beside her. "Our beautiful—our brave, he is gone." It was the formal wail. It rose to a high piercing whine and subsided to a moan. Mama raised it three times and then she turned and went into the house and shut the door.

Emilio and Rosy stood wondering in the dawn. They heard Mama whimpering in the house. They went out to sit on the cliff above the ocean. They touched shoulders. "When did Pepé come to be a man?" Emilio said.

"Last night," said Rosy. "Last night in Monterey." The ocean clouds turned red with the sun that was behind the mountains.

"We will have no breakfast," said Emilio. "Mama will not want to cook." Rosy did not answer him. "Where is Pepé gone?" he asked.

Rosy looked around at him. She drew her knowledge from the quiet air. "He has gone on a journey. He will never come back."

"Is he dead? Do you think he is dead?"

Rosy looked back at the ocean again. A little steamer, drawing a line of smoke sat on the edge of the horizon. "He is not dead," Rosy explained. "Not yet."

Pepé rested the big rifle across the saddle in front of him. He let the horse walk up the hill and he didn't look back. The stony slope took on a coat of short brush so that Pepé found the entrance to a trail and entered it.

When he came to the canyon opening, he swung once in his saddle and looked back, but the houses were swallowed in the misty light. Pepé jerked forward again. The high shoulder of the canyon closed in on him. His horse stretched out its neck and sighed and settled to the trail.

It was a well-worn path, dark soft leaf-mould earth strewn with broken pieces of sandstone. The trail rounded the shoulder of the canyon and dropped steeply into the bed of the stream. In the shallows the water ran smoothly, glinting in the first morning sun. Small round stones on the bottom were as brown as rust with sun moss. In the sand along the edges of the stream the tall, rich wild mint grew, while in the water itself the cress, old and tough, had gone to heavy seed.

The path went into the stream and emerged on the other side. The horse sloshed into the water and stopped. Pepé dropped his bridle and let the beast drink of the running water.

Soon the canyon sides became steep and the first giant sentinel redwoods guarded the trail, great round red trunks bearing foliage as green and lacy as ferns. Once Pepé was among the trees, the sun was lost. A perfumed and purple light lay in the pale green of the underbrush. Gooseberry bushes and blackberries and tall ferns lined the stream, and overhead the branches of the redwoods met and cut off the sky.

Pepé drank from the water bag, and he reached into the flour sack and brought out a black string of jerky. His white teeth gnawed at the string until the tough meat parted. He chewed slowly and drank occasionally from the water bag. His little eyes were slumberous and tired, but the muscles of his face were hard set. The earth of the trail was black now. It gave up a hollow sound under the walking hoofbeats.

The stream fell more sharply. Little waterfalls splashed on the stones. Five-fingered ferns hung over the water and dripped spray from their fingertips. Pepé rode half over in his saddle, dangling one leg loosely. He picked a bay leaf from a tree beside the way and put it into his mouth for a moment to flavor the dry jerky. He held the gun loosely across the pommel.

Suddenly he squared in his saddle, swung the horse from the trail and kicked it hurriedly up behind a big redwood tree. He pulled up the reins tight against the bit to keep the horse from whinnying. His face was intent and his nostrils quivered a little.

A hollow pounding came down the trail, and a horseman rode by, a fat man with red cheeks and a white stubble beard. His horse put down its head and blubbered at the trail when it came to the place where Pepé had turned off. "Hold up!" said the man and he pulled up his horse's head.

When the last sound of the hooves died away, Pepé came back into the trail again. He did not relax in the saddle any more. He lifted the big rifle and swung the lever to throw a shell into the chamber, and then he let down the hammer to half cock.

The trail grew very steep. Now the redwood trees were smaller and their tops were dead, bitten dead where the wind reached them. The horse plodded on; the sun went slowly overhead and started down toward the afternoon.

Where the stream came out of a side canyon, the trail left it. Pepé dismounted and watered his horse and filled up his water bag. As soon as the trail had parted from the stream, the trees were gone and only the thick brittle sage and manzanita and chaparral edged the trail. And the soft black earth was gone, too, leaving only the light tan broken rock for the trail bed. Lizards scampered away into the brush as the horse rattled over the little stones.

Pepé turned in his saddle and looked back. He was in the open now: he could be seen from a distance. As he ascended the trail the country grew more rough and terrible and dry. The way wound about the bases of the great square rocks. Little grey rabbits skittered in the brush. A bird made a monotonous high creaking. Eastward the bare rock mountaintops were pale and powder-dry under the dropping sun. The horse plodded up and up the trail toward a little V in the ridge which was the pass.

Pepé looked suspiciously back every minute or so, and his eyes sought the tops of the ridges ahead. Once, on a white barren spur, he saw a black figure for a moment, but he looked quickly away, for it was one of the dark watchers. No one knew who the watchers were, nor where they lived, but it was better to ignore them and never to show interest in them. They did not bother one who stayed on the trail and minded his own business.

The air was parched and full of light dust blown by the breeze from the eroding mountains. Pepé drank sparingly from his bag and corked it tightly and hung it on the horn again. The trail moved up the dry shale hillside, avoiding rocks, dropping under clefts, climbing in and out of old water scars. When he arrived at the little pass he stopped and looked back for a long time. No dark watchers were to be seen now. The trail behind was empty. Only the high tops of the redwoods indicated where the stream flowed.

Pepé rode on through the pass. His little eyes were nearly closed with weariness, but his face was stern, relentless and manly. The high mountain wind coasted sighing through the pass and whistled on the edges of the big blocks of broken granite. In the air, a red-tailed hawk sailed over close to the ridge and screamed angrily. Pepé went slowly through the broken jagged pass and looked down on the other side.

The trail dropped quickly, staggering among broken rock. At the bottom of the slope there was a dark crease, thick with brush, and on the other side of the crease a little flat, in which a grove of oak trees grew. A scar of green grass cut across the flat. And behind the flat another mountain rose, desolate with dead rocks and starving little black bushes. Pepé drank from the bag again for the air was so dry that it encrusted his nostrils and burned his lips. He put the horse down the trail. The hooves slipped and struggled on the steep way, starting little stones that rolled off into the brush. The sun was gone behind the westward mountain now, but still it glowed brilliantly on the oaks and on the grassy flat. The rocks and the hillsides still sent up waves of the heat they had gathered from the day's sun.

Pepé looked up to the top of the next dry withered ridge. He saw a dark form against the sky, a man's figure standing on top of a rock, and he glanced away quickly not to appear curious. When a moment later he looked up again, the figure was gone.

Downward the trail was quickly covered. Sometimes the horse floundered for footing, sometimes set his feet and slid a little way. They came at last to the bottom where the dark chaparral was higher than Pepé's head. He held up his rifle on one side and his arm on the other to shield his face from the sharp brittle fingers of the brush.

Up and out of the crease he rode, and up a little cliff. The grassy flat was before him, and the round comfortable oaks. For a moment he studied the trail down which he had come, but there was no movement and no sound from it. Finally he rode out over the flat, to the green streak, and at the upper end of the damp he found a little spring welling out of the earth and dropping into a dug basin before it seeped out over the flat.

Pepé filled his bag first, and then he let the thirsty horse drink out of the pool. He led the horse to the clump of oaks, and in the middle of the grove, fairly protected from sight on all sides, he took off the saddle and the bridle and laid them on the ground. The horse stretched his jaws sideways and yawned. Pepé knotted the lead rope about the horse's neck and tied him to a sapling among the oaks, where he could graze in a fairly large circle.

When the horse was gnawing hungrily at the dry grass, Pepé went to the saddle and took a black string of jerky from the sack and strolled to an oak tree on the edge of the grove, from under which he could watch the trail. He sat down in the crisp dry oak leaves and automatically felt for his big black knife to cut the jerky, but he had no knife. He leaned back on his elbow and gnawed at the tough strong meat. His face was blank, but it was a man's face.

The bright evening light washed the eastern ridge, but the valley was darkening. Doves flew down from the hills to the spring, and the quail came running out of the brush and joined them, calling clearly to one another.

Out of the corner of his eye Pepé saw a shadow grow out of the bushy crease. He turned his head slowly. A big spotted wildcat was creeping toward the spring, belly to the ground, moving like thought.

Pepé cocked his rifle and edged the muzzle slowly around. Then he looked apprehensively up the trail and dropped the hammer again. From the ground beside him he picked an oak twig and threw it toward the spring. The quail flew up with a roar and the doves whistled away. The big cat stood up: for a long moment he looked at Pepé with cold yellow eyes, and then fearlessly walked back into the gulch.

The dusk gathered quickly in the deep valley. Pepé muttered his prayers, put his head down on his arm and went instantly to sleep.

The moon came up and filled the valley with cold blue light, and the wind swept rustling down from the peaks. The owls worked up and down the slopes looking for rabbits. Down in the brush of the gulch a coyote gabbled. The oak trees whispered softly in the night breeze.

Pepé started up, listening. His horse had whinnied. The moon was just slipping behind the western ridge, leaving the valley in darkness behind it. Pepé sat tensely gripping his rifle. From far up the trail he heard an answering whinny and the crash of shod hooves on the broken rock. He jumped to his feet, ran to his horse and led it under the trees. He threw on the saddle and cinched it tight for the steep trail, caught the unwilling head and forced the bit into the mouth. He felt the saddle to make sure the water bag and the sack of jerky were there. Then he mounted and turned up the hill.

It was velvet dark. The horse found the entrance to the trail where it left the flat, and started up, stumbling and slipping on the rocks. Pepé's hand rose up to his head. His hat was gone. He had left it under the oak tree.

The horse had struggled far up the trail when the first change of dawn came into the air, a steel greyness as light mixed thoroughly with dark. Gradually the sharp snaggled edge of the ridge stood out above them, rotten granite tortured and eaten by the winds of time. Pepé had dropped his reins on the horn, leaving direction to the horse. The brush grabbed at his legs in the dark until one knee of his jeans was ripped.

Gradually the light flowed down over the ridge. The starved brush and rocks stood out in the half light, strange and lonely in high perspective. Then there came warmth into the light. Pepé drew up and looked back, but he could see nothing in the darker valley below. The sky turned blue over the coming sun. In the waste of the mountainside, the poor dry brush grew only three feet high. Here and there, big outcroppings of unrotted granite stood up like mouldering houses. Pepé relaxed a little. He drank from his water bag and bit off a piece of jerky. A single eagle flew over, high in the light.

Without warning Pepé's horse screamed and fell on its side. He was almost down before the rifle crash echoed up from the valley. From a hole behind the struggling shoulder, a stream of bright crimson blood pumped and stopped and pumped and stopped. The hooves threshed on the ground. Pepé lay half stunned beside the horse. He looked slowly down the hill. A piece of sage clipped off beside his head and another crash echoed up from side to side of the canyon. Pepé flung himself frantically behind a bush.

He crawled up the hill on his knees and one hand. His right hand held the rifle up off the ground and pushed it ahead of him. He moved with the instinctive care of an animal. Rapidly he wormed his way toward one of the big outcroppings of granite on the hill above him. Where the brush was high he doubled up and ran, but where the cover was slight he wriggled forward on his stomach, pushing the rifle ahead of him. In the last little distance there was no cover at all. Pepé poised and then he darted across the space and flashed around the corner of the rock.

He leaned panting against the stone. When his breath came easier he moved behind the big rock until he came to a narrow split that offered a thin section of vision down the hill. Pepé lay on his stomach and pushed the rifle barrel through the slit and waited.

The sun reddened the western ridges now. Already the buzzards were settling down toward the place where the horse lay. A small brown bird scratched in the dead sage leaves directly in front of the rifle muzzle. The coasting eagle flew back toward the rising sun.

Pepé saw a little movement in the brush far below. His grip tightened on the gun. A little brown doe stepped daintily out on the trail and crossed it and disappeared into the brush again. For a long time Pepé waited. Far below he could see the little flat and the oak trees and the slash of green. Suddenly his eyes flashed back at the trail again. A quarter of a mile down there had been a quick movement in the chaparral. The rifle swung over. The front sight nestled in the

V of the rear sight. Pepé studied for a moment and then raised the rear sight a notch. The little movement in the brush came again. The sight settled on it. Pepé squeezed the trigger. The explosion crashed down the mountain and up the other side, and came rattling back. The whole side of the slope grew still. No more movement. And then a white streak cut into the granite of the slit and a bullet whined away and a crash sounded up from below. Pepé felt a sharp pain in his right hand. A sliver of granite was sticking out from between his first and second knuckles and the point protruded from his palm. Carefully he pulled out the sliver of stone. The wound bled evenly and gently. No vein nor artery was cut.

Pepé looked into a little dusty cave in the rock and gathered a handful of spider web, and he pressed the mass into the cut, plastering the soft web into the blood. The flow stopped almost at once.

The rifle was on the ground. Pepé picked it up, levered a new shell into the chamber. And then he slid into the brush on his stomach. Far to the right he crawled, and then up the hill, moving slowly and carefully, crawling to cover and resting and then crawling again.

In the mountains the sun is high in its arc before it penetrates the gorges. The hot face looked over the hill and brought instant heat with it. The white light beat on the rocks and reflected from them and rose up quivering from the earth again, and the rocks and bushes seemed to quiver behind the air.

Pepé crawled in the general direction of the ridge peak, zig-zagging for cover. The deep cut between his knuckles began to throb. He crawled close to a rattlesnake before he saw it, and when it raised its dry head and made a soft beginning whirr, he backed up and took another way. The quick grey lizards flashed in front of him, raising a tiny line of dust. He found another mass of spider web and pressed it against his throbbing hand.

Pepé was pushing the rifle with his left hand now. Little drops of sweat ran to the ends of his coarse black hair and rolled down his cheeks. His lips and tongue were growing thick and heavy. His lips writhed to draw saliva into his mouth. His little dark eyes were uneasy and suspicious. Once when a grey lizard paused in front of him on the parched ground and turned its head sideways he crushed it flat with a stone.

When the sun slid past noon he had not gone a mile. He crawled exhaustedly a last hundred yards to a patch of high sharp manzanita, crawled desperately, and when the patch was reached he wriggled in among the tough gnarly trunks and dropped his head on his left arm. There was little shade in the meager brush, but there was cover and safety. Pepé went to sleep as he lay and the sun beat on his back. A few little birds hopped close to him and peered and hopped away. Pepé squirmed in his sleep and he raised and dropped his wounded hand again and again.

The sun went down behind the peaks and the cool evening came, and then the dark. A coyote yelled from the hillside, Pepé started awake and looked about with misty eyes. His hand was swollen and heavy; a little thread of pain ran up the inside of his arm and settled in a pocket in his armpit. He peered about and then stood up, for the mountains were black and the moon had not yet risen. Pepé stood up in the dark. The coat of his father pressed on his arm. His tongue was swollen until it nearly filled his mouth. He wriggled out of the coat and dropped it in the brush, and then he struggled up the hill, falling over rocks and tearing his way through the brush. The rifle knocked against stones as he went. Little dry avalanches of gravel and shattered stone went whispering down the hill behind him.

After a while the old moon came up and showed the jagged ridge top ahead of him. By moonlight Pepé traveled more easily. He bent forward so that his throbbing arm hung away from his body. The journey uphill was made in dashes and rests, a frantic rush up a few yards and then a rest. The wind coasted down the slope rattling the dry stems of the bushes.

The moon was at meridian when Pepé came at last to the sharp backbone of the ridge top. On the last hundred yards of the rise no soil had clung under the wearing winds. The way was on solid rock. He clambered to the top and looked down on the other side. There was a draw like the last below him, misty with moonlight, brushed with dry struggling sage and chaparral. On the other side the hill rose up sharply and at the top the jagged rotten teeth of the mountain showed against the sky. At the bottom of the cut the brush was thick and dark.

Pepé stumbled down the hill. His throat was almost closed with thirst. At first he tried to run, but immediately he fell and rolled. After that he went more carefully. The moon was just disappearing behind the mountains when he came to the bottom. He crawled into the heavy brush feeling with his fingers for water.

There was no water in the bed of the stream, only damp earth. Pepé laid his gun down and scooped up a handful of mud and put it in his mouth, and then he spluttered and scraped the earth from his tongue with his finger, for the mud drew at his mouth like a poultice. He dug a hole in the stream bed with his fingers, dug a little basin to catch water; but before it was very deep his head fell forward on the damp ground and he slept.

The dawn came and the heat of the day fell on the earth, and still Pepé slept. Late in the afternoon his head jerked up. He looked slowly around. His eyes were slits of wariness. Twenty feet away in the heavy brush a big tawny mountain lion stood looking at him. Its long thick tail waved gracefully, its ears were erect with interest, now laid back dangerously. The lion squatted down on its stomach and watched him.

Pepé looked at the hole he had dug in the earth. A half inch of muddy water had collected in the bottom. He tore the sleeve from his hurt arm, with his teeth ripped out a little square, soaked it in the water and put it in his mouth. Over and over he filled the cloth and sucked it.

Still the lion sat and watched him. The evening came down but there was no movement on the hills. No birds visited the dry bottom of the cut. Pepé looked occasionally at the lion. The eyes of the yellow beast drooped as though he were about to sleep. He yawned and his long thin red tongue curled out. Suddenly his head jerked around and his nostrils quivered. His big tail lashed. He stood up and slunk like a tawny shadow into the thick brush.

A moment later Pepé heard the sound, the faint far

crash of horses' hooves on gravel. And he heard something else, a high whining yelp of a dog.

Pepé took his rifle in his left hand and he glided into the brush almost as quietly as the lion had. In the darkening evening he crouched up the hill toward the next ridge. Only when the dark came did he stand up. His energy was short. Once it was dark he fell over the rocks and slipped to his knees on the steep slope, but he moved on and on up the hill, climbing and scrabbling over the broken hillside.

When he was far up toward the top, he lay down and slept for a little while. The withered moon, shining on his face, awakened him. He stood up and moved up the hill. Fifty yards away he stopped and turned back, for he had forgotten his rifle. He walked heavily down and poked about in the brush, but he could not find his gun. At last he lay down to rest. The pocket of pain in his armpit had grown more sharp. His arm seemed to swell out and fall with every heartbeat. There was no position lying down where the heavy arm did not press against his armpit.

With the effort of a hurt beast, Pepé got up and moved again toward the top of the ridge. He held his swollen arm away from his body with his left hand. Up the steep hill he dragged himself, a few steps and a rest, and a few more steps. At last he was nearing the top. The moon showed the uneven sharp back of it against the sky.

Pepé's brain spun in a big spiral up and away from him. He slumped to the ground and lay still. The rock ridge top was only a hundred feet above him.

The moon moved over the sky. Pepé half turned on his back. His tongue tried to make words, but only a thick hissing came from between his lips.

When the dawn came, Pepé pulled himself up. His eyes were sane again. He drew his great puffed arm in front of him and looked at the angry wound. The black line ran up from his wrist to his armpit. Automatically he reached in his pocket for the big black knife, but it was not there. His eyes searched the ground. He picked up a sharp blade of stone and scraped at the wound, sawed at the proud flesh and then squeezed the green juice out in big drops. Instantly he threw back his head and whined like a dog. His whole right side shuddered at the pain, but the pain cleared his head.

In the grey light he struggled up the last slope to the ridge and crawled over and lay down behind a line of rocks. Below him lay a deep canyon exactly like the last, waterless and desolate. There was no flat, no oak trees, not even heavy brush in the bottom of it. And on the other side a sharp ridge stood up, thinly brushed with starving sage, littered with broken granite. Strewn over the hill there were giant outcroppings, and on the top the granite teeth stood out against the sky.

The new day was light now. The flame of the sun came over the ridge and fell on Pepé where he lay on the ground. His coarse black hair was littered with twigs and bits of spider web. His eyes had retreated back into his head. Between his lips the tip of his black tongue showed.

He sat up and dragged his great arm into his lap and nursed it, rocking his body and moaning in his throat. He threw back his head and looked up into the pale sky. A big black bird circled nearly out of sight, and far to the left another was sailing near.

He lifted his head to listen, for a familiar sound had

come to him from the valley he had climbed out of; it was the crying yelp of hounds, excited and feverish, on a trail.

Pepé bowed his head quickly. He tried to speak rapid words but only a thick hiss came from his lips. He drew a shaky cross on his breast with his left hand. It was a long struggle to get to his feet. He crawled slowly and mechanically to the top of a big rock on the ridge peak. Once there, he arose slowly, swaying to his feet, and stood erect. Far below he could see the dark brush where he had slept. He braced his feet and stood there, black against the morning sky.

There came a ripping sound at his feet. A piece of stone flew up and a bullet droned off into the next gorge. The hollow crash echoed up from below. Pepé looked down for a moment and then pulled himself straight again.

His body jarred back. His left hand fluttered helplessly toward his breast. The second crash sounded from below. Pepé swung forward and toppled from the rock. His body struck and rolled over and over, starting a little avalanche. And when at last he stopped against a bush, the avalanche slid slowly down and covered up his head.

THE SNAKE

THE SNAKE

It was almost dark when young Dr. Phillips swung his sack to his shoulder and left the tide pool. He climbed up over the rocks and squashed along the street in his rubber boots. The street lights were on by the time he arrived at his little commercial laboratory on the cannery street of Monterey. It was a tight little building, standing partly on piers over the bay water and partly on the land. On both sides the big corrugated-iron sardine canneries crowded in on it.

Dr. Phillips climbed the wooden steps and opened the door. The white rats in their cages scampered up and down the wire, and the captive cats in their pens mewed for milk. Dr. Phillips turned on the glaring light over the dissection table and dumped his clammy sack on the floor. He walked to the glass cages by the window where the rattlesnakes lived, leaned over and looked in.

The snakes were bunched and resting in the corners of the cage, but every head was clear; the dusty eyes seemed to look at nothing, but as the young man leaned over the cage the forked tongues, black on the ends and pink behind, twittered out and waved slowly up and down. Then the snakes recognized the man and pulled in their tongues.

Dr. Phillips threw off his leather coat and built a fire in the tin stove; he set a kettle of water on the stove and dropped a can of beans into the water. Then he stood staring down at the sack on the floor. He was a slight young man with the mild, preoccupied eyes of one who looks through a microscope a great deal. He wore a short blond beard.

The draft ran breathily up the chimney and a glow of warmth came from the stove. The little waves washed quietly about the piles under the building. Arranged on shelves about the room were tier above tier of museum jars containing the mounted marine specimens the laboratory dealt in.

Dr. Phillips opened a side door and went into his bedroom, a book-lined cell containing an army cot, a reading light and an uncomfortable wooden chair. He pulled off his rubber boots and put on a pair of sheepskin slippers. When he went back to the other room the water in the kettle was already beginning to hum.

He lifted his sack to the table under the white light and emptied out two dozen common starfish. These he laid out side by side on the table. His preoccupied eyes turned to the busy rats in the wire cages. Taking grain from a paper sack, he poured it into the feeding troughs. Instantly the rats scrambled down from the wire and fell upon the food. A bottle of milk stood on a glass shelf between a small mounted octopus and a jellyfish. Dr. Phillips lifted down the milk and walked to the cat cage, but before he filled the containers he reached in the cage and gently picked out a big rangy alley tabby. He stroked her for a moment and then dropped her in a small black painted box, closed the lid and bolted it and then turned on a petcock which admitted gas into the killing chamber. While the short soft struggle went on in the black box he filled the saucers with milk. One of the cats arched against his hand and he smiled and petted her neck.

The box was quiet now. He turned off the petcock, for the airtight box would be full of gas.

On the stove the pan of water was bubbling furiously about the can of beans. Dr. Phillips lifted out the can with a big pair of forceps, opened it, and emptied the beans into a glass dish. While he ate he watched the starfish on the table. From between the rays little drops of milky fluid were exuding. He bolted his beans and when they were gone he put the dish in the sink and stepped to the equipment cupboard. From this he took a microscope and a pile of little glass dishes. He filled the dishes one by one with sea water from a tap and arranged them in a line beside the starfish. He took out his watch and laid it on the table under the pouring white light. The waves washed with little sighs against the piles under the floor. He took an eye-dropper from a drawer and bent over the starfish.

At that moment there were quick soft steps on the wooden stairs and a strong knocking at the door. A slight grimace of annoyance crossed the young man's face as he went to open. A tall, lean woman stood in the doorway. She was dressed in a severe dark suit—her straight black hair, growing low on a flat forehead, was mussed as though the wind had been blowing it. Her black eyes glittered in the strong light.

She spoke in a soft throaty voice, "May I come in? I want to talk to you."

"I'm very busy just now," he said half-heartedly. "I have to do things at times." But he stood away from the door. The tall woman slipped in.

"I'll be quiet until you can talk to me."

He closed the door and brought the uncomfortable chair from the bedroom. "You see," he apologized, "the process is started and I must get to it." So many people wandered in and asked questions. He had little routines of explanations for the commoner processes. He could say them without thinking. "Sit here. In a few minutes I'll be able to listen to you."

The tall woman leaned over the table. With the eye-dropper the young man gathered fluid from between the rays of the starfish and squirted it into a bowl of water, and then he drew some milky fluid and squirted it in the same bowl and stirred the water gently with the eye-dropper. He began his little patter of explanation.

"When starfish are sexually mature they release sperm and ova when they are exposed at low tide. By choosing mature specimens and taking them out of the water, I give them a condition of low tide. Now I've mixed the sperm and eggs. Now I put some of the mixture in each one of these ten watch glasses. In ten minutes I will kill those in the first glass with menthol, twenty minutes later I will kill the second group and then a new group every twenty minutes. Then I will have arrested the process in stages, and I will mount the series on microscope slides for biologic study." He paused. "Would you like to look at this first group under the microscope?"

"No, thank you."

He turned quickly to her. People always wanted to look through the glass. She was not looking at the table at all, but at him. Her black eyes were on him, but they did not seem to see him. He realized why—the irises were as dark as the pupils, there was no color line between the two. Dr. Phillips was piqued at her answer. Although answering questions bored him, a lack of interest in what he was doing irritated him. A desire to arouse her grew in him.

"While I'm waiting the first ten minutes I have something to do. Some people don't like to see it. Maybe you'd better step into that room until I finish."

"No," she said in her soft flat tone. "Do what you wish. I will wait until you can talk to me." Her hands rested side by side on her lap. She was completely at rest. Her eyes were bright but the rest of her was almost in a state of suspended animation. He thought, "Low metabolic rate, almost as low as a frog's, from the looks." The desire to shock her out of her inanition possessed him again.

He brought a little wooden cradle to the table, laid out scalpels and scissors and rigged a big hollow needle to a pressure tube. Then from the killing chamber he brought the limp dead cat and laid it in the cradle and tied its legs to hooks in the sides. He glanced sidewise at the woman. She had not moved. She was still at rest.

The cat grinned up into the light, its pink tongue stuck out between its needle teeth. Dr. Phillips deftly snipped open the skin at the throat; with a scalpel he slit through and found an artery. With flawless technique he put the needle in the vessel and tied it in with gut. "Embalming fluid," he explained. "Later I'll inject yellow mass into the veinous system and red mass into the arterial system—for bloodstream dissection—biology classes."

He looked around at her again. Her dark eyes seemed veiled with dust. She looked without expression at the cat's open throat. Not a drop of blood had escaped. The incision was clean. Dr. Phillips looked at his watch. "Time for the first group." He shook a few crystals of menthol into the first watch glass.

The woman was making him nervous. The rats climbed about on the wire of their cage again and squeaked softly. The waves under the building beat with little shocks on the piles.

The young man shivered. He put a few lumps of coal in the stove and sat down. "Now," he said. "I haven't anything to do for twenty minutes." He noticed how short her chin was between lower lip and point. She seemed to awaken slowly, to come up out of some deep pool of consciousness. Her head raised and her dark dusty eyes moved about the room and then came back to him.

"I was waiting," she said. Her hands remained side by side on her lap. "You have snakes?"

"Why, yes," he said rather loudly. "I have about two dozen rattlesnakes. I milk out the venom and send it to the anti-venom laboratories."

She continued to look at him but her eyes did not center on him, rather they covered him and seemed to see in a big circle all around him. "Have you a male snake, a male rattlesnake?"

"Well, it just happens I know I have. I came in one morning and found a big snake in–in coition with a smaller one. That's very rare in captivity. You see, I do know I have a male snake."

"Where is he?"

"Why, right in the glass cage by the window there."

Her head swung slowly around but her two quiet hands did not move. She turned back toward him. "May I see?"

He got up and walked to the case by the window. On the sand bottom the knot of rattlesnakes lay entwined, but their heads were clear. The tongues came out and flickered a moment and then waved up and down feeling the air for vibrations. Dr. Phillips nervously turned his head. The woman was standing beside him. He had not heard her get up from the chair. He had heard only the splash of water among the piles and the scampering of the rats on the wire screen.

She said softly, "Which is the male you spoke of?"

He pointed to a thick, dusty grey snake lying by itself in one corner of the cage. "That one. He's nearly five feet long. He comes from Texas. Our Pacific coast snakes are usually smaller. He's been taking all the rats, too. When I want the others to eat I have to take him out."

The woman stared down at the blunt dry head. The forked tongue slipped out and hung quivering for a long moment. "And you're sure he's a male."

"Rattlesnakes are funny," he said glibly. "Nearly every generalization proves wrong. I don't like to say anything definite about rattlesnakes, but—yes—I can assure you he's a male."

Her eyes did not move from the flat head. "Will you sell him to me?"

"Sell him?" he cried. "Sell him to you?"

"You do sell specimens, don't you?"

"Oh—yes. Of course I do. Of course I do."

"How much? Five dollars? Ten?"

"Oh! Not more than five. But—do you know anything about rattlesnakes? You might be bitten."

She looked at him for a moment. "I don't intend to take him. I want to leave him here, but—I want him to be mine. I want to come here and look at him and feed him and to know he's mine." She opened a little purse and took out a five-dollar bill. "Here! Now he is mine."

Dr. Phillips began to be afraid. "You could come to look at him without owning him."

"I want him to be mine."

"Oh, Lord!" he cried. "I've forgotten the time." He ran to the table. "Three minutes over. It won't matter much." He shook menthol crystals into the second watch glass. And then he was drawn back to the cage where the woman still stared at the snake.

She asked, "What does he eat?"

"I feed them white rats, rats from the cage over there."

"Will you put him in the other cage? I want to feed him."

"But he doesn't need food. He's had a rat already this week. Sometimes they don't eat for three or four months. I had one that didn't eat for over a year."

In her low monotone she asked, "Will you sell me a rat?"

He shrugged his shoulders. "I see. You want to watch how rattlesnakes eat. All right. I'll show you. The rat will cost twenty-five cents. It's better than a bullfight if you look at it one way, and it's simply a snake eating his dinner if you look at it another." His tone had become acid. He hated people who made sport of natural processes. He was not a sportsman but a biologist. He could kill a thousand animals for knowledge, but not an insect for pleasure. He'd been over this in his mind before.

She turned her head slowly toward him and the beginning of a smile formed on her thin lips. "I want to feed my snake," she said. "I'll put him in the other cage." She had opened the top of the cage and dipped her hand in before he knew what she was doing. He leaped forward and pulled her back. The lid banged shut.

"Haven't you any sense," he asked fiercely. "Maybe he wouldn't kill you, but he'd make you damned sick in spite of what I could do for you."

"You put him in the other cage then," she said quietly.

Dr. Phillips was shaken. He found that he was avoiding the dark eyes that didn't seem to look at anything. He felt that it was profoundly wrong to put a rat into the cage, deeply sinful; and he didn't know why. Often he had put rats in the cage when someone or other had wanted to see it, but this desire tonight sickened him. He tried to explain himself out of it.

"It's a good thing to see," he said. "It shows you how a snake can work. It makes you have a respect for a rattlesnake. Then, too, lots of people have dreams about the terror of snakes making the kill. I think because it is a subjective rat. The person is the rat. Once you see it the whole matter is objective. The rat is only a rat and the terror is removed."

He took a long stick equipped with a leather noose from the wall. Opening the trap he dropped the noose over the big snake's head and tightened the thong. A piercing dry rattle filled the room. The thick body writhed and slashed about the handle of the stick as he lifted the snake out and dropped it in the feeding cage. It stood ready to strike for a time, but the buzzing gradually ceased. The snake crawled into a corner, made a big figure eight with its body and lay still.

"You see," the young man explained, "these snakes are quite tame. I've had them a long time. I suppose I could handle them if I wanted to, but everyone who does handle rattlesnakes gets bitten sooner or later. I just don't want to take the chance." He glanced at the woman. He hated to put in the rat. She had moved over in front of the new cage; her black eyes were on the stony head of the snake again.

She said, "Put in a rat."

Reluctantly he went to the rat cage. For some reason he was sorry for the rat, and such a feeling had never come to him before. His eyes went over the mass of swarming white bodies climbing up the screen toward him. "Which one?" he thought. "Which one shall it be?" Suddenly he turned angrily to the woman. "Wouldn't you rather I put in a cat? Then you'd see a real fight. The cat might even win, but if it did it might kill the snake. I'll sell you a cat if you like."

She didn't look at him. "Put in a rat," she said. "I want him to eat."

He opened the rat cage and thrust his hand in. His fingers found a tail and he lifted a plump, red-eyed rat out of the cage. It struggled up to try to bite his fingers and, failing, hung spread out and motionless from its tail. He walked quickly across the room, opened the feeding cage and dropped the rat in on the sand floor. "Now, watch it," he cried.

The woman did not answer him. Her eyes were on the snake where it lay still. Its tongue, flicking in and out rapidly, tasted the air of the cage.

The rat landed on its feet, turned around and sniffed at its pink naked tail and then unconcernedly trotted across the sand, smelling as it went. The room was silent. Dr. Phillips did not know whether the water sighed among the piles or whether the woman sighed. Out of the corner of his eyes he saw her body crouch and stiffen.

The snake moved out smoothly, slowly. The tongue flicked in and out. The motion was so gradual, so smooth that it didn't seem to be motion at all. In the other end of the cage the rat perked up in a sitting position and began to lick down the fine white hair on its chest. The snake moved on, keeping always a deep S curve in its neck.

The silence beat on the young man. He felt the blood drifting up in his body. He said loudly, "See! He keeps the striking curve ready. Rattlesnakes are cautious, almost cowardly animals. The mechanism is so delicate. The snake's dinner is to be got by an operation as deft as a surgeon's job. He takes no chances with his instruments."

The snake had flowed to the middle of the cage by now. The rat looked up, saw the snake and then unconcernedly went back to licking its chest.

"It's the most beautiful thing in the world," the young man said. His veins were throbbing. "It's the most terrible thing in the world."

The snake was close now. Its head lifted a few inches from the sand. The head weaved slowly back and forth, aiming, getting distance, aiming. Dr. Phillips glanced again at the woman. He turned sick. She was weaving too, not much, just a suggestion.

The rat looked up and saw the snake. It dropped to four feet and back up, and then—the stroke. It was impossible to see, simply a flash. The rat jarred as though under an invisible blow. The snake backed hurriedly into the corner from which it had come, and settled down, its tongue working constantly.

"Perfect!" Dr. Phillips cried. "Right between the shoulder blades. The fangs must almost have reached the heart."

The rat stood still, breathing like a little white bellows. Suddenly it leaped in the air and landed on its side. Its legs kicked spasmodically for a second and it was dead.

The woman relaxed, relaxed sleepily.

"Well," the young man demanded, "it was an emotional bath, wasn't it?"

She turned her misty eyes to him. "Will he eat it now?" she asked.

"Of course he'll eat it. He didn't kill it for a thrill. He killed it because he was hungry."

The corners of the woman's mouth turned up a trifle again. She looked back at the snake. "I want to see him eat it."

Now the snake came out of its corner again. There was no striking curve in its neck, but it approached the rat gingerly, ready to jump back in case it attacked. It nudged the body gently with its blunt nose, and drew away. Satisfied that it was dead, the snake touched the body all over with its chin, from head to tail. It seemed to measure the body and to kiss it. Finally it opened its mouth and unhinged its jaws at the corners.

Dr. Phillips put his will against his head to keep it from turning toward the woman. He thought, "If she's opening her mouth, I'll be sick. I'll be afraid." He succeeded in keeping his eyes away.

The snake fitted its jaws over the rat's head and then with a slow peristaltic pulsing, began to engulf the rat. The jaws gripped and the whole throat crawled up, and the jaws gripped again.

Dr. Phillips turned away and went to his work table. "You've made me miss one of the series," he said bitterly. "The set won't be complete." He put one of the watch glasses under a low-power microscope and looked at it, and then angrily he poured the contents of all the dishes into the sink. The waves had fallen so that only a wet whisper came up through the floor. The young man lifted a trapdoor at his feet and dropped the starfish down into the black water. He paused at the cat, crucified in the cradle and grinning comically into the light. Its body was puffed with embalming fluid. He shut off the pressure, withdrew the needle and tied the vein.

"Would you like some coffee?" he asked.

"No, thank you. I shall be going pretty soon."

He walked to her where she stood in front of the snake cage. The rat was swallowed, all except an inch of pink tail that stuck out of the snake's mouth like a sardonic tongue. The throat heaved again and the tail disappeared. The jaws snapped back into their sockets, and the big snake crawled heavily to the corner, made a big eight and dropped its head on the sand.

"He's asleep now," the woman said. "I'm going now. But I'll come back and feed my snake every little while. I'll pay for the rats. I want him to have plenty. And sometime—I'll take him away with me." Her eyes came out of their dusty dream for a moment. "Remember, he's mine. Don't take his poison. I want him to have it. Good-night." She walked swiftly to the door and went out. He heard her footsteps on the stairs, but he could not hear her walk away on the pavement.

Dr. Phillips turned a chair around and sat down in front of the snake cage. He tried to comb out his thought as he looked at the torpid snake. "I've read so much about psychological sex symbols," he thought. "It doesn't seem to explain. Maybe I'm too much alone. Maybe I should kill the snake. If I knew—no, I can't pray to anything."

For weeks he expected her to return. "I will go out and leave her alone here when she comes," he decided. "I won't see the damned thing again."

She never came again. For months he looked for her when he walked about in the town. Several times he ran after some tall woman thinking it might be she. But he never saw her again—ever.

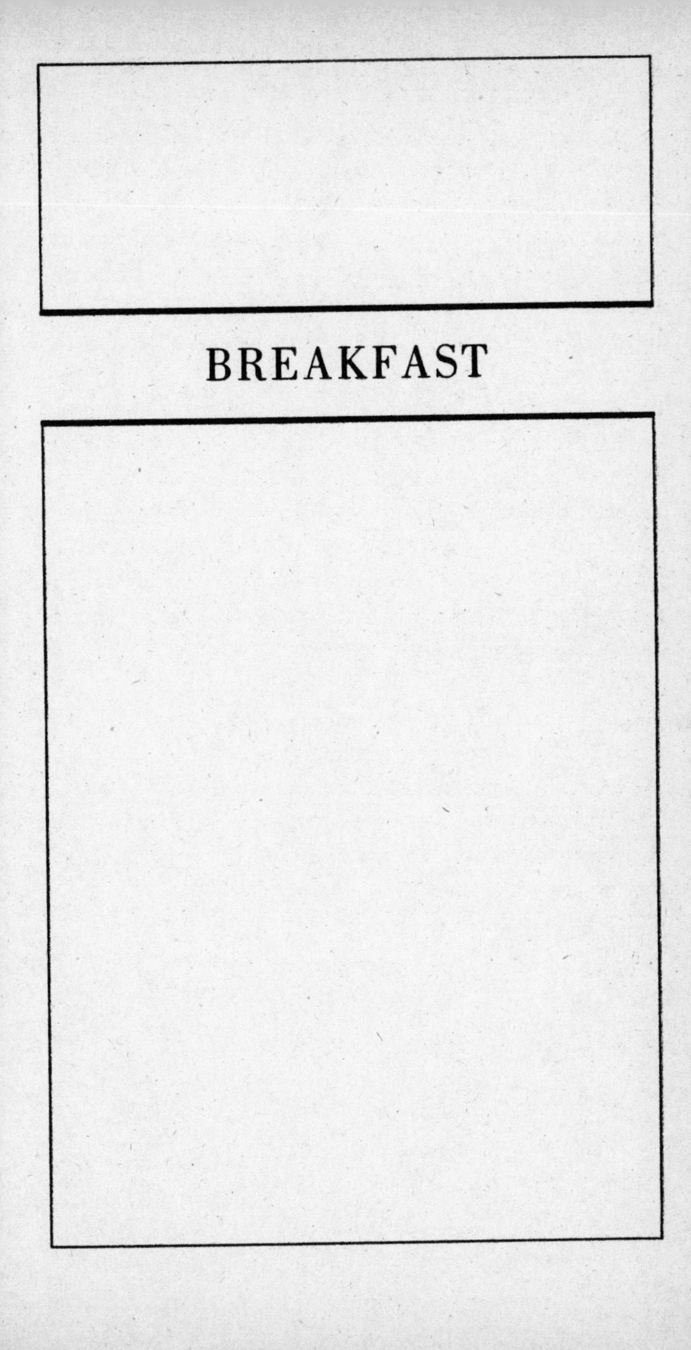

BREAKFAST

BREAKFAST

This thing fills me with pleasure. I don't know why, I can see it in the smallest detail. I find myself recalling it again and again, each time bringing more detail out of sunken memory, remembering brings the curious warm pleasure.

It was very early in the morning. The eastern mountains were black-blue, but behind them the light stood up faintly colored at the mountain rims with a washed red, growing colder, greyer and darker as it went up and overhead until, at a place near the west, it merged with pure night.

And it was cold, not painfully so, but cold enough so that I rubbed my hands and shoved them deep into my pockets, and I hunched my shoulders up and scuffled my feet on the ground. Down in the valley where I was, the earth was that lavender grey of dawn. I walked along a country road and ahead of me I saw a tent that was only a little lighter grey than the ground. Beside the tent there was a flash of orange fire seeping out of the cracks of an old rusty iron stove. Grey smoke spurted up out of the stubby stovepipe, spurted up a long way before it spread out and dissipated.

I saw a young woman beside the stove, really a girl. She was dressed in a faded cotton skirt and waist. As I came close I saw that she carried a baby in a crooked arm and the baby was nursing, its head under her waist out of the cold. The mother moved about, poking the fire, shifting the rusty lids of the stove to make a greater draft, opening the oven door; and all the time the baby was nursing, but that didn't interfere with the mother's work, nor with the light quick gracefulness of her movements. There was something very precise and practiced in her movements. The orange fire flicked out of the cracks in the stove and threw dancing reflections on the tent.

I was close now and I could smell frying bacon and baking bread, the warmest, pleasantest odors I know. From the east the light grew swiftly. I came near to the stove and stretched my hands out to it and shivered all over when the warmth struck me. Then the tent flap jerked up and a young man came out and an older man followed him. They were dressed in new blue dungarees and in new dungaree coats with brass buttons shining. They were sharp-faced men, and they looked much alike.

The younger had a dark stubble beard and the older had a grey stubble beard. Their heads and faces were wet, their hair dripped with water, and water stood out on their stiff beards and their cheeks shone with water. Together they stood looking quietly at the lightening east; they yawned together and looked at the light on the hill rims. They turned and saw me.

"Morning," said the older man. His face was neither friendly nor unfriendly.

"Morning, sir," I said.

"Morning," said the young man.

The water was slowly drying on their faces. They came to the stove and warmed their hands at it.

The girl kept to her work, her face averted and her eyes on what she was doing. Her hair was tied back out of her eyes with a string and it hung down her back and swayed as she worked. She set tin cups on a big packing box, set tin plates and knives and forks out too. Then she scooped fried bacon out of the deep grease and laid it on a big tin platter, and the bacon cricked and rustled as it grew crisp. She opened the rusty oven door and took out a square pan full of high big biscuits.

When the smell of that hot bread came out, both of the men inhaled deeply. The young man said softly, "Keerist!"

The elder man turned to me, "Had you breakfast?"

"No."

"Well, sit down with us, then."

That was the signal. We went to the packing case and squatted on the ground about it. The young man asked, "Picking cotton?"

"No."

"We have twelve days' work so far," the young man said.

The girl spoke from the stove. "They even got new clothes."

The two men looked down at their new dungarees and they both smiled a little.

The girl set out the platter of bacon, the brown high biscuits, a bowl of bacon gravy and a pot of coffee, and then she squatted down by the box too. The baby was still nursing, its head up under her waist out of the cold. I could hear the sucking noises it made.

We filled our plates, poured bacon gravy over our biscuits and sugared our coffee. The older man filled his mouth full and he chewed and chewed and swallowed. Then he said, "God Almighty, it's good," and he filled his mouth again.

The young man said, "We been eating good for twelve days."

We all ate quickly, frantically, and refilled our plates and ate quickly again until we were full and warm. The hot bitter coffee scalded our throats. We threw the last little bit with the grounds in it on the earth and refilled our cups.

There was color in the light now, a reddish gleam that made the air seem colder. The two men faced the east and their faces were lighted by the dawn, and I looked up for a moment and saw the image of the mountain and the light coming over it reflected in the older man's eyes.

Then the two men threw the grounds from their cups on the earth and they stood up together. "Got to get going," the older man said.

The younger turned to me. " 'Fyou want to pick cotton, we could maybe get you on."

"No. I got to go along. Thanks for breakfast."

The older man waved his hand in a negative. "O.K. Glad to have you." They walked away together. The air was blazing with light at the eastern skyline. And I walked away down the country road.

That's all. I know, of course, some of the reasons why it was pleasant. But there was some element of great beauty there that makes the rush of warmth when I think of it.

THE RAID

THE RAID

I

It was dark in the little California town when the two men stepped from the lunch car and strode arrogantly through the back streets. The air was full of the sweet smell of fermenting fruit from the packing plants. High over the corners, blue arc lights swung in the wind and put moving shadows of telephone wires on the ground. The old wooden buildings were silent and resting. The dirty windows dismally reflected the street lights.

The two men were about the same size, but one was much older than the other. Their hair was cropped, they wore blue jeans. The older man had on a pea-jacket, while the younger wore a blue turtle-neck sweater. As they swung down the dark street, footsteps echoed back loudly from the wooden buildings. The younger man began to whistle *Come to Me My Melancholy Baby*. He stopped abruptly. "I wish that damn tune would get out of my head. It's been going all day. It's an old tune, too."

His companion turned toward him. "You're scared, Root. Tell the truth. You're scared as hell."

They were passing under one of the blue street lights. Root's face put on its toughest look, the eyes squinted, the mouth went crooked and bitter. "No, I ain't scared." They were out of the light. His face relaxed again. "I wish I knew the ropes better. You been out before, Dick. You know what to expect. But I ain't ever been out."

"The way to learn is to do," Dick quoted sententiously. "You never really learn nothing from books."

They crossed a railroad track. A block tower up the line a little was starred with green lights. "It's awful dark," said Root. "I wonder if the moon will come up later. Usually does when it's so dark. You going to make the first speech, Dick?"

"No, you make it. I had more experience than you. I'll watch them while you talk and then I can smack them where I know they bite. Know what you're going to say?"

"Sure I do. I got it all in my head, every word. I wrote it out and learned it. I heard guys tell how they got up and couldn't think of a thing to say, and then all of a sudden they just started in like it was somebody else, and the words came out like water out of a hydrant. Big Mike Sheane said it was like that with him. But I wasn't taking no chances, so I wrote it out."

A train hooted mournfully, and in a moment it rounded a bend and pushed its terrible light down the track. The lighted coaches rattled past. Dick turned to watch it go by. "Not many people on that one," he said with satisfaction. "Didn't you say your old man worked on the railroad?"

Root tried to keep the bitterness out of his voice. "Sure, he works on the road. He's a brakeman. He kicked me out when he found out what I was doing. He was scared he'd lose his job. He couldn't see. I talked to him, but he just couldn't see. He kicked me right out." Root's voice was lonely. Suddenly he realized how he had weakened and how he sounded homesick. "That's the trouble with them," he went on harshly. "They can't see beyond their jobs. They can't see what's happening to them. They hang on to their chains."

"Save it," said Dick. "That's good stuff. Is that part of your speech?"

"No, but I guess I'll put it in if you say it's good."

The street lights were fewer now. A line of locust trees grew along the road, for the town was beginning to thin and the country took control. Along the unpaved road there were a few little houses with ill-kept gardens.

"Jesus! It's dark," Root said again. "I wonder if there'll be any trouble. It's a good night to get away if anything happens."

Dick snorted into the collar of his peajacket. They walked along in silence for a while.

"Do you think you'd try to get away, Dick?" Root asked.

"No, by God! It's against orders. If anything happens we got to stick. You're just a kid. I guess you'd run if I let you!"

Root blustered: "You think you're hell on wheels just because you been out a few times. You'd think you was a hundred to hear you talk."

"I'm dry behind the ears, anyway," said Dick.

Root walked with his head down. He said softly, "Dick, are you sure you wouldn't run? Are you sure you could just stand there and take it?"

"Of course I'm sure. I've done it before. It's the orders, ain't it? Why, it's good publicity." He peered through the darkness at Root. "What makes you ask, kid? You scared you'll run? If you're scared you got no business here."

Root shivered. "Listen, Dick, you're a good guy. You won't tell nobody what I say, will you? I never been tried. How do I know what I'll do if somebody smacks me in the face with a club? How can anybody tell what he'd do? I don't think I'd run. I'd try not to run."

"All right, kid. Let it go at that. But you try running, and I'll turn your name in. We got no place for yellow bastards. You remember that, kid."

"Oh, lay off that kid stuff. You're running that in the ground."

The locust trees grew closer together as they went. The wind rustled gently in the leaves. A dog growled in one of the yards as the men went by. A light fog began to drift down through the air, and the stars were swallowed in it. "You sure you got everything ready?" Dick asked. "Got the lamps? Got the lit'ature? I left all that to you."

"I did it all this afternoon," said Root. "I didn't put the posters up yet, but I got them in a box out there."

"Got oil in the lamps?"

"They had plenty in. Say, Dick, I guess some bastard has squealed, don't you?"

"Sure. Somebody always squeals."

"Well, you didn't hear nothing about no raid, did you?"

"How the hell would I hear. You think they'd come and tell me they was going to knock my can off? Get hold of yourself, Root. You got the pants scared off you. You're going to make me nervous if you don't cut it out."

II

They approached a low, square building, black and heavy in the darkness. Their feet pounded on a wooden sidewalk. "Nobody here, yet," said Dick. "Let's open her up and get some light." They had come to a deserted store. The old show-windows were opaque with dirt. A Lucky Strike poster was stuck to the glass on one side while a big cardboard Coca-Cola lady stood like a ghost in the other. Dick threw open the double doors and walked in. He struck a match and lighted a kerosene lamp, got the chimney back in place, and set the lamp on an up-ended apple box. "Come on, Root, we got to get things ready."

The walls of the building were scabrous with streaked whitewash. A pile of dusty newspapers had been kicked into a corner. The two back windows were laced with cobwebs. Except for three apple boxes, there was nothing at all in the store.

Root walked to one of the boxes and took out a large poster bearing a portrait of a man done in harsh reds and blacks. He tacked the portrait to the whitewashed wall behind the lamp. Then he tacked another poster beside it, a large red symbol on a white background. Last he up-ended another apple box and piled leaflets and little paper-bound books on it. His footsteps were loud on the bare wooden floor. "Light the other lamp, Dick! It's too damned dark in here."

"Scared of the dark, too, kid?"

"No. The men will be here pretty soon. We want to have more light when they come. What time is it?"

Dick looked at his watch. "Quarter to eight. Some of the guys ought to be here pretty soon now." He put his hands in the breast pockets of his peajacket and stood loosely by the box of pamphlets. There was nothing to sit on. The black and red portrait stared harshly out at the room. Root leaned against the wall.

The light from one of the lamps yellowed, and the flame slowly sank down. Dick stepped over to it. "I thought you said there was plenty of oil. This one's dry."

"I thought there was plenty. Look! The other one's nearly full. We can pour some of that oil in this lamp."

"How we going to do that? We got to put them both out to pour the oil. You got any matches?"

Root felt through his pockets. "Only two."

"Now, you see? We got to hold this meeting with only one lamp. I should've looked things over this afternoon. I was busy in town, though. I thought I could leave it to you."

"Maybe we could quick pour some of this oil in a can and then pour it into the other lamp."

"Yeah, and then set the joint on fire. You're a hell of a helper."

Root leaned back against the wall again. "I wish they'd come. What time is it, Dick?"

"Five after eight."

"Well, what's keeping them? What are they waiting for? Did you tell them eight o'clock?"

"Oh! Shut up, kid. You'll get my goat pretty soon. I

don't know what's keeping them. Maybe they got cold feet. Now shut up for a little while." He dug his hands into the pockets of his jacket again. "Got a cigarette, Root?"

"No."

It was very still. Nearer the center of the town, automobiles were moving; the mutter of their engines and an occasional horn sounded. A dog barked unexcitedly at one of the houses nearby. The wind ruffled the locust trees in whishing gusts.

"Listen, Dick! Do you hear voices? I think they're coming." They turned their heads and strained to listen.

"I don't hear nothing. You just thought you heard it."

Root walked to one of the dirty windows and looked out. Coming back, he paused at the pile of pamphlets and straightened them neatly. "What time is it now, Dick?"

"Keep still, will you? You'll drive me nuts. You got to have guts for this job. For God's sake show some guts."

"Well, I never been out before, Dick."

"Do you think anybody couldn't tell that? You sure make it plain enough."

The wind gusted sharply in the locust trees. The front doors clicked and one of them opened slowly, squeaking a little at the hinges. The breeze came in, ruffled the pile of dusty newspapers in the corner and sailed the posters out from the wall like curtains.

"Shut that door, Root. . . . No, leave it open. Then we can hear them coming better." He looked at his watch. "It's nearly half-past eight."

"Do you think they'll come? How long we going to wait, if they don't show up?"

The older man stared at the open door. "We ain't going to leave here before nine-thirty at the earliest. We got orders to hold this meeting."

The night sounds came in more clearly through the open door—the dance of dry locust leaves on the road, the slow steady barking of the dog. On the wall the red and black portrait was menacing in the dim light. It floated out at the bottom again. Dick looked around at it. "Listen, kid," he said quietly. "I know you're scared. When you're scared, just take a look at him." He indicated the picture with his thumb. "He wasn't scared. Just remember about what he did."

The boy considered the portrait. "You suppose he wasn't ever scared?"

Dick reprimanded him sharply. "If he was, nobody ever found out about it. You take that for a lesson and don't go opening up for everybody to show them how you feel."

"You're a good guy, Dick. I don't know what I'll do when I get sent out alone."

"You'll be all right kid. You got stuff in you. I can tell that. You just never been under fire."

Root glanced quickly at the door. "Listen! You hear somebody coming?"

"Lay off that stuff! When they get here, they'll get here."

"Well—let's close the door. It's kind of cold in here. Listen! There *is* somebody coming."

Quick footsteps sounded on the road, broke into a run and crossed the wooden sidewalk. A man in overalls and a painter's cap ran into the room. He was panting and winded. "You guys better scram," he said. "There's a raiding party coming. None of the boys is coming to the meeting. They was going to let you take it, but I wouldn't do that. Come on! Get your stuff together and get out. That party's on the way."

Root's face was pale and tight. He looked nervously at Dick. The older man shivered. He thrust his hands into his breast pockets and slumped his shoulders. "Thanks," he said. "Thanks for telling us. You run along. We'll be all right."

"The others was just going to leave you take it," the man said.

Dick nodded. "Sure, they can't see the future. They can't see beyond their nose. Run along now before you get caught."

"Well, ain't you guys coming? I'll help carry some of your stuff."

"We're going to stay," Dick said woodenly. "We got orders to stay. We got to take it."

The man was moving toward the door. He turned back. "Want me to stay with you?"

"No, you're a good guy. No need for you to stay. We could maybe use you some other time."

"Well, I did what I could."

III

Dick and Root heard him cross the wooden sidewalk and trot off into the darkness. The night resumed its sounds. The dead leaves scraped along the ground. The motors hummed from the center of the town.

Root looked at Dick. He could see that the man's

fists were doubled up in his breast pockets. The face muscles were stiff, but he smiled at the boy. The posters drifted out from the wall and settled back again.

"Scared, kid?"

Root bristled to deny it, and then gave it up. "Yes, I'm scared. Maybe I won't be no good at this."

"Take hold, kid!" Dick said fiercely. "You take hold!"

Dick quoted to him, " 'The men of little spirit must have an example of stead—steadfastness. The people at large must have an example of injustice.' There it is, Root. That's orders." He relapsed into silence. The barking dog increased his tempo.

"I guess that's them," said Root. "Will they kill us, do you think?"

"No, they don't very often kill anybody."

"But they'll hit us and kick us, won't they? They'll hit us in the face with sticks and break our nose. Big Mike, they broke his jaw in three places."

"Take hold, kid! You take hold! And listen to me; if some one busts you, it isn't him that's doing it, it's the System. And it isn't you he's busting. He's taking a crack at the Principle. Can you remember that?"

"I don't want to run, Dick. Honest to God I don't. If I start to run, you hold me, will you?"

Dick walked near and touched him on the shoulder. "You'll be all right. I can tell a guy that will stick."

"Well, hadn't we better hide the lit'ature so it won't all get burned?"

"No—somebody might put a book in his pocket and read it later. Then it would be doing some good. Leave the books there. And shut up now! Talking only makes it worse."

The dog had gone back to his slow, spiritless barking. A rush of wind brought a scurry of dead leaves in the open door. The portrait poster blew out and came loose at one corner. Root walked over and pinned it back. Somewhere in the town, an automobile squealed its brakes.

"Hear anything, Dick? Hear them coming yet?"

"No."

"Listen, Dick. Big Mike lay two days with his jaw broke before anybody'd help him."

The older man turned angrily on him. One doubled fist came out of his peajacket pocket. His eyes narrowed as he looked at the boy. He walked close and put an arm about his shoulders. "Listen to me close, kid," he said. "I don't know much, but I been through this mill before. I can tell you this for sure. When it comes—it won't hurt. I don't know why, but it won't. Even if they kill you it won't hurt." He dropped his arm and moved toward the front door. He looked out and listened in two directions before he came back into the room.

"Hear anything?"

"No. Not a thing."

"What—do you think is keeping them?"

"How do you suppose I'd know?"

Root swallowed thickly. "Maybe they won't come. Maybe it was all a lie that fella told us, just a joke."

"Maybe."

"Well, are—we going to wait all night to get our cans knocked off?"

Dick mimicked him. "Yes, we're going to wait all night to get our cans knocked off."

The wind sounded in one big fierce gust and then

dropped away completely. The dog stopped barking. A train screamed for the crossing and went crashing by, leaving the night more silent than before. In a house nearby, an alarm clock went off. Dick said, "Somebody goes to work early. Night watchman, maybe." His voice was too loud in the stillness. The front door squeaked slowly shut.

"What time is it now, Dick?"

"Quarter-past nine."

"Jesus! Only that? I thought it was about morning. . . . Don't you wish they'd come and get it over, Dick? Listen, Dick!—I thought I heard voices."

They stood stiffly, listening. Their heads were bent forward. "You hear voices, Dick?"

"I think so. Like they're talking low."

The dog barked again, fiercely this time. A little quiet murmur of voices could be heard. "Look, Dick! I thought I saw somebody out the back window."

The older man chuckled uneasily. "That's so we can't get away. They got the place surrounded. Take hold, kid! They're coming now. Remember about it's not them, it's the System."

There came a rushing clatter of footsteps. The doors burst open. A crowd of men thronged in, roughly dressed men, wearing black hats. They carried clubs and sticks in their hands. Dick and Root stood erect, their chins out, their eyes dropped and nearly closed.

Once inside, the raiders were uneasy. They stood in a half-circle about the two men, scowling, waiting for some one to move.

Young Root glanced sidewise at Dick and saw that the older man was looking at him coldly, critically, as though he judged his deportment. Root shoved his trembling hands in his pockets. He forced himself forward. His voice was shrill with fright. "Comrades," he shouted, "you're just men like we are. We're all brothers——" A piece of two-by-four lashed out and struck him on the side of the head with a fleshy thump. Root went down to his knees and steadied himself with his hands.

The men stood still, glaring.

Root climbed slowly to his feet. His split ear spilled a red stream down his neck. The side of his face was mushy and purple. He got himself erect again. His breath burst passionately. His hands were steady now, his voice sure and strong. His eyes were hot with an ecstasy. "Can't you see?" he shouted. "It's all for you. We're doing it for you. All of it. You don't know what you're doing."

"Kill the red rats!"

Some one giggled hysterically. And then the wave came. As he went down, Root caught a moment's glimpse of Dick's face smiling a tight, hard smile.

IV

He came near the surface several times, but didn't quite make it into consciousness. At last he opened his eyes and knew things. His face and head were heavy with bandages. He could only see a line of light between his puffed eyelids. For a time he lay, trying to think his way out. Then he heard Dick's voice near to him.

"You awake, kid?"

Root tried his voice and found that it croaked pretty badly. "I guess so."

"They sure worked out on your head. I thought you was gone. You was right about your nose. It ain't going to be very pretty."

"What'd they do to you, Dick?"

"Oh, they bust my arm and a couple of ribs. You got to learn to turn your face down to the ground. That saves your eyes." He paused and drew a careful breath. "Hurts some to breathe when you get a rib bust. We are lucky. The cops picked us up and took us in."

"Are we in jail, Dick?"

"Yeah! Hospital cell."

"What they got on the book?"

He heard Dick try to chuckle, and gasp when it hurt him. "Inciting to riot. We'll get six months, I guess. The cops got the lit'ature."

"You won't tell them I'm under age, will you, Dick?"

"No. I won't. You better shut up. Your voice don't sound so hot. Take it easy."

Root lay silent, muffled in a coat of dull pain. But in a moment he spoke again. "It didn't hurt, Dick. It was funny. I felt all full up—and good."

"You done fine, kid. You done as good as anybody I ever seen. I'll give you a blow to the committee. You just done fine."

Root struggled to get something straight in his head. "When they was busting me I wanted to tell them I didn't care."

"Sure, kid. That's what I told you. It wasn't them. It was the System. You don't want to hate them. They don't know no better."

Root spoke drowsily. The pain was muffling him

under. "You remember in the Bible, Dick, how it says something like 'Forgive them because they don't know what they're doing'?"

Dick's reply was stern. "You lay off that religion stuff, kid." He quoted, " 'Religion is the opium of the people.' "

"Sure, I know," said Root. "But there wasn't no religion to it. It was just—I felt like saying that. It was just kind of the way I felt."

THE HARNESS

THE HARNESS

Peter Randall was one of the most highly respected farmers of Monterey County. Once, before he was to make a little speech at a Masonic convention, the brother who introduced him referred to him as an example for young Masons of California to emulate. He was nearing fifty; his manner was grave and restrained, and he wore a carefully tended beard. From every gathering he reaped the authority that belongs to the bearded man. Peter's eyes were grave, too; blue and grave almost to the point of sorrowfulness. People knew there was force in him, but force held caged. Sometimes, for no apparent reason, his eyes grew sullen and mean, like the eyes of a bad dog; but that look soon passed, and the restraint and probity came back into his face. He was tall and broad. He held his shoulders back as though they were braced, and he sucked in his stomach like a soldier. Inasmuch as farmers are usually slouchy men, Peter gained an added respect because of his posture.

Concerning Peter's wife, Emma, people generally agreed that it was hard to see how such a little skin-

and-bones woman could go on living, particularly when she was sick most of the time. She weighed eighty-seven pounds. At forty-five, her face was as wrinkled and brown as that of an old, old woman, but her dark eyes were feverish with a determination to live. She was a proud woman, who complained very little. Her father had been a thirty-third degree Mason and Worshipful Master of the Grand Lodge of California. Before he died he had taken a great deal of interest in Peter's Masonic career.

Once a year Peter went away for a week, leaving his wife alone on the farm. To neighbors who called to keep her company she invariably explained, "He's away on a business trip."

Each time Peter returned from a business trip, Emma was ailing for a month or two, and this was hard on Peter, for Emma did her own work and refused to hire a girl. When she was ill, Peter had to do the housework.

The Randall ranch lay across the Salinas River, next to the foothills. It was an ideal balance of bottom and upland. Forty-five acres of rich level soil brought from the cream of the county by the river in old times and spread out as flat as a board; and eighty acres of gentle upland for hay and orchard. The white farmhouse was as neat and restrained as its owners. The immediate yard was fenced, and in the garden, under Emma's direction, Peter raised button dahlias and immortelles, carnations and pinks.

From the front porch one could look down over the flat to the river with its sheath of willows and cottonwoods, and across the river to the beet fields, and past the fields to the bulbous dome of the Salinas courthouse. Often in the afternoon Emma sat in a rocking-chair on the front porch, until the breeze drove her in. She knitted constantly, looking up now and then to watch Peter working on the flat or in the orchard, or on the slope below the house.

The Randall ranch was no more encumbered with mortgage than any of the others in the valley. The crops, judiciously chosen and carefully tended, paid the interest, made a reasonable living and left a few hundred dollars every year toward paying off the principal. It was no wonder that Peter Randall was respected by his neighbors and that his seldom spoken words were given attention even when they were about the weather or the way things were going. Let Peter say, "I'm going to kill a pig Saturday," and nearly every one of his hearers went home and killed a pig on Saturday. They didn't know why, but if Peter Randall was going to kill a pig, it seemed like a good, safe, conservative thing to do.

Peter and Emma were married for twenty-one years. They collected a houseful of good furniture, a number of framed pictures, vases of all shapes, and books of a sturdy type. Emma had no children. The house was unscarred, uncarved, unchalked. On the front and back porches footscrapers and thick cocoa-fiber mats kept dirt out of the house.

In the intervals between her illnesses, Emma saw to it that the house was kept up. The hinges of doors and cupboards were oiled, and no screws were gone from the catches. The furniture and woodwork were freshly varnished once a year. Repairs were usually made after Peter came home from his yearly business trips.

Whenever the word went around among the farms

that Emma was sick again, the neighbors waylaid the doctor as he drove by on the river road.

"Oh, I guess she'll be all right," he answered their questions. "She'll have to stay in bed for a couple of weeks."

The good neighbors took cakes to the Randall farm, and they tiptoed into the sickroom, where the little skinny bird of a woman lay in a tremendous walnut bed. She looked at them with her bright little dark eyes.

"Wouldn't you like the curtains up a little, dear?" they asked.

"No, thank you. The light worries my eyes."

"Is there anything we can do for you?"

"No, thank you. Peter does for me very well."

"Just remember, if there's anything you think of—"

Emma was such a tight woman. There was nothing you could do for her when she was ill, except to take pies and cakes to Peter. Peter would be in the kitchen, wearing a neat, clean apron. He would be filling a hot water bottle or making junket.

And so, one fall, when the news traveled that Emma was down, the farm-wives baked for Peter and prepared to make their usual visits.

Mrs. Chappell, the next farm neighbor, stood on the river road when the doctor drove by. "How's Emma Randall, doctor?"

"I don't think she's so very well, Mrs. Chappell. I think she's a pretty sick woman."

Because to Dr. Marn anyone who wasn't actually a corpse was well on the road to recovery, the word went about among the farms that Emma Randall was going to die.

It was a long, terrible illness. Peter himself gave enemas and carried bedpans. The doctor's suggestion that a nurse be employed met only beady, fierce refusal in the eyes of the patient; and, ill as she was, her demands were respected. Peter fed her and bathed her, and made up the great walnut bed. The bedroom curtains remained drawn.

It was two months before the dark, sharp bird eyes veiled, and the sharp mind retired into unconsciousness. And only then did a nurse come to the house. Peter was lean and sick himself, not far from collapse. The neighbors brought him cakes and pies, and found them uneaten in the kitchen when they called again.

Mrs. Chappell was in the house with Peter the afternoon Emma died. Peter became hysterical immediately. Mrs. Chappell telephoned the doctor, and then she called her husband to come and help her, for Peter was wailing like a crazy man, and beating his bearded cheeks with his fists. Ed Chappell was ashamed when he saw him.

Peter's beard was wet with his tears. His loud sobbing could be heard throughout the house. Sometimes he sat by the bed and covered his head with a pillow, and sometimes he paced the floor of the bedroom bellowing like a calf. When Ed Chappell self-consciously put a hand on his shoulder and said, "Come on, Peter, come on, now," in a helpless voice, Peter shook his hand off. The doctor drove out and signed the certificate.

When the undertaker came, they had a devil of a time with Peter. He was half mad. He fought them when they tried to take the body away. It was only after Ed Chappell and the undertaker held him down while the doctor stuck him with a hypodermic, that they were able to remove Emma.

The morphine didn't put Peter to sleep. He sat hunched in the corner, breathing heavily and staring at the floor.

"Who's going to stay with him?" the doctor asked. "Miss Jack?" to the nurse.

"I couldn't handle him, doctor, not alone."

"Will you stay, Chappell?"

"Sure, I'll stay."

"Well, look. Here are some triple bromides. If he gets going again, give him one of these. And if they don't work, here's some sodium amytal. One of these capsules will calm him down."

Before they went away, they helped the stupefied Peter into the sitting-room and laid him gently down on a sofa. Ed Chappell sat in an easy-chair and watched him. The bromides and a glass of water were on the table beside him.

The little sitting-room was clean and dusted. Only that morning Peter had swept the floor with pieces of damp newspaper. Ed built a little fire in the grate, and put on a couple of pieces of oak when the flames were well started. The dark had come early. A light rain spattered against the windows when the wind drove it. Ed trimmed the kerosene lamps and turned the flames low. In the grate the blaze snapped and crackled and the flames curled like hair over the oak. For a long time Ed sat in his easy-chair watching Peter where he lay drugged on the couch. At last Ed dozed off to sleep.

It was about ten o'clock when he awakened. He started up and looked toward the sofa. Peter was sitting up, looking at him. Ed's hand went out toward the bromide bottle, but Peter shook his head.

"No need to give me anything, Ed. I guess the doctor slugged me pretty hard, didn't he? I feel all right now, only a little dopey."

"If you just take one of these you'll get some sleep."

"I don't want sleep." He fingered his draggled beard and then stood up. "I'll go out and wash my face, then I'll feel better."

Ed heard him running water in the kitchen. In a moment he came back into the living-room, still drying his face on a towel. Peter was smiling curiously. It was an expression Ed had never seen on him before, a quizzical, wondering smile. "I guess I kind of broke loose when she died, didn't I?" Peter said.

"Well—yes, you carried on some."

"It seemed like something snapped inside of me," Peter explained. "Something like a suspender strap. It made me all come apart. I'm all right, now, though."

Ed looked down at the floor and saw a little brown spider crawling, and stretched out his foot and stomped it.

Peter asked suddenly, "Do you believe in an after-life?"

Ed Chappell squirmed. He didn't like to talk about such things, for to talk about them was to bring them up in his mind and think about them. "Well, yes. I suppose if you come right down to it, I do."

"Do you believe that somebody that's—passed on—can look down and see what we're doing?"

"Oh, I don't know as I'd go that far—I don't know."

Peter went on as though he were talking to himself. "Even if she could see me, and I didn't do what she wanted, she ought to feel good because I did it when she was here. It ought to please her that she made a good man of me. If I wasn't a good man when she wasn't here, that'd prove she did it all, wouldn't it? I was a good man, wasn't I, Ed?"

"What do you mean, 'was'?"

"Well, except for one week a year I was good. I don't know what I'll do now. . . ." His face grew angry. "Except one thing." He stood up and stripped off his coat and his shirt. Over his underwear there was a web harness that pulled his shoulders back. He unhooked the harness and threw it off. Then he dropped his trousers, disclosing a wide elastic belt. He shucked this off over his feet, and then he scratched his stomach luxuriously before he put on his clothes again. He smiled at Ed, the strange, wondering smile, again. "I don't know how she got me to do things, but she did. She didn't seem to boss me, but she always made me do things. You know, I don't think I believe in an after-life. When she was alive, even when she was sick, I had to do things she wanted, but just the minute she died, it was—why like that harness coming off! I couldn't stand it. It was all over. I'm going to have to get used to going without that harness." He shook his finger in Ed's direction. "My stomach's going to stick out," he said positively. "I'm going to let it stick out. Why, I'm fifty years old."

Ed didn't like that. He wanted to get away. This sort of thing wasn't very decent. "If you'll just take one of these, you'll get some sleep," he said weakly.

Peter had not put his coat on. He was sitting on the sofa in an open shirt. "I don't want to sleep. I want to talk. I guess I'll have to put that belt and harness on for the funeral, but after that I'm going to burn them. Listen, I've got a bottle of whiskey in the barn. I'll go get it."

"Oh no," Ed protested quickly. "I couldn't drink now, not at a time like this."

Peter stood up. "Well, I could. You can sit and watch me if you want. I tell you, it's all over." He went out the door, leaving Ed Chappell unhappy and scandalized. It was only a moment before he was back. He started talking as he came through the doorway with the whiskey. "I only got one thing in my life, those trips. Emma was a pretty bright woman. She knew I'd've gone crazy if I didn't get away once a year. God, how she worked on my conscience when I came back!" His voice lowered confidentially. "You know what I did on those trips?"

Ed's eyes were wide open now. Here was a man he didn't know, and he was becoming fascinated. He took the glass of whiskey when it was handed to him. "No, what did you do?"

Peter gulped his drink and coughed, and wiped his mouth with his hand. "I got drunk," he said. "I went to fancy houses in San Francisco. I was drunk for a week, and I went to a fancy house every night." He poured his glass full again. "I guess Emma knew, but she never said anything. I'd've *busted* if I hadn't got away."

Ed Chappell sipped his whiskey gingerly. "She always said you went on business."

Peter looked at his glass and drank it, and poured it full again. His eyes had begun to shine. "Drink your drink, Ed. I know you think it isn't right—so soon, but no one'll know but you and me. Kick up the fire. I'm not sad."

Chappell went to the grate and stirred the glowing wood until lots of sparks flew up the chimney like little shining birds. Peter filled the glasses and retired to the sofa again. When Ed went back to the chair he sipped from his glass and pretended he didn't know it was filled up. His cheeks were flushing. It didn't seem so terrible, now, to be drinking. The afternoon and the death had receded into an indefinite past.

"Want some cake?" Peter asked. "There's half a dozen cakes in the pantry."

"No, I don't think I will thank you for some."

"You know," Peter confessed, "I don't think I'll eat cake again. For ten years, every time Emma was sick, people sent cakes. It was nice of 'em, of course, only now cake means sickness to me. Drink your drink."

Something happened in the room. Both men looked up, trying to discover what it was. The room was somehow different than it had been a moment before. Then Peter smiled sheepishly. "It was that mantel clock stopped. I don't think I'll start it any more. I'll get a little quick alarm clock that ticks fast. That clack-clack-clack is too mournful." He swallowed his whiskey. "I guess you'll be telling around that I'm crazy, won't you?"

Ed looked up from his glass, and smiled and nodded. "No, I will not. I can see pretty much how you feel about things. I didn't know you wore that harness and belt."

"A man ought to stand up straight," Peter said. "I'm a natural sloucher." Then he exploded: "I'm a natural fool! For twenty years I've been pretending I was a wise, good man—except for that one week a year." He said loudly, "Things have been dribbled to me. My life's been dribbled out to me. Here, let me fill your glass. I've got another bottle out in the barn, way down under a pile of sacks."

Ed held out his glass to be filled. Peter went on, "I thought how it would be nice to have my whole river flat in sweet peas. Think how it'd be to sit on the front porch and see all those acres of blue and pink, just solid. And when the wind came up over them, think of the big smell. A big smell that would almost knock you over."

"A lot of men have gone broke on sweet peas. 'Course you get a big price for the seed, but too many things can happen to your crop."

"I don't give a damn," Peter shouted. "I want a lot of everything. I want forty acres of color and smell. I want fat women, with breasts as big as pillows. I'm hungry, I tell you, I'm hungry for everything, for a lot of everything."

Ed's face became grave under the shouting. "If you'd just take one of these, you'd get some sleep."

Peter looked ashamed. "I'm all right. I didn't mean to yell like that. I'm not just thinking these things for the first time. I been thinking about them for years, the way a kid thinks of vacation. I was always afraid I'd be too old. Or that I'd go first and miss everything. But I'm only fifty, I've got plenty of vinegar left. I told Emma about the sweet peas, but she wouldn't let me. I don't know how she made me do things," he said wonderingly. "I can't remember. She had a way of doing it. But she's gone. I can feel she's gone just like that harness is gone. I'm going to slouch, Ed—slouch all over the place. I'm going to track dirt into the house. I'm going to get a big fat housekeeper—a big fat one from San Francisco. I'm going to have a bottle of brandy on the shelf all the time."

Ed Chappell stood up and stretched his arms over his head. "I guess I'll go home now, if you feel all right. I got to get some sleep. You better wind that clock, Peter. It don't do a clock any good to stand not running."

The day after the funeral Peter Randall went to work on his farm. The Chappells, who lived on the next place, saw the lamp in his kitchen long before daylight, and they saw his lantern cross the yard to the barn half an hour before they even got up.

Peter pruned his orchard in three days. He worked from first light until he couldn't see the twigs against the sky any more. Then he started to shape the big piece of river flat. He plowed and rolled and harrowed. Two strange men dressed in boots and riding breeches came out and looked at his land. They felt the dirt with their fingers and ran a post-hole digger deep down under the surface, and when they went away they took little paper bags of the dirt with them.

Ordinarily, before planting time, the farmers did a good deal of visiting back and forth. They sat on their haunches, picking up handsful of dirt and breaking little clods between their fingers. They discussed markets and crops, recalled other years when beans had done well in a good market, and other years when field peas didn't bring enough to pay for the seed hardly. After a great number of these discussions it usually happened that all the farmers planted the same things. There were certain men whose ideas carried weight. If Peter Randall or Clark DeWitt thought they would put in pink beans and barley, most of the crops would turn out to be pink beans and barley that year; for, since such men were respected and fairly successful, it was conceded that their plans must be based on something besides chance choice. It was generally believed but never stated that Peter Randall and Clark DeWitt had extra reasoning powers and special prophetic knowledge.

When the usual visits started, it was seen that a change had taken place in Peter Randall. He sat on his plow and talked pleasantly enough. He said he hadn't decided yet what to plant, but he said it in such a guilty way that it was plain he didn't intend to tell. When he had rebuffed a few inquiries, the visits to his place stopped and the farmers went over in a body to Clark DeWitt. Clark was putting in Chevalier barley. His decision dictated the major part of the planting in the vicinity.

But because the questions stopped, the interest did not. Men driving by the forty-five acre flat of the Randall place studied the field to try to figure out from the type of work what the crop was going to be. When Peter drove the seeder back and forth across the land no one came in, for Peter had made it plain that his crop was a secret.

Ed Chappell didn't tell on him, either. Ed was a little ashamed when he thought of that night; ashamed of Peter for breaking down, and ashamed of himself for having sat there and listened. He watched Peter narrowly to see whether his vicious intentions were really there or whether the whole conversation had been the result of loss and hysteria. He did notice that Peter's shoulders weren't back and that his stomach stuck out a little. He went to Peter's house and was relieved when he saw no dirt on the floor and when he heard the mantel clock ticking away.

Mrs. Chappell spoke often of the afternoon. "You'd've thought he lost his mind the way he carried on. He just howled. Ed stayed with him part of the night, until he quieted down. Ed had to give him some whiskey to get him to sleep. But," she said brightly, "hard work is the thing to kill sorrow. Peter Randall is getting up at three o'clock every morning. I can see the light in his kitchen window from my bedroom."

The pussywillows burst out in silver drops, and the little weeds sprouted up along the roadside. The Salinas River ran dark water, flowed for a month, and then subsided into green pools again. Peter Randall had shaped his land beautifully. It was smooth and black; no clod was larger than a small marble, and under the rains it looked purple with richness.

And then the little weak lines of green stretched out across the black field. In the dusk a neighbor crawled under the fence and pulled one of the tiny plants. "Some kind of legume," he told his friends. "Field peas, I guess. What did he want to be so quiet about it for? I asked him right out what he was planting, and he wouldn't tell me."

The word ran through the farms, "It's sweet peas. The whole God-damn' forty-five acres is in sweet peas!" Men called on Clark DeWitt then, to get his opinion.

His opinion was this: "People think because you can get twenty to sixty cents a pound for sweet peas you can get rich on them. But it's the most ticklish crop in the world. If the bugs don't get it, it might do good. And then come a hot day and bust the pods and lose your crop on the ground. Or it might come up a little rain and spoil the whole kaboodle. It's all right to put in a few acres and take a chance, but not the whole place. Peter's touched in the head since Emma died."

This opinion was widely distributed. Every man used it as his own. Two neighbors often said it to each other, each one repeating half of it. When too many people said it to Peter Randall he became angry. One day he cried, "Say, whose land is this? If I want to go broke, I've got a damn good right to, haven't I?" And that changed the whole feeling. Men remembered that Peter was a good farmer. Perhaps he had special knowledge. Why, that's who those two men in boots were—soil chemists! A good many of the farmers wished they'd put in a few acres of sweet peas.

They wished it particularly when the vines spread out, when they met each other across the rows and hid the dark earth from sight, when the buds began to form and it was seen the crop was rich. And then the blooms came; forty-five acres of color, forty-five acres of perfume. It was said that you could smell them in Salinas, four miles away. Busses brought the school children out to look at them. A group of men from a seed company spent all day looking at the vines and feeling the earth.

Peter Randall sat on his porch in a rocking-chair every afternoon. He looked down on the great squares of pink and blue, and on the mad square of mixed colors. When the afternoon breeze came up, he inhaled deeply. His blue shirt was open at the throat, as though he wanted to get the perfume down next to his skin.

Men called on Clark DeWitt to get his opinion now. He said, "There's about ten things that can happen to spoil that crop. He's welcome to his sweet peas." But the men knew from Clark's irritation that he was a little jealous. They looked up over the fields of color to where Peter sat on his porch, and they felt a new admiration and respect for him.

Ed Chappell walked up the steps to him one afternoon. "You got a crop there, mister."

"Looks that way," said Peter.

"I took a look. Pods are setting fine."

Peter sighed. "Blooming's nearly over," he said. "I'll hate to see the petals drop off."

"Well, I'd be glad to see 'em drop. You'll make a lot of money, if nothing happens."

Peter took out a bandana handkerchief and wiped his nose, and jiggled it sideways to stop an itch. "I'll be sorry when the smell stops," he said.

Then Ed made his reference to the night of the death. One of his eyes drooped secretly. "Found somebody to keep house for you?"

"I haven't looked," said Peter. "I haven't had time." There were lines of worry about his eyes. But who wouldn't worry, Ed thought, when a single shower could ruin his whole year's crop.

If the year and the weather had been manufactured for sweet peas, they couldn't have been better. The fog lay close to the ground in the mornings when the vines were pulled. When the great piles of vines lay safely on spread canvasses, the hot sun shone down and crisped the pods for the threshers. The neighbors watched the long cotton sacks filling with round black seeds, and they went home and tried to figure out how much money

Peter would make on his tremendous crop. Clark De-Witt lost a good part of his following. The men decided to find out what Peter was going to plant next year if they had to follow him around. How did he know, for instance, that this year'd be good for sweet peas? He *must* have some kind of special knowledge.

When a man from the upper Salinas Valley goes to San Francisco on business trips or for a vacation, he takes a room in the Ramona Hotel. This is a nice arrangement, for in the lobby he can usually find someone from home. They can sit in the soft chairs of the lobby and talk about the Salinas Valley.

Ed Chappell went to San Francisco to meet his wife's cousin who was coming out from Ohio for a trip. The train was not due until the next morning. In the lobby of the Ramona, Ed looked for someone from the Salinas Valley, but he could see only strangers sitting in the soft chairs. He went out to a moving picture show. When he returned, he looked again for someone from home, and still there were only strangers. For a moment he considered glancing over the register, but it was quite late. He sat down to finish his cigar before he went to bed.

There was a commotion at the door. Ed saw the clerk motion with his hand. A bellhop ran out. Ed squirmed around in his chair to look. Outside a man was being helped out of a taxicab. The bellhop took him from the driver and guided him in the door. It was Peter Randall. His eyes were glassy, and his mouth open and wet. He had no hat on his mussed hair. Ed jumped up and strode over to him.

"Peter!"

Peter was batting helplessly at the bellhop. "Let me alone," he explained. "I'm all right. You let me alone, and I'll give you two bits."

Ed called again, "Peter!"

The glassy eyes turned slowly to him, and then Peter fell into his arms. "My old friend," he cried. "Ed Chappell, my old, good friend. What you doing here? Come up to my room and have a drink."

Ed set him back on his feet. "Sure I will," he said. "I'd like a little night-cap."

"Night-cap, hell. We'll go out and see a show, or something."

Ed helped him into the elevator and got him to his room. Peter dropped heavily to the bed and struggled up to a sitting position. "There's a bottle of whiskey in the bathroom. Bring me a drink, too."

Ed brought out the bottle and glasses. "What you doing, Peter, celebrating the crop? You must've made a pile of money."

Peter put out his palm and tapped it impressively with a forefinger. "Sure I made money—but it wasn't a bit better than gambling. It was just like straight gambling."

"But you got the money."

Peter scowled thoughtfully. "I might've lost my pants," he said. "The whole time, all the year, I been worrying. It was just like gambling."

"Well, you got it, anyway."

Peter changed the subject, then. "I been sick," he said. "I been sick right in the taxicab. I just came from a fancy house on Van Ness Avenue," he explained apologetically, "I just had to come up to the city. I'd'a busted if I hadn't come up and got some of the vinegar out of my system."

Ed looked at him curiously. Peter's head was hanging loosely between his shoulders. His beard was draggled and rough. "Peter—" Ed began, "the night Emma—passed on, you said you was going to—change things."

Peter's swaying head rose up slowly. He stared owlishly at Ed Chappell. "She didn't die dead," he said thickly. "She won't let me do things. She's worried me all year about those peas." His eyes were wondering. "I don't know how she does it." Then he frowned. His palm came out, and he tapped it again. "But you mark, Ed Chappell, I won't wear that harness, and I damn well won't ever wear it. You remember that." His head dropped forward again. But in a moment he looked up. "I been drunk," he said seriously. "I been to fancy houses." He edged out confidentially toward Ed. His voice dropped to a heavy whisper. "But it's all right, I'll fix it. When I get back, you know what I'm going to do? I'm going to put in electric lights. Emma always wanted electric lights." He sagged sideways on the bed.

Ed Chappell stretched Peter out and undressed him before he went to his own room.

THE VIGILANTE

THE VIGILANTE

The great surge of emotion, the milling and shouting of the people fell gradually to silence in the town park. A crowd of people still stood under the elm trees, vaguely lighted by a blue street light two blocks away. A tired quiet settled on the people; some members of the mob began to sneak away into the darkness. The park lawn was cut to pieces by the feet of the crowd.

Mike knew it was all over. He could feel the letdown in himself. He was as heavily weary as though he had gone without sleep for several nights, but it was a dream-like weariness, a grey comfortable weariness. He pulled his cap down over his eyes and moved away, but before leaving the park he turned for one last look.

In the center of the mob someone had lighted a twisted newspaper and was holding it up. Mike could see how the flame curled about the feet of the grey naked body hanging from the elm tree. It seemed curious to him that negroes turn a bluish grey when they are dead. The burning newspaper lighted the heads of the up-looking men, silent men and fixed; they didn't move their eyes from the hanged man.

Mike felt a little irritation at whoever it was who was trying to burn the body. He turned to a man who stood beside him in the near-darkness. "That don't do no good," he said.

The man moved away without replying.

The newspaper torch went out, leaving the park almost black by contrast. But immediately another twisted paper was lighted and held up against the feet. Mike moved to another watching man. "That don't do no good," he repeated. "He's dead now. They can't hurt him none."

The second man grunted but did not look away from the flaming paper. "It's a good job," he said. "This'll save the county a lot of money and no sneaky lawyers getting in."

"That's what I say," Mike agreed. "No sneaky lawyers. But it don't do no good to try to burn him."

The man continued staring toward the flame. "Well, it can't do much harm, either."

Mike filled his eyes with the scene. He felt that he was dull. He wasn't seeing enough of it. Here was a thing he would want to remember later so he could tell about it, but the dull tiredness seemed to cut the sharpness off the picture. His brain told him this was a terrible and important affair, but his eyes and his feelings didn't agree. It was just ordinary. Half an hour before, when he had been howling with the mob and fighting for a chance to help pull on the rope, then his chest had been so full that he had found he was crying. But now everything was dead, everything unreal;

the dark mob was made up of stiff lay-figures. In the flamelight the faces were as expressionless as wood. Mike felt the stiffness, the unreality in himself, too. He turned away at last and walked out of the park.

The moment he left the outskirts of the mob a cold loneliness fell upon him. He walked quickly along the street wishing that some other man might be walking beside him. The wide street was deserted, empty, as unreal as the park had been. The two steel lines of the car tracks stretched glimmering away down the street under the electroliers, and the dark store windows reflected the midnight globes.

A gentle pain began to make itself felt in Mike's chest. He felt with his fingers; the muscles were sore. Then he remembered. He was in the front line of the mob when it rushed the closed jail door. A driving line forty men deep had crushed Mike against the door like the head of a ram. He had hardly felt it then, and even now the pain seemed to have the dull quality of loneliness.

Two blocks ahead the burning neon word BEER hung over the sidewalk. Mike hurried toward it. He hoped there would be people there, and talk, to remove this silence; and he hoped the men wouldn't have been to the lynching.

The bartender was alone in his little bar, a small, middle-aged man with a melancholy moustache and an expression like an aged mouse, wise and unkempt and fearful.

He nodded quickly as Mike came in. "You look like you been walking in your sleep," he said.

Mike regarded him with wonder. "That's just how I feel, too, like I been walking in my sleep."

"Well, I can give you a shot if you want."

Mike hesitated. "No—I'm kind of thirsty. I'll take a beer. . . . Was you there?"

The little man nodded his mouse-like head again. "Right at the last, after he was all up and it was all over. I figured a lot of the fellas would be thirsty, so I came back and opened up. Nobody but you so far. Maybe I was wrong."

"They might be along later," said Mike. "There's a lot of them still in the park. They cooled off, though. Some of them trying to burn him with newspapers. That don't do no good."

"Not a bit of good," said the little bartender. He twitched his thin moustache.

Mike knocked a few grains of celery salt into his beer and took a long drink. "That's good," he said. "I'm kind of dragged out."

The bartender leaned close to him over the bar, his eyes were bright. "Was you there all the time—to the jail and everything?"

Mike drank again and then looked through his beer and watched the beads of bubbles rising from the grains of salt in the bottom of the glass. "Everything," he said. "I was one of the first in the jail, and I helped pull on the rope. There's times when citizens got to take the law in their own hands. Sneaky lawyer comes along and gets some fiend out of it."

The mousy head jerked up and down. "You God-dam' right," he said. "Lawyers can get them out of anything. I guess the nigger was guilty all right."

"Oh, sure! Somebody said he even confessed."

The head came close over the bar again. "How did it

start, mister? I was only there after it was all over, and then I only stayed a minute and then came back to open up in case any of the fellas might want a glass of beer."

Mike drained his glass and pushed it out to be filled. "Well, of course everybody knew it was going to happen. I was in a bar across from the jail. Been there all afternoon. A guy came in and says, 'What are we waiting for?' So we went across the street, and a lot more guys was there and a lot more come. We all stood there and yelled. Then the sheriff come out and made a speech, but we yelled him down. A guy with a twenty-two rifle went along the street and shot out the street lights. Well, then we rushed the jail doors and bust them. The sheriff wasn't going to do nothing. It wouldn't do him no good to shoot a lot of honest men to save a nigger fiend."

"And election coming on, too," the bartender put in.

"Well, the sheriff started yelling, 'Get the right man, boys, for Christ's sake get the right man. He's in the fourth cell down.'

"It was kind of pitiful," Mike said slowly. "The other prisoners were so scared. We could see them through the bars. I never seen such faces."

The bartender excitedly poured himself a small glass of whiskey and poured it down. "Can't blame 'em much. Suppose you was in for thirty days and a lynch mob came through. You'd be scared they'd get the wrong man."

"That's what I say. It was kind of pitiful. Well, we got to the nigger's cell. He just stood stiff with his eyes closed like he was dead drunk. One of the guys slugged him down and he got up, and then somebody else socked him and he went over and hit his head on the cement floor." Mike leaned over the bar and tapped the polished wood with his forefinger. " 'Course this is only my idea, but I think that killed him. Because I helped get his clothes off, and he never made a wiggle, and when we strung him up he didn't jerk around none. No, sir. I think he was dead all the time, after that second guy smacked him."

"Well, it's all the same in the end."

"No, it ain't. You like to do the thing right. He had it coming to him, and he should have got it." Mike reached into his trousers pocket and brought out a piece of torn blue denim. "That's a piece of the pants he had on."

The bartender bent close and inspected the cloth. He jerked his head up at Mike. "I'll give you a buck for it."

"Oh no, you won't!"

"All right. I'll give you two bucks for half of it."

Mike looked suspiciously at him. "What you want it for?"

"Here! Give me your glass! Have a beer on me. I'll pin it up on the wall with a little card under it. The fellas that come in will like to look at it."

Mike haggled the piece of cloth in two with his pocket knife and accepted two silver dollars from the bartender.

"I know a show card writer," the little man said. "Comes in every day. He'll print me up a nice little card to go under it." He looked wary. "Think the sheriff will arrest anybody?"

" 'Course not. What's he want to start any trouble for? There was a lot of votes in that crowd tonight.

Soon as they all go away, the sheriff will come and cut the nigger down and clean up some."

The bartender looked toward the door. "I guess I was wrong about the fellas wanting a drink. It's getting late."

"I guess I'll get along home. I feel tired."

"If you go south, I'll close up and walk a ways with you. I live on south Eighth."

"Why, that's only two blocks from my house. I live on south Sixth. You must go right past my house. Funny I never saw you around."

The bartender washed Mike's glass and took off the long apron. He put on his hat and coat, walked to the door and switched off the red neon sign and the house lights. For a moment the two men stood on the sidewalk looking back toward the park. The city was silent. There was no sound from the park. A policeman walked along a block away, turning his flash into the store windows.

"You see?" said Mike. "Just like nothing happened."

"Well, if the fellas wanted a glass of beer they must have gone someplace else."

"That's what I told you," said Mike.

They swung along the empty street and turned south, out of the business district. "My name's Welch," the bartender said. "I only been in this town about two years."

The loneliness had fallen on Mike again. "It's funny—" he said, and then, "I was born right in this town, right in the house I live in now. I got a wife but no kids. Both of us born right in this town. Everybody knows us."

They walked on for a few blocks. The stores dropped behind and the nice houses with bushy gardens and cut lawns lined the street. The tall shade trees were shadowed on the sidewalk by the street lights. Two night dogs went slowly by, smelling at each other.

Welch said softly—"I wonder what kind of a fella he was—the nigger, I mean."

Mike answered out of his loneliness. "The papers all said he was a fiend. I read all the papers. That's what they all said."

"Yes, I read them, too. But it makes you wonder about him. I've known some pretty nice niggers."

Mike turned his head and spoke protestingly. "Well, I've knew some dam' fine niggers myself. I've worked right 'longside some niggers and they was as nice as any white man you could want to meet. —But not no fiends."

His vehemence silenced little Welch for a moment. Then he said, "You couldn't tell, I guess, what kind of a fella he was?"

"No—he just stood there stiff, with his mouth shut and his eyes tight closed and his hands right down at his sides. And then one of the guys smacked him. It's my idea he was dead when we took him out."

Welch sidled close on the walk. "Nice gardens along here. Must take a lot of money to keep them up." He walked even closer, so that his shoulder touched Mike's arm. "I never been to a lynching. How's it make you feel—afterwards?"

Mike shied away from the contact. "It don't make you feel nothing." He put down his head and increased his pace. The little bartender had nearly to trot to keep up. The street lights were fewer. It was darker and safer. Mike burst out, "Makes you feel kind of cut off and tired, but kind of satisfied, too.

Like you done a good job—but tired and kind of sleepy." He slowed his steps. "Look, there's a light in the kitchen. That's where I live. My old lady's waiting up for me." He stopped in front of his little house.

Welch stood nervously beside him. "Come into my place when you want a glass of beer—or a shot. Open till midnight. I treat my friends right." He scampered away like an aged mouse.

Mike called, "Good night."

He walked around the side of his house and went in the back door. His thin, petulant wife was sitting by the open gas oven warming herself. She turned complaining eyes on Mike where he stood in the doorway.

Then her eyes widened and hung on his face. "You been with a woman," she said hoarsely. "What woman you been with?"

Mike laughed. "You think you're pretty slick, don't you? You're a slick one, ain't you? What makes you think I been with a woman?"

She said fiercely, "You think I can't tell by the look on your face that you been with a woman?"

"All right," said Mike. "If you're so slick and know-it-all, I won't tell you nothing. You can just wait for the morning paper."

He saw doubt come into the dissatisfied eyes. "Was it the nigger?" she asked. "Did they get the nigger? Everybody said they was going to."

"Find out for yourself if you're so slick. I ain't going to tell you nothing."

He walked through the kitchen and went into the bathroom. A little mirror hung on the wall. Mike took off his cap and looked at his face. "By God, she was right," he thought. "That's just exactly how I do feel."

Like you done it. And those [illegible]
[illegible]
[illegible]
up for her [illegible]
Well, she'd [illegible] nervously [illegible]
place when you [illegible]
[illegible]
[illegible]
She called, 'Good night.'
He [illegible] moved [illegible]
[illegible]
[illegible]
[illegible]
Then he [illegible]
[illegible] with a woman [illegible]
[illegible]
[illegible] 'you're really sure [illegible]
[illegible]
that I been [illegible]
[illegible]
[illegible]
[illegible]
[illegible] the [illegible]
[illegible] money?'
He saw [illegible]
[illegible]
[illegible]
[illegible]
[illegible] you [illegible]
He [illegible]
[illegible]
[illegible]
[illegible]

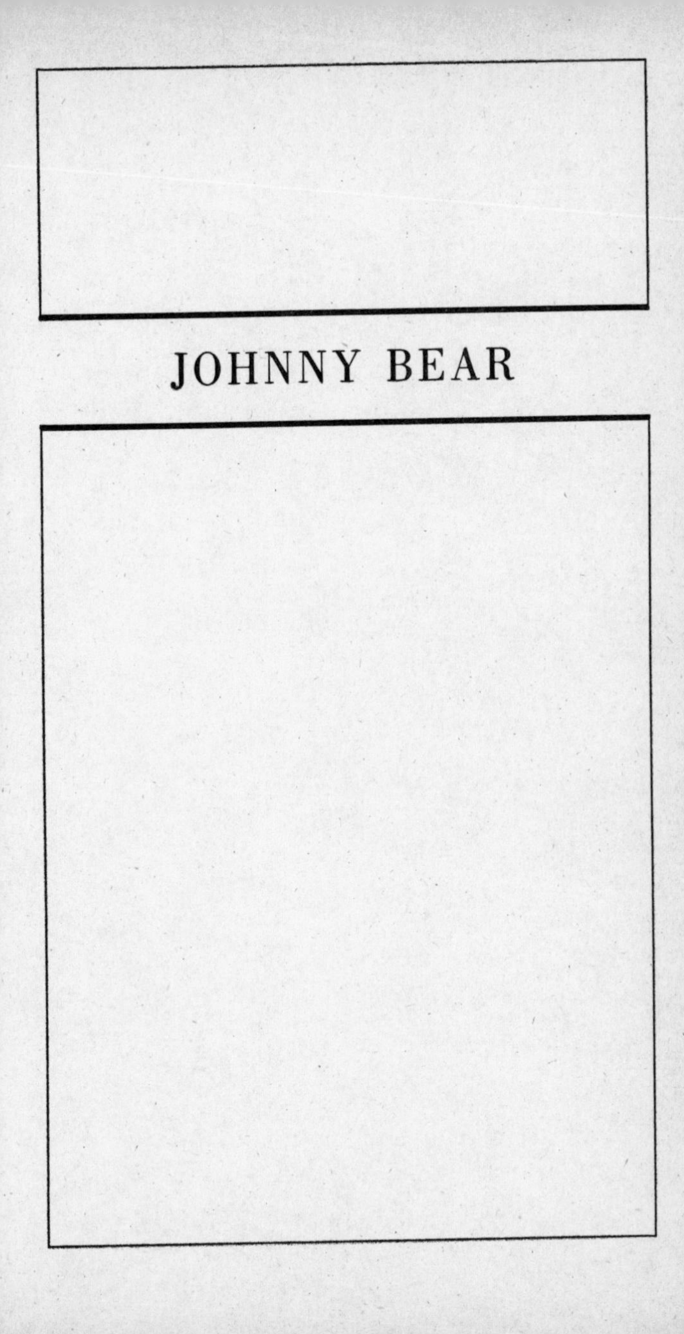

JOHNNY BEAR

JOHNNY BEAR

The village of Loma is built, as its name implies, on a low round hill that rises like an island out of the flat mouth of the Salinas Valley in central California. To the north and east of the town a black tule swamp stretches for miles, but to the south the marsh has been drained. Rich vegetable land has been the result of the draining, land so black with wealth that the lettuce and cauliflowers grow to giants.

The owners of the swamp to the north of the village began to covet the black land. They banded together and formed a reclamation district. I work for the company which took the contract to put a ditch through. The floating clam-shell digger arrived, was put together and started eating a ditch of open water through the swamp.

I tried living in the floating bunkhouse with the crew for a while, but the mosquitoes that hung in banks over the dredger and the heavy pestilential mist that sneaked out of the swamp every night and slid near to the ground drove me into the village of Loma, where I took a furnished room, the most dismal I have ever seen, in the house of Mrs. Ratz. I might have looked farther, but the idea of having my mail come in care of Mrs. Ratz decided me. After all, I only slept in the bare cold room. I ate my meals in the galley of the floating bunkhouse.

There aren't more than two hundred people in Loma. The Methodist church has the highest place on the hill; its spire is visible for miles. Two groceries, a hardware store, an ancient Masonic Hall and the Buffalo Bar comprise the public buildings. On the side of the hills are the small wooden houses of the population, and on the rich southern flats are the houses of the landowners, small yards usually enclosed by high walls of clipped cypress to keep out the driving afternoon winds.

There was nothing to do in Loma in the evening except to go to the saloon, an old board building with swinging doors and a wooden sidewalk awning. Neither prohibition nor repeal had changed its business, its clientele, or the quality of its whiskey. In the course of an evening every male inhabitant of Loma over fifteen years old came at least once to the Buffalo Bar, had a drink, talked a while and went home.

Fat Carl, the owner and bartender, greeted every newcomer with a phlegmatic sullenness which nevertheless inspired familiarity and affection. His face was sour, his tone downright unfriendly, and yet—I don't know how he did it. I know I felt gratified and warm when Fat Carl knew me well enough to turn his sour pig face to me and say with some impatience, "Well, what's it going to be?" He always asked that although he served only whiskey, and only one kind of whiskey. I have seen him flatly refuse to squeeze some lemon juice in it for a stranger. Fat Carl didn't like fumadiddles. He wore a big towel tied about his middle and he polished the glasses on it as he moved about. The floor was bare wood sprinkled with sawdust, the bar an old store counter, the chairs were hard and straight; the only decorations were the posters and cards and pictures stuck to the wall by candidates for county elections, salesmen and auctioneers. Some of these were many years old. The card of Sheriff Rittal still begged for re-election although Rittal had been dead for seven years.

The Buffalo Bar sounds, even to me, like a terrible place, but when you walked down the night street, over the wooden sidewalks, when the long streamers of swamp fog, like waving, dirty bunting, flapped in your face, when finally you pushed open the swinging doors of Fat Carl's and saw men sitting around talking and drinking, and Fat Carl coming along toward you, it seemed pretty nice. You couldn't get away from it.

There would be a game of the mildest kind of poker going on. Timothy Ratz, the husband of my landlady, would be playing solitaire, cheating pretty badly because he took a drink only when he got it out. I've seen him get it out five times in a row. When he won he piled the cards neatly, stood up and walked with great dignity to the bar. Fat Carl, with a glass half filled before he arrived, asked, "What'll it be?"

"Whiskey," said Timothy gravely.

In the long room, men from the farms and the town sat in the straight hard chairs or stood against the old counter. A soft, monotonous rattle of conversation went on except at times of elections or big prize fights, when there might be orations or loud opinions.

I hated to go out into the damp night, and to hear far off in the swamp the chuttering of the Diesel engine on the dredger and the clang of the bucket, and then to go to my own dismal room at Mrs. Ratz'.

Soon after my arrival in Loma I scraped an acquaintance with Mae Romero, a pretty half-Mexican girl. Sometimes in the evenings I walked with her down the south side of the hill, until the nasty fog drove us back into town. After I escorted her home I dropped in at the bar for a while.

I was sitting in the bar one night talking to Alex Hartnell, who owned a nice little farm. We were talking about black bass fishing, when the front doors opened and swung closed. A hush fell on the men in the room. Alex nudged me and said, "It's Johnny Bear." I looked around.

His name described him better than I can. He looked like a great, stupid, smiling bear. His black matted head bobbed forward and his long arms hung out as though he should have been on all fours and was only standing upright as a trick. His legs were short and bowed, ending with strange, square feet. He was dressed in dark blue denim, but his feet were bare; they didn't seem to be crippled or deformed in any way, but they were square, just as wide as they were long. He stood in the doorway, swinging his arms jerkily the way half-wits do. On his face there was a foolish happy smile. He moved forward and for all his bulk and clumsiness, he seemed to creep. He didn't move like a man, but like some prowling night animal. At the bar he stopped, his little bright eyes went about from face to face expectantly, and he asked, "Whiskey?"

Loma was not a treating town. A man might buy a

drink for another if he were pretty sure the other would immediately buy one for him. I was surprised when one of the quiet men laid a coin on the counter. Fat Carl filled the glass. The monster took it and gulped the whiskey.

"What the devil——" I began. But Alex nudged me and said, "Sh."

There began a curious pantomime. Johnny Bear moved to the door and then he came creeping back. The foolish smile never left his face. In the middle of the room he crouched down on his stomach. A voice came from his throat, a voice that seemed familiar to me.

"But you are too beautiful to live in a dirty little town like this."

The voice rose to a soft throaty tone, with just a trace of accent in his words. "You just tell me that."

I'm sure I nearly fainted. The blood pounded in my ears. I flushed. It was my voice coming out of the throat of Johnny Bear, my words, my intonation. And then it was the voice of Mae Romero—exact. If I had not seen the crouching man on the floor I would have called to her. The dialogue went on. Such things sound silly when someone else says them. Johnny Bear went right on, or rather I should say I went right on. He said things and made sounds. Gradually the faces of the men turned from Johnny Bear, turned toward me, and they grinned at me. I could do nothing. I knew that if I tried to stop him I would have a fight on my hands, and so the scene went on, to a finish. When it was over I was cravenly glad Mae Romero had no brothers. What obvious, forced, ridiculous words had come from Johnny Bear. Finally he stood up, still smiling the foolish smile, and he asked again, "Whiskey?"

I think the men in the bar were sorry for me. They looked away from me and talked elaborately to one another. Johnny Bear went to the back of the room, crawled under a round card table, curled up like a dog and went to sleep.

Alex Hartnell was regarding me with compassion. "First time you ever heard him?"

"Yes, what in hell is he?"

Alex ignored my question for a moment. "If you're worrying about Mae's reputation, don't. Johnny Bear has followed Mae before."

"But how did he hear us? I didn't see him."

"No one sees or hears Johnny Bear when he's on business. He can move like no movement at all. Know what our young men do when they go out with girls? They take a dog along. Dogs are afraid of Johnny and they can smell him coming."

"But good God! Those voices——"

Alex nodded. "I know. Some of us wrote up to the university about Johnny, and a young man came down. He took a look and then he told us about Blind Tom. Ever hear of Blind Tom?"

"You mean the negro piano player? Yes, I've heard of him."

"Well, Blind Tom was a half-wit. He could hardly talk, but he could imitate anything he heard on the piano, long pieces. They tried him with fine musicians and he reproduced not only the music but every little personal emphasis. To catch him they made little mistakes, and he played the mistakes. He photographed the playing in the tiniest detail. The man says Johnny

Bear is the same, only he can photograph words and voices. He tested Johnny with a long passage in Greek and Johnny did it exactly. He doesn't know the words he's saying, he just says them. He hasn't brains enough to make anything up, so you know that what he says is what he heard."

"But why does he do it? Why is he interested in listening if he doesn't understand?"

Alex rolled a cigarette and lighted it. "He isn't, but he loves whiskey. He knows if he listens in windows and comes here and repeats what he hears, someone will give him whiskey. He tries to palm off Mrs. Ratz' conversation in the store, or Jerry Noland arguing with his mother, but he can't get whiskey for such things."

I said, "It's funny somebody hasn't shot him while he was peeking in windows."

Alex picked at his cigarette. "Lots of people have tried, but you just don't see Johnny Bear, and you don't catch him. You keep your windows closed, and even then you talk in a whisper if you don't want to be repeated. You were lucky it was dark tonight. If he had seen you, he might have gone through the action too. You should see Johnny Bear screw up his face to look like a young girl. It's pretty awful."

I looked toward the sprawled figure under the table. Johnny Bear's back was turned to the room. The light fell on his black matted hair. I saw a big fly land on his head, and then I swear I saw the whole scalp shiver the way the skin of a horse shivers under flies. The fly landed again and the moving scalp shook it off. I shuddered too, all over.

Conversation in the room had settled to the bored monotone again. Fat Carl had been polishing a glass on his apron towel for the last ten minutes. A little group of men near me was discussing fighting dogs and fighting cocks, and they switched gradually to bullfighting.

Alex, beside me, said, "Come have a drink."

We walked to the counter. Fat Carl put out two glasses. "What'll it be?"

Neither of us answered. Carl poured out the brown whiskey. He looked sullenly at me and one of his thick, meaty eyelids winked at me solemnly. I don't know why, but I felt flattered. Carl's head twitched back toward the card table. "Got you, didn't he?"

I winked back at him. "Take a dog next time." I imitated his clipped sentences. We drank our whiskey and went back to our chairs. Timothy Ratz won a game of solitaire and piled his cards and moved up on the bar.

I looked back at the table under which Johnny Bear lay. He had rolled over on his stomach. His foolish, smiling face looked out at the room. His head moved and he peered all about, like an animal about to leave its den. And then he came sliding out and stood up. There was a paradox about his movement. He looked twisted and shapeless, and yet he moved with complete lack of effort.

Johnny Bear crept up the room toward the bar, smiling about at the men he passed. In front of the bar his insistent question arose. "Whiskey? Whiskey?" It was like a bird call. I don't know what kind of bird, but I've heard it—two notes on a rising scale, asking a question over and over, "Whiskey? Whiskey?"

The conversation in the room stopped, but no one came forward to lay money on the counter. Johnny smiled plaintively. "Whiskey?"

Then he tried to cozen them. Out of his throat an angry woman's voice issued. "I tell you it was all bone. Twenty cents a pound, and half bone." And then a man, "Yes, ma'am. I didn't know it. I'll give you some sausage to make it up."

Johnny Bear looked around expectantly. "Whiskey?" Still none of the men offered to come forward. Johnny crept to the front of the room and crouched. I whispered, "What's he doing?"

Alex said, "Sh. Looking through a window. Listen!"

A woman's voice came, a cold, sure voice, the words clipped. "I can't quite understand it. Are you some kind of monster? I wouldn't have believed it if I hadn't seen you."

Another woman's voice answered her, a voice low and hoarse with misery. "Maybe I am a monster. I can't help it. I can't help it."

"You *must* help it," the cold voice broke in. "Why you'd be better dead."

I heard a soft sobbing coming from the thick smiling lips of Johnny Bear. The sobbing of a woman in hopelessness. I looked around at Alex. He was sitting stiffly, his eyes wide open and unblinking. I opened my mouth to whisper a question, but he waved me silent. I glanced about the room. All the men were stiff and listening. The sobbing stopped. "Haven't you ever felt that way, Emalin?"

Alex caught his breath sharply at the name. The cold voice announced, "Certainly not."

"Never in the night? Not ever—ever in your life?"

"If I had," the cold voice said, "if ever I had, I would cut that part of me away. Now stop your whining, Amy. I won't stand for it. If you don't get control of your nerves I'll see about having some medical treatment for you. Now go to your prayers."

Johnny Bear smiled on. "Whiskey?"

Two men advanced without a word and put down coins. Fat Carl filled two glasses and, when Johnny Bear tossed off one after the other, Carl filled one again. Everyone knew by that how moved he was. There were no drinks on the house at the Buffalo Bar. Johnny Bear smiled about the room and then he went out with that creeping gait of his. The doors folded together after him, slowly without a sound.

Conversation did not spring up again. Everyone in the room seemed to have a problem to settle in his own mind. One by one they drifted out and the back-swing of the doors brought in little puffs of tule fog. Alex got up and walked out and I followed him.

The night was nasty with the evil-smelling fog. It seemed to cling to the buildings and to reach out with free arms into the air. I doubled my pace and caught up with Alex. "What was it?" I demanded. "What was it all about?"

For a moment I thought he wouldn't answer. But then he stopped and turned to me. "Oh, damn it. Listen! Every town has its aristocrats, its family above reproach. Emalin and Amy Hawkins are our aristocrats, maiden ladies, kind people. Their father was a congressman. I don't like this. Johnny Bear shouldn't do it. Why! they feed him. Those men shouldn't give him whiskey. He'll haunt that house now. . . . Now he knows he can get whiskey for it."

I asked, "Are they relatives of yours?"

"No, but they're—why, they aren't like other people. They have the farm next to mine. Some Chinese farm it on shares. You see, it's hard to explain. The Hawkins women, they're symbols. They're what we tell our kids when we want to—well, to describe good people."

"Well," I protested, "Nothing Johnny Bear said would hurt them, would it?"

"I don't know. I don't know what it means. I mean, I kind of know. Oh! Go on to bed. I didn't bring the Ford. I'm going to walk out home." He turned and hurried into that slow squirming mist.

I walked along to Mrs. Ratz' boarding house. I could hear the chuttering of the Diesel engine off in the swamp and the clang of the big steel mouth that ate its way through the ground. It was Saturday night. The dredger would stop at seven Sunday morning and rest until midnight Sunday. I could tell by the sound that everything was all right. I climbed the narrow stairs to my room. Once in bed I left the light burning for a while and stared at the pale insipid flowers on the wallpaper. I thought of those two voices speaking out of Johnny Bear's mouth. They were authentic voices, not reproductions. Remembering the tones, I could see the women who had spoken, the chill-voiced Emalin, and the loose, misery-broken face of Amy. I wondered what caused the misery. Was it just the lonely suffering of a middle-aged woman? It hardly seemed so to me, for there was too much fear in the voice. I went to sleep with the light on and had to get up later and turn it off.

About eight the next morning I walked down across the swamp to the dredger. The crew was busy bending some new wire to the drums and coiling the worn cable for removal. I looked over the job and at about eleven o'clock walked back to Loma. In front of Mrs. Ratz' boarding house Alex Hartnell sat in a model T Ford touring car. He called to me, "I was just going to the dredger to get you. I knocked off a couple of chickens this morning. Thought you might like to come out and help with them."

I accepted joyfully. Our cook was a good cook, a big pasty man; but lately I had found a dislike for him arising in me. He smoked Cuban cigarettes in a bamboo holder. I didn't like the way his fingers twitched in the morning. His hands were clean—floury like a miller's hands. I never knew before why they called them moth millers, those little flying bugs. Anyway I climbed into the Ford beside Alex and we drove down the hill to the rich land of the southwest. The sun shone brilliantly on the black earth. When I was little, a Catholic boy told me that the sun always shone on Sunday, if only for a moment, because it was God's day. I always meant to keep track to see if it were true. We rattled down to the level plain.

Alex shouted, "Remember about the Hawkinses?"

"Of course I remember."

He pointed ahead. "That's the house."

Little of the house could be seen, for a high thick hedge of cypress surrounded it. There must be a small garden inside the square too. Only the roof and the tops of the windows showed over the hedge. I could see that the house was painted tan, trimmed with dark brown, a combination favored for railroad stations and schools in California. There were two wicket gates in the front and side of the hedge. The barn was outside the green barrier to the rear of the house. The hedge was clipped square. It looked incredibly thick and strong.

"The hedge keeps the wind out," Alex shouted above the roar of the Ford.

"It doesn't keep Johnny Bear out," I said.

A shadow crossed his face. He waved at a white-washed square building standing out in the field. "That's where the Chink share-croppers live. Good workers. I wish I had some like them."

At that moment from behind the corner of the hedge a horse and buggy appeared and turned into the road. The grey horse was old but well groomed, the buggy shiny and the harness polished. There was a big silver H on the outside of each blinder. It seemed to me that the check-rein was too short for such an old horse

Alex cried, "There they are now, on their way to church."

We took off our hats and bowed to the women as they went by, and they nodded formally to us. I had a good look at them. It was a shock to me. They looked almost exactly as I thought they would. Johnny Bear was more monstrous even than I had known, if by the tone of voice he could describe the features of his people. I didn't have to ask which was Emalin and which was Amy. The clear straight eyes, the sharp sure chin, the mouth cut with the precision of a diamond, the stiff, curveless figure, that was Emalin. Amy was very like her, but so unlike. Her edges were soft. Her eyes were warm, her mouth full. There was a swell to her breast, and yet she did look like Emalin. But whereas Emalin's mouth was straight by nature, Amy *held* her mouth straight. Emalin must have been fifty or fifty-five and Amy about ten years younger. I had only a moment to look at them, and I never saw them again. It seems strange that I don't know anyone in the world better than those two women.

Alex was shouting, "You see what I meant about aristocrats?"

I nodded. It was easy to see. A community would feel kind of—safe, having women like that about. A place like Loma with its fogs, with its great swamp like a hideous sin, needed, really needed, the Hawkins women. A few years there might do things to a man's mind if those women weren't there to balance matters.

It was a good dinner. Alex's sister fried the chicken in butter and did everything else right. I grew more suspicious and uncharitable toward our cook. We sat around in the dining-room and drank really good brandy.

I said, "I can't see why you ever go into the Buffalo. That whiskey is——"

"I know," said Alex. "But the Buffalo is the mind of Loma. It's our newspaper, our theatre and our club."

This was so true that when Alex started the Ford and prepared to take me back I knew, and he knew, we would go for an hour or two to the Buffalo Bar.

We were nearly into town. The feeble lights of the car splashed about on the road. Another car rattled toward us. Alex swung across the road and stopped. "It's the doctor, Doctor Holmes," he explained. The oncoming car pulled up because it couldn't get around us. Alex called, "Say, Doc, I was going to ask you to take a look at my sister. She's got a swelling on her throat."

Doctor Holmes called back, "All right, Alex, I'll take a look. Pull out, will you? I'm in a hurry."

Alex was deliberate. "Who's sick, Doc?"

"Why, Miss Amy had a little spell. Miss Emalin phoned in and asked me to hurry. Get out of the way, will you?"

Alex squawked his car back and let the doctor by. We drove on. I was about to remark that the night was clear when, looking ahead, I saw the rags of fog creeping around the hill from the swamp side and climbing like slow snakes on the top of Loma. The Ford shuddered to a stop in front of the Buffalo. We went in.

Fat Carl moved toward us, wiping a glass on his apron. He reached under the bar for the nearby bottle. "What'll it be?"

"Whiskey."

For a moment a faint smile seemed to flit over the fat sullen face. The room was full. My dredger crew was there, all except the cook. He was probably on the scow, smoking his Cuban cigarettes in a bamboo holder. He didn't drink. That was enough to make me suspicious of him. Two deck hands and an engineer and three levermen were there. The levermen were arguing about a cutting. The old lumber adage certainly held for them: "Women in the woods and logging in the honky-tonk."

That was the quietest bar I ever saw. There weren't any fights, not much singing and no tricks. Somehow the sullen baleful eyes of Fat Carl made drinking a quiet, efficient business rather than a noisy game. Timothy Ratz was playing solitaire at one of the round tables. Alex and I drank our whiskey. No chairs were available, so we just stayed leaning against the bar, talking about sports and markets and adventures we had had or pretended we had—just a casual barroom conversation. Now and then we bought another drink.

I guess we hung around for a couple of hours. Alex had already said he was going home, and I felt like it. The dredger crew trooped out, for they had to start work at midnight.

The doors unfolded silently, and Johnny Bear crept into the room, swinging his long arms, nodding his big hairy head and smiling foolishly about. His square feet were like cats' feet.

"Whiskey?" he chirruped. No one encouraged him. He got out his wares. He was down on his stomach the way he had been when he got to me. Sing-song nasal words came out, Chinese I thought. And then it seemed to me that the same words were repeated in another voice, slower and not nasally. Johnny Bear raised his shaggy head and asked, "Whiskey?" He got to his feet with effortless ease. I was interested. I wanted to see him perform. I slid a quarter along the bar. Johnny gulped his drink. A moment later I wished I hadn't. I was afraid to look at Alex, for Johnny Bear crept to the middle of the room and took that window pose of his.

The chill voice of Emalin said, "She's in here, doctor." I closed my eyes against the looks of Johnny Bear, and the moment I did he went out. It was Emalin Hawkins who had spoken.

I had heard the doctor's voice in the road, and it was his veritable voice that replied, "Ah—you said a fainting fit?"

"Yes, doctor."

There was a little pause, and then the doctor's voice again, very softly, "Why did she do it, Emalin?"

"Why did she do what?" There was almost a threat in the question.

"I'm your doctor, Emalin. I was your father's doctor. You've got to tell me things. Don't you think I've seen that kind of a mark on the neck before? How long was she hanging before you got her down?"

There was a longer pause then. The chill left the woman's voice. It was soft, almost a whisper. "Two or three minutes. Will she be all right, doctor?"

"Oh, yes, she'll come around. She's not badly hurt. Why did she do it?"

The answering voice was even colder than it had been at first. It was frozen. "I don't know, sir."

"You mean you won't tell me?"

"I mean what I say."

Then the doctor's voice went on giving directions for treatment, rest, milk and a little whiskey. "Above all, be gentle," he said. "Above everything, be gentle with her."

Emalin's voice trembled a little. "You would never—tell, doctor?"

"I'm your doctor," he said softly. "Of course I won't tell. I'll send down some sedatives tonight."

"Whiskey?" My eyes jerked open. There was the horrible Johnny Bear smiling around the room.

The men were silent, ashamed. Fat Carl looked at the floor. I turned apologetically to Alex, for I was really responsible. "I didn't know he'd do that," I said. "I'm sorry."

I walked out the door and went to the dismal room at Mrs. Ratz'. I opened the window and looked out into that coiling, pulsing fog. Far off in the marsh I heard the Diesel engine start slowly and warm up. And after a while I heard the clang of the big bucket as it went to work on the ditch.

The next morning one of those series of accidents so common in construction landed on us. One of the new wires parted on the in-swing and dropped the bucket on one of the pontoons, sinking it and the works in eight feet of ditch water. When we sunk a dead man and got a line out to it to pull us from the water, the line parted and clipped the legs neatly off one of the deck hands. We bound the stumps and rushed him to Salinas. And then little accidents happened. A lever-man developed blood poisoning from a wire scratch. The cook finally justified my opinion by trying to sell a little can of marijuana to the engineer. Altogether there wasn't much peace in the outfit. It was two weeks before we were going again with a new pontoon, a new deck hand and a new cook.

The new cook was a sly, dark, little long-nosed man, with a gift for subtle flattery.

My contact with the social life of Loma had gone to pot, but when the bucket was clanging into the mud again and the big old Diesel was chuttering away in the swamp I walked out to Alex Hartnell's farm one night. Passing the Hawkins place, I peered in through one of the little wicket gates in the cypress hedge. The house was dark, more than dark because a low light glowed in one window. There was a gentle wind that night, blowing balls of fog like tumbleweeds along the ground. I walked in the clear a moment, and then was swallowed in a thick mist, and then was in the clear again. In the starlight I could see those big silver fog balls moving like elementals across the fields. I thought I heard a soft moaning in the Hawkins yard behind the hedge, and once when I came suddenly out of the fog I saw a dark figure hurrying along in the field, and I knew from the dragging footsteps that it was one of the Chinese field hands walking in sandals. The Chinese eat a great many things that have to be caught at night.

Alex came to the door when I knocked. He seemed glad to see me. His sister was away. I sat down by his stove and he brought out a bottle of that nice brandy. "I heard you were having some trouble," he said.

I explained the difficulty. "It seems to come in series. The men have it figured out that accidents come in groups of three, five, seven and nine."

Alex nodded. "I kind of feel that way myself."

"How are the Hawkins sisters?" I asked. "I thought I heard someone crying as I went by."

Alex seemed reluctant to talk about them, and at the same time eager to talk about them. "I stopped over about a week ago. Miss Amy isn't feeling very well. I didn't see her. I only saw Miss Emalin." Then Alex broke out, "There's something hanging over those people, something——"

"You almost seem to be related to them," I said.

"Well, their father and my father were friends. We called the girls Aunt Amy and Aunt Emalin. They can't do anything bad. It wouldn't be good for any of us if the Hawkins sisters weren't the Hawkins sisters."

"The community conscience?" I asked.

"The safe thing," he cried. "The place where a kid can get gingerbread. The place where a girl can get reassurance. They're proud, but they believe in things we hope are true. And they live as though—well, as though honesty really is the best policy and charity really is its own reward. We need them."

"I see."

"But Miss Emalin is fighting something terrible and—I don't think she's going to win."

"What do you mean?"

"I don't know what I mean. But I've thought I should shoot Johnny Bear and throw him in the swamp. I've really thought about doing it."

"It's not his fault," I argued. "He's just a kind of recording and reproducing device, only you use a glass of whiskey instead of a nickel."

We talked of some other things then, and after a while I walked back to Loma. It seemed to me that that fog was clinging to the cypress hedge of the Hawkins house, and it seemed to me that a lot of the fog balls were slowly moving in. I smiled as I walked along at the way a man's thought can rearrange nature to fit his thoughts. There was no light in the house as I went by.

A nice steady routine settled on my work. The big bucket cut out the ditch ahead of it. The crew felt the trouble was over too, and that helped, and the new cook flattered the men so successfully that they would have eaten fried cement. The personality of a cook has a lot more to with the happiness of a dredger crew than his cooking has.

In the evening of the second day after my visit to Alex I walked down the wooden sidewalk trailing a streamer of fog behind me and went into the Buffalo Bar. Fat Carl moved toward me polishing a whiskey glass. I cried, "Whiskey," before he had a chance to ask what it would be. I took my glass and went to one of the straight chairs. Alex was not there. Timothy Ratz was playing solitaire and having a phenomenal run of luck. He got it out four times in a row and had a drink each time. More and more men arrived. I don't know what we would have done without the Buffalo Bar.

At about ten o'clock the news came. Thinking about such things afterwards, you never can remember quite what transpired. Someone comes in; a whisper starts; suddenly everyone knows what has happened, knows details. Miss Amy had committed suicide. Who brought in the story? I don't know. She had hanged herself. There wasn't much talk in the barroom about it. I could see the men were trying to get straight on it. It was a thing that didn't fit into their schemes. They stood in groups, talking softly.

The swinging doors opened slowly and Johnny Bear crept in, his great hairy head rolling, and that idiot smile on his face. His square feet slid quietly over the floor. He looked about and chirruped, "Whiskey? Whiskey for Johnny?"

Now those men really wanted to know. They were ashamed of wanting to know, but their whole mental system required the knowledge. Fat Carl poured out a drink. Timothy Ratz put down his cards and stood up. Johnny Bear gulped the whiskey. I closed my eyes.

The doctor's tone was harsh. "Where is she, Emalin?"

I've never heard a voice like that one that answered, cold control, layer and layer of control, but cold penetrated by the most awful heartbreak. It was a monotonous tone, emotionless, and yet the heartbreak got into the vibrations. "She's in here, doctor."

"H-m-m." A long pause. "She was hanging a long time."

"I don't know how long, doctor."

"Why did she do it, Emalin?"

The monotone again. "I don't—know, doctor."

A longer pause, and then, "H-m-m. Emalin, did you know she was going to have a baby?"

The chill voice cracked and a sigh came through. "Yes, doctor," very softly.

"If that was why you didn't find her for so long—— No, Emalin, I didn't mean that, poor dear."

The control was back in Emalin's voice. "Can you make out the certificate without mentioning——"

"Of course I can, sure I can. And I'll speak to the undertaker, too. You needn't worry."

"Thank you, doctor."

"I'll go and telephone now. I won't leave you here alone. Come into the other room, Emalin. I'm going to fix you a sedative. . . ."

"Whiskey? Whiskey for Johnny?" I saw the smile and the rolling hairy head. Fat Carl poured out another glass. Johnny Bear drank it and then crept to the back of the room and crawled under a table and went to sleep.

No one spoke. The men moved up to the bar and laid down their coins silently. They looked bewildered, for a system had fallen. A few minutes later Alex came into the silent room. He walked quickly over to me. "You've heard?" he asked softly.

"Yes."

"I've been afraid," he cried. "I told you a couple of nights ago. I've been afraid."

I said, "Did you know she was pregnant?"

Alex stiffened. He looked around the room and then back at me. "Johnny Bear?" he asked.

I nodded.

Alex ran his palm over his eyes. "I don't believe it." I was about to answer when I heard a little scuffle and looked to the back of the room. Johnny Bear crawled like a badger out of his hole and stood up and crept toward the bar.

"Whiskey?" He smiled expectantly at Fat Carl.

Then Alex stepped out and addressed the room. "Now you guys listen! This has gone far enough. I don't want any more of it." If he had expected opposition he was disappointed. I saw the men nodding to one another.

"Whiskey for Johnny?"

Alex turned on the idiot. "You ought to be ashamed. Miss Amy gave you food, and she gave you all the clothes you ever had."

Johnny smiled at him. "Whiskey?"

He got out his tricks. I heard the sing-song nasal language that sounded like Chinese. Alex looked relieved.

And then the other voice, slow, hesitant, repeating the words without nasal quality.

Alex sprang so quickly that I didn't see him move. His fist splatted into Johnny Bear's smiling mouth. "I told you there was enough of it," he shouted.

Johnny Bear recovered his balance. His lips were split and bleeding, but the smile was still there. He moved slowly and without effort. His arms enfolded Alex as the tentacles of an anemone enfold a crab. Alex bent backward. Then I jumped and grabbed one of the arms and wrenched at it, and could not tear it loose. Fat Carl came rolling over the counter with a bung-starter in his hand. And he beat the matted head until the arms relaxed and Johnny Bear crumpled. I caught Alex and helped him to a chair. "Are you hurt?"

He tried to get his breath. "My back's wrenched, I guess," he said. "I'll be all right."

"Got your Ford outside? I'll drive you home."

Neither of us looked at the Hawkins place as we went by. I didn't lift my eyes off the road. I got Alex to his own dark house and helped him to bed and poured a hot brandy into him. He hadn't spoken all the way home. But after he was propped in the bed he demanded, "You don't think anyone noticed, do you? I caught him in time, didn't I?"

"What are you talking about? I don't know yet why you hit him."

"Well, listen," he said. "I'll have to stay close for a little while with this back. If you hear anyone say anything, you stop it, won't you? Don't let them say it."

"I don't know what you're talking about."

He looked into my eyes for a moment. "I guess I can trust you," he said. "That second voice—that was Miss Amy."

THE MURDER

THE MURDER

This happened a number of years ago in Monterey County, in central California. The Cañon del Castillo is one of those valleys in the Santa Lucia range which lie between its many spurs and ridges. From the main Cañon del Castillo a number of little arroyos cut back into the mountains, oak-wooded canyons, heavily brushed with poison oak and sage. At the head of the canyon there stands a tremendous stone castle, buttressed and towered like those strongholds the Crusaders put up in the path of their conquests. Only a close visit to the castle shows it to be a strange accident of time and water and erosion working on soft, stratified sandstone. In the distance the ruined battlements, the gates, the towers, even the arrow slits, require little imagination to make out.

Below the castle, on the nearly level floor of the canyon, stand the old ranch house, a weathered and mossy barn and a warped feeding-shed for cattle. The house is deserted; the doors, swinging on rusted hinges, squeal and bang on nights when the wind courses down from the castle. Not many people visit the house. Sometimes a crowd of boys tramp through the rooms, peering into empty closets and loudly defying the ghosts they deny.

Jim Moore, who owns the land, does not like to have people about the house. He rides up from his new house, farther down the valley, and chases the boys away. He has put "No Trespassing" signs on his fences to keep curious and morbid people out. Sometimes he thinks of burning the old house down, but then a strange and powerful relation with the swinging doors, the blind and desolate windows, forbids the destruction. If he should burn the house he would destroy a great and important piece of his life. He knows that when he goes to town with his plump and still pretty wife, people turn and look at his retreating back with awe and some admiration.

Jim Moore was born in the old house and grew up in it. He knew every grained and weathered board of the barn, every smooth, worn manger-rack. His mother and father were both dead when he was thirty. He celebrated his majority by raising a beard. He sold the pigs and decided never to have any more. At last he brought a fine Guernsey bull to improve his stock, and he began to go to Monterey on Saturday nights, to get drunk and to talk with the noisy girls of the Three Star.

Within a year Jim Moore married Jelka Sepic, a Jugo-Slav girl, daughter of a heavy and patient farmer of Pine Canyon. Jim was not proud of her foreign family, of her many brothers and sisters and cousins, but he delighted in her beauty. Jelka had eyes as large and questioning as a doe's eyes. Her nose was thin and sharply faceted, and her lips were deep and soft. Jelka's skin always startled Jim, for between night and night he forgot how beautiful it was. She was so smooth and quiet and gentle, such a good housekeeper, that Jim often thought with disgust of her father's advice on the wedding day. The old man, bleary and bloated with festival beer, elbowed Jim in the ribs and grinned suggestively, so that his little dark eyes almost disappeared behind puffed and wrinkled lids.

"Don't be big fool, now," he said. "Jelka is Slav girl. He's not like American girl. If he is bad, beat him. If he's good too long, beat him too. I beat his mama. Papa beat my mama. Slav girl! He's not like a man that don't beat hell out of him."

"I wouldn't beat Jelka," Jim said.

The father giggled and nudged him again with his elbow. "Don't be big fool," he warned. "Sometime you see." He rolled back to the beer barrel.

Jim found soon enough that Jelka was not like American girls. She was very quiet. She never spoke at first, but only answered his questions, and then with soft short replies. She learned her husband as she learned passages of Scripture. After they had been married a while, Jim never wanted for any habitual thing in the house but Jelka had it ready for him before he could ask. She was a fine wife, but there was no companionship in her. She never talked. Her great eyes followed him, and when he smiled, sometimes she smiled too, a distant and covered smile. Her knitting and mending and sewing were interminable. There she sat, watching her wise hands, and she seemed to regard with wonder and pride the little white hands that could do such nice and useful things. She was so much like an animal that sometimes Jim patted her head and neck under the same impulse that made him stroke a horse.

In the house Jelka was remarkable. No matter what time Jim came in from the hot dry range or from the bottom farm land, his dinner was exactly, steamingly ready for him. She watched while he ate, and pushed the dishes close when he needed them, and filled his cup when it was empty.

Early in the marriage he told her things that happened on the farm, but she smiled at him as a foreigner does who wishes to be agreeable even though he doesn't understand.

"The stallion cut himself on the barbed wire," he said.

And she replied, "Yes," with a downward inflection that held neither question nor interest.

He realized before long that he could not get in touch with her in any way. If she had a life apart, it was so remote as to be beyond his reach. The barrier in her eyes was not one that could be removed, for it was neither hostile nor intentional.

At night he stroked her straight black hair and her unbelievably smooth golden shoulders, and she whimpered a little with pleasure. Only in the climax of embrace did she seem to have a life apart, fierce and passionate. And then immediately she lapsed into the alert and painfully dutiful wife.

"Why don't you ever talk to me?" he demanded. "Don't you want to talk to me?"

"Yes," she said. "What do you want me to say?"

She spoke the language of his race out of a mind that was foreign to his race.

When a year had passed, Jim began to crave the company of women, the chattery exchange of small talk, the shrill pleasant insults, the shame-sharpened vulgarity. He began to go again to town, to drink and play with the noisy girls of the Three Star. They liked him there for his firm, controlled face and for his readiness to laugh.

"Where's your wife?" they demanded.

"Home in the barn," he responded. It was a never-failing joke.

Saturday afternoons he saddled a horse and put a rifle in the scabbard in case he should see a deer. Always he asked, "You don't mind staying alone?"

"No. I don't mind."

At once he asked, "Suppose someone should come?"

Her eyes sharpened for a moment, and then she smiled. "I would send them away," she said.

"I'll be back about noon tomorrow. It's too far to ride in the night." He felt that she knew where he was going, but she never protested nor gave any sign of disapproval. "You should have a baby," he said.

Her face lighted up. "Some time God will be good," she said eagerly.

He was sorry for her loneliness. If only she visited with the other women of the canyon she would be less lonely, but she had no gift for visiting. Once every month or so she put horses to the buckboard and went to spend an afternoon with her mother, and with the brood of brothers and sisters and cousins who lived in her father's house.

"A fine time you'll have," Jim said to her. "You'll gabble your crazy language like ducks for a whole afternoon. You'll giggle with that big grown cousin of yours with the embarrassed face. If I could find any fault with you, I'd call you a damn foreigner." He remembered how she blessed the bread with the sign of the cross before she put it in the oven, how she knelt at the bedside every night, how she had a holy picture tacked to the wall in the closet.

One Saturday of a hot dusty June, Jim cut oats in the farm flat. The day was long. It was after six o'clock when the mower tumbled the last band of oats. He drove the clanking machine up into the barnyard and backed it into the implement shed, and there he unhitched the horses and turned them out to graze on the hills over Sunday. When he entered the kitchen Jelka was just putting his dinner on the table. He washed his hands and face and sat down to eat.

"I'm tired," he said, "but I think I'll go to Monterey anyway. There'll be a full moon."

Her soft eyes smiled.

"I'll tell you what I'll do," he said. "If you would like to go, I'll hitch up a rig and take you with me."

She smiled again and shook her head. "No, the stores would be closed. I would rather stay here."

"Well, all right, I'll saddle the horse then. I didn't think I was going. The stock's all turned out. Maybe I can catch a horse easy. Sure you don't want to go?"

"If it was early, and I could go to the stores—but it will be ten o'clock when you get there."

"Oh, no—well, anyway, on horseback I'll make it a little after nine."

Her mouth smiled to itself, but her eyes watched

him for the development of a wish. Perhaps because he was tired from the long day's work, he demanded, "What are you thinking about?"

"Thinking about? I remember, you used to ask that nearly every day when we were first married."

"But what are you?" he insisted irritably.

"Oh—I'm thinking about the eggs under the black hen." She got up and went to the big calendar on the wall. "They will hatch tomorrow or maybe Monday."

It was almost dusk when he had finished shaving and putting on his blue serge suit and his new boots. Jelka had the dishes washed and put away. As Jim went through the kitchen he saw that she had taken the lamp to the table near the window, and that she sat beside it knitting a brown wool sock.

"Why do you sit there tonight?" he asked. "You always sit over here. You do funny things sometimes."

Her eyes arose slowly from her flying hands. "The moon," she said quietly. "You said it would be full tonight. I want to see the moon rise."

"But you're silly. You can't see it from that window. I thought you knew direction better than that."

She smiled remotely. "I will look out of the bedroom window, then."

Jim put on his black hat and went out. Walking through the dark empty barn, he took a halter from the rack. On the grassy sidehill he whistled high and shrill. The horses stopped feeding and moved slowly in towards him, and stopped twenty feet away. Carefully he approached his bay gelding and moved his hand from its rump along its side and up over its neck. The halter-strap clicked in its buckle. Jim turned and led the horse back to the barn. He threw his saddle on and cinched it tight, put his silver-bound bridle over the stiff ears, buckled the throat latch, knotted the tie-rope about the gelding's neck and fastened the neat coil-end to the saddle string. Then he slipped the halter and led the horse to the house. A radiant crown of soft red light lay over the eastern hills. The full moon would rise before the valley had completely lost daylight.

In the kitchen Jelka still knitted by the window. Jim strode to the corner of the room and took up his 30-30 carbine. As he rammed cartridges into the magazine, he said, "The moon glow is on the hills. If you are going to see it rise, you better go outside now. It's going to be a good red one at rising."

"In a moment," she replied, "when I come to the end here." He went to her and patted her sleek head.

"Good night. I'll probably be back by noon tomorrow." Her dusky black eyes followed him out of the door.

Jim thrust the rifle into his saddle-scabbard, and mounted and swung his horse down the canyon. On his right, from behind the blackening hills, the great red moon slid rapidly up. The double light of the day's last afterglow and the rising moon thickened the outlines of the trees and gave a mysterious new perspective to the hills. The dusty oaks shimmered and glowed, and the shade under them was black as velvet. A huge, long-legged shadow of a horse and half a man rode to the left and slightly ahead of Jim. From the ranches near and distant came the sound of dogs tuning up for a night of song. And the roosters crowed, thinking a new dawn had come too quickly. Jim lifted the gelding to a trot. The spattering hoof-steps echoed back from the castle behind him. He thought of blond May at the Three Star in Monterey. "I'll be late. Maybe someone else'll have her," he thought. The moon was clear of the hills now.

Jim had gone a mile when he heard the hoofbeats of a horse coming towards him. A horseman cantered up and pulled to a stop. "That you, Jim?"

"Yes. Oh, hello, George."

"I was just riding up to your place. I want to tell you—you know the springhead at the upper end of my land?"

"Yes, I know."

"Well, I was up there this afternoon. I found a dead campfire and a calf's head and feet. The skin was in the fire, half burned, but I pulled it out and it had your brand."

"The hell," said Jim. "How old was the fire?"

"The ground was still warm in the ashes. Last night, I guess. Look, Jim, I can't go up with you. I've got to go to town, but I thought I'd tell you, so you could take a look around."

Jim asked quietly, "Any idea how many men?"

"No. I didn't look close."

"Well, I guess I better go up and look. I was going to town too. But if there are thieves working, I don't want to lose any more stock. I'll cut up through your land if you don't mind, George."

"I'd go with you, but I've got to go to town. You got a gun with you?"

"Oh yes, sure. Here under my leg. Thanks for telling me."

"That's all right. Cut through any place you want. Good night." The neighbour turned his horse and cantered back in the direction from which he had come.

For a few moments Jim sat in the moonlight, looking down at his stilted shadow. He pulled his rifle from its scabbard, levered a cartridge into the chamber, and held the gun across the pommel of his saddle. He turned left from the road, went up the little ridge, through the oak grove, over the grassy hogback and down the other side into the next canyon.

In half an hour he had found the deserted camp. He turned over the heavy, leathery calf's head and felt its dusty tongue to judge by the dryness how long it had been dead. He lighted a match and looked at his brand on the half-burned hide. At last he mounted his horse again, rode over the bald grassy hills and crossed into his own land.

A warm summer wind was blowing on the hilltops. The moon, as it quartered up the sky, lost its redness and turned the colour of strong tea. Among the hills the coyotes were singing, and the dogs at the ranch houses below joined them with broken-hearted howling. The dark green oaks below and the yellow summer grass showed their colours in the moonlight.

Jim followed the sound of the cowbells to his herd, and found them eating quietly, and a few deer feeding with them. He listened for the sound of hoofbeats or the voices of men on the wind.

It was after eleven when he turned his horse towards home. He rounded the west tower of the sandstone castle, rode through the shadow and out into the moonlight again. Below, the roofs of his barn and house shone dully. The bedroom window cast back a streak of reflection.

The feeding horses lifted their heads as Jim came down through the pasture. Their eyes glinted redly when they turned their heads.

Jim had almost reached the corral fence—he heard a horse stamping in the barn. His hand jerked the gelding down. He listened. It came again, the stamping from the barn. Jim lifted his rifle and dismounted silently. He turned his horse loose and crept towards the barn.

In the blackness he could hear the grinding of the horse's teeth as it chewed hay. He moved along the barn until he came to the occupied stall. After a moment of listening he scratched a match on the butt of his rifle. A saddled and bridled horse was tied in the stall. The bit was slipped under the chin and the cinch loosened. The horse stopped eating and turned its head towards the light.

Jim blew out the match and walked quickly out of the barn. He sat on the edge of the horse trough and looked into the water. His thoughts came so slowly that he put them into words and said them under his breath.

"Shall I look through the window? No. My head would throw a shadow in the room."

He regarded the rifle in his hand. Where it had been rubbed and handled, the black gun finish had worn off, leaving the metal silvery.

At last he stood up with decision and moved towards the house. At the steps, an extended foot tried each board tenderly before putting his weight on it. The three ranch dogs came out from under the house and shook themselves, stretched and sniffed, wagged their tails and went back to bed.

The kitchen was dark, but Jim knew where every piece of furniture was. He put out his hand and touched the corner of the table, a chair back, the towel hanger, as he went along. He crossed the room so silently that even he could hear only his breath and the whisper of his trouser legs together, and the beating of his watch in his pocket. The bedroom door stood open and spilled a patch of moonlight on the kitchen floor. Jim reached the door at last and peered through.

The moonlight lay on the white bed. Jim saw Jelka lying on her back, one soft bare arm flung across her forehead and eyes. He could not see who the man was, for his head was turned away. Jim watched, holding his breath. Then Jelka twitched in her sleep and the man rolled his head and sighed—Jelka's cousin, her grown, embarrassed cousin.

Jim turned and quickly stole back across the kitchen and down the back steps. He walked up the yard to the water-trough again, and sat down on the edge of it. The moon was white as chalk, and it swam in the water, and lighted the straws and barley dropped by the horses' mouths. Jim could see the mosquito wigglers, tumbling up and down, end over end, in the water, and he could see a newt lying in the sun moss in the bottom of the trough.

He cried a few dry, hard, smothered sobs, and wondered why, for his thought was of the grassed hill-tops and of the lonely summer wind whisking along.

His thought turned to the way his mother used to hold a bucket to catch the throat blood when his father killed a pig. She stood as far away as possible and held the bucket at arms'-length to keep her clothes from getting spattered.

Jim dipped his hand into the trough and stirred the moon to broken, swirling streams of light. He wetted his forehead with his damp hands and stood up. This time he did not move so quietly, but he crossed the kitchen on tiptoe and stood in the bedroom door. Jelka moved her arm and opened her eyes a little. Then the eyes sprang wide, then they glistened with moisture. Jim looked into her eyes; his face was empty of expression. A little drop ran out of Jelka's nose and lodged in the hollow of her upper lip. She stared back at him.

Jim cocked the rifle. The steel click sounded through the house. The man on the bed stirred uneasily in his sleep. Jim's hands were quivering. He raised the gun to his shoulder and held it tightly to keep from shaking. Over the sights he saw the little white square between the man's brows and hair. The front sight wavered a moment and then came to rest.

The gun crash tore the air. Jim, still looking down the barrel, saw the whole bed jolt under the blow. A small, black, bloodless hole was in the man's forehead. But behind, the hollow-point took brain and bone and splashed them on the pillow.

Jelka's cousin gurgled in his throat. His hands came crawling out from under the covers like big white spiders, and they walked for a moment, then shuddered and fell quiet.

Jim looked slowly back at Jelka. Her nose was running. Her eyes had moved from him to the end of the rifle. She whined softly, like a cold puppy.

Jim turned in panic. His boot heels beat on the kitchen floor, but outside, he moved slowly towards the water-trough again. There was the taste of salt in his throat, and his heart heaved painfully. He pulled his hat off and dipped his head into the water. Then he leaned over and vomited on the ground. In the house he could hear Jelka moving about. She whimpered like a puppy. Jim straightened up, weak and dizzy.

He walked tiredly through the corral and into the pasture. His saddled horse came at his whistle. Automatically he tightened the cinch, mounted and rode away, down the road to the valley. The squat black shadow traveled under him. The moon sailed high and white. The uneasy dogs barked monotonously.

At daybreak a buckboard and pair trotted up to the ranch yard, scattering the chickens. A deputy sheriff and a coroner sat in the seat. Jim Moore half reclined against his saddle in the wagon-box. His tired gelding followed behind. The deputy sheriff set the brake and wrapped the lines around it. The men dismounted.

Jim asked, "Do I have to go in? I'm too tired and wrought up to see it now."

The coroner pulled his lip and studied. "Oh, I guess not. We'll tend to things and look around."

Jim sauntered away towards the water-trough. "Say," he called, "kind of clean up a little, will you? You know."

The men went into the house.

In a few minutes they emerged, carrying the stiffened body between them. It was wrapped up in a comforter. They eased it up into the wagon-box. Jim walked back towards them. "Do I have to go with you now?"

"Where's your wife, Mr. Moore?" the deputy sheriff demanded.

"I don't know," he said wearily. "She's somewhere around."

"You're sure you didn't kill her too?"

"No. I didn't touch her. I'll find her and bring her in this afternoon. That is, if you don't want me to go in with you now."

"We've got your statement," the coroner said. "And by God, we've got eyes, haven't we, Will? Of course there's a technical charge of murder against you, but it'll be dismissed. Always is in this part of the country. Go kind of light on your wife, Mr. Moore."

"I won't hurt her," said Jim.

He stood and watched the buckboard jolt away. He kicked his feet reluctantly in the dust. The hot June sun showed its face over the hills and flashed viciously on the bedroom window.

Jim went slowly into the house, and brought out a nine-foot, loaded bull whip. He crossed the yard and walked into the barn. And as he climbed the ladder to the hayloft, he heard the high, puppy whimpering start.

When Jim came out of the barn again, he carried Jelka over his shoulder. By the water-trough he set her tenderly on the ground. Her hair was littered with bits of hay. The back of her shirtwaist was streaked with blood.

Jim wetted his bandana at the pipe and washed her bitten lips, and washed her face and brushed back her hair. Her dusky black eyes followed every move he made.

"You hurt me," she said. "You hurt me bad."

He nodded gravely. "Bad as I could without killing you."

The sun shone hotly on the ground. A few blowflies buzzed about, looking for the blood.

Jelka's thickened lips tried to smile. "Did you have any breakfast at all?"

"No," he said. "None at all."

"Well, then, I'll fry you up some eggs." She struggled painfully to her feet.

"Let me help you," he said. "I'll help you get your shirtwaist off. It's drying stuck to your back. It'll hurt."

"No. I'll do it myself." Her voice had a peculiar resonance in it. Her dark eyes dwelt warmly on him for a moment, and then she turned and limped into the house.

Jim waited, sitting on the edge of the water-trough. He saw the smoke start out of the chimney and sail straight up into the air. In a very few moments Jelka called him from the kitchen door.

"Come, Jim. Your breakfast."

Four fried eggs and four thick slices of bacon lay on a warmed plate for him. "The coffee will be ready in a minute," she said.

"Won't you eat?"

"No. Not now. My mouth's too sore."

He ate his eggs hungrily and then looked up at her. Her black hair was combed smooth. She had on a fresh, white shirtwaist. "We're going to town this afternoon," he said. "I'm going to order lumber. We'll build a new house farther down the canyon."

Her eyes darted to the closed bedroom door and then back to him. "Yes," she said. "That will be good." And then, after a moment, "Will you whip me any more—for this?"

"No, not any more, for this."

Her eyes smiled. She sat down on a chair beside him, and Jim put out his hand and stroked her hair and the back of her neck.

SAINT KATY THE VIRGIN

SAINT KATY THE VIRGIN

In P—— (as the French say), in the year 13—, there lived a bad man who kept a bad pig. He was a bad man because he laughed too much at the wrong times and at the wrong people. He laughed at the good brothers of M—— when they came to the door for a bit of whiskey or a piece of silver, and he laughed at tithe time. When Brother Clement fell in the mill pond and drowned because he would not drop the sack of salt he was carrying, the bad man, Roark, laughed until he had to go to bed for it. When you think of the low, nasty kind of laughter it was, you'll see what a bad man this Roark was, and you'll not be surprised that he didn't pay his tithes and got himself talked about for excommunication. You see, Roark didn't have the proper kind of a face for a laugh to come out of. It was a dark, tight face, and when he laughed it looked as though Roark's leg had just been torn off and his face was getting ready to scream about it. In addition he called people fools, which is unkind and unwise even if they are. Nobody knew what made Roark so bad except that he had been a traveler and seen bad things about the world.

You see the atmosphere the bad pig, Katy, grew up in, and maybe it's no wonder. There are books written how Katy came from a long line of bad pigs; how Katy's father was a chicken eater and everybody knew it, and how Katy's mother would make a meal out of her own litter if she was let. But that isn't true. Katy's mother and father were good modest pigs insofar as nature has provided pigs with equipment for modesty, which isn't far. But still, they had the spirit of modesty as a lot of people have.

Katy's mother had litter after litter of nice red hungry pigs, as normal and decent as you could wish. You must see that the badness of Katy wasn't anything she got by inheritance, so she must have picked it up from the man Roark.

There was Katy lying in the straw with her eyes squinted shut and her pink nose wrinkled, as fine and quiet a piglet as you ever saw, until the day when Roark went out to the sty to name the litter. "You'll be Brigid," he said, "And you're Rory and—turn over you little devil!—you're Katy," and from that minute Katy was a bad pig, the worst pig, in fact, that was ever in the County of P——.

She began by stealing most of the milk; what dugs she couldn't suck on, she put her back against, so that poor Rory and Brigid and the rest turned out runts. Pretty soon, Katy was twice as big as her brothers and sisters and twice as strong. And for badness, can you equal this: one at a time, Katy caught Brigid and Rory and the rest and ate them. With such a start, you might expect almost any kind of a sin out of Katy; and sure enough, it wasn't long before she began eating chickens and ducks, until at last Roark interfered. He put her in a strong sty; at least it was strong on his side. After that, what chickens Katy ate she got from the neighbors.

You should have seen the face of Katy. From the beginning it was a wicked face. The evil yellow eyes of her would frighten you even if you had a stick to knock her on the nose with. She became the terror of the neighborhood. At night, Katy would go stealing out of a hole in her sty to raid hen roosts. Now and then even a child disappeared and was heard of no more. And Roark, who should have been ashamed and sad, grew fonder and fonder of Katy. He said she was the best pig he ever owned, and had more sense than any pig in the county.

After a while the whisper went around that it was a were-pig that wandered about in the night and bit people on the legs and rooted in the gardens and ate ducks. Some even went so far as to say it was Roark himself who changed into a pig and stole through the hedges at night. That was the kind of reputation Roark had with his neighbors.

Well, Katy was a big pig now, and it came time for her to be bred. The boar was sterile from that day on and went about with a sad suspicious look on his face and was perplexed and distrustful. But Katy swelled up and swelled up until one night she had her litter. She cleaned them all up and licked them off the way you'd think motherhood had changed her ways. When she got them all dry and clean, she placed them in a row and ate every one of them. It was too much even for a bad man like Roark, for as everyone knows, a sow that will eat her own young is depraved beyond human ability to conceive wickedness.

Reluctantly Roark got ready to slaughter Katy. He was just getting the knife ready when along the path came Brother Colin and Brother Paul on their way collecting tithes. They were sent out from the Monastery of M—— and, while they didn't expect to get anything out of Roark, they thought they'd give him a try anyhow, the way a man will. Brother Paul was a thin, strong man, with a thin strong face and a sharp eye and unconditional piety written all over him, while Brother Colin was a short, round man with a wide round face. Brother Paul looked forward to trying the graces of God in Heaven but Brother Colin was all for testing them on earth. The people called Colin a fine man and Paul a good man. They went tithing together, because what Brother Colin couldn't get by persuasion, Brother Paul dug out with threatenings and descriptions of the fires of Hell.

"Roark!" says Brother Paul, "we're out tithing. You won't go pickling your soul in sulphur the way you've been in the habit, will you?"

Roark stopped whetting the knife, and his eyes for evilness might have been Katy's own eyes. He started out to laugh, and then the beginning of it stuck in his throat. He got a look on his face like the look Katy had when she was eating her litter. "I have a pig for you," said Roark, and he put the knife away.

The Brothers were amazed, for up to that time they'd got nothing out of Roark except the dog sic'd on them, and Roark laughing at the way they tripped over their skirts getting to the gate. "A pig?" said Brother Colin suspiciously. "What kind of a pig?"

"The pig that's in the sty alone there," said Roark, and his eyes seemed to turn yellow.

The Brothers hurried over to the sty and looked in. They noted the size of Katy and the fat on her, and they stared incredulously. Colin could think of nothing but the great hams she had and the bacon she wore about like a top coat. "We'll get a sausage for ourselves from this," he whispered. But Brother Paul was thinking of the praise from Father Benedict when he heard they'd got a pig out of Roark. Paul turned away.

"When will you send this pig over?" he asked.

"I'll bring nothing," Roark cried. "It's your pig there. You take her with you or she will stay here."

The Brothers did not argue. They were too glad to get anything. Paul slipped a cord throught the nose-ring of Katy and led her out of the sty; and for a moment Katy followed them as though she were a really good pig. As the three went through the gate, Roark called after them, "Her name is Katy," and the laugh that had been cooped up in his throat so long cackled out.

"It's a fine big sow," Brother Paul remarked uneasily.

Brother Colin was about to answer him, when something like a wolf trap caught him by the back of the leg. Colin yelled and spun about. There was Katy contentedly chewing up a piece of the calf of his leg, and the look on her face like the devil's own look. Katy chewed slowly and swallowed; then she started forward to get another piece of Brother Colin, but in that instant Brother Paul stepped forward and landed a fine big kick on the end of her snout. If there had been evil in Katy's face before, there were demons in her eyes then. She braced herself and growled down deep in her throat; she moved forward snorting and clicking her teeth like a bulldog. The Brothers didn't wait for her; they ran to a thorn tree beside the way and up they climbed with grunts and strainings until at last they were out of reach of the terrible Katy.

Roark had come down to his gate to see them off, and he stood there laughing the way they knew they'd get no help from him. Beneath them, on the ground, Katy paced back and forth; she pawed the ground and rooted out great pieces of turf to show her strength. Brother Paul threw a branch at her, and she tore it to pieces and ground the pieces into the earth under her sharp hooves, all the time looking up at them with her slanty yellow eyes and grinning to herself.

The two Brothers seated themselves miserably in the tree, their heads between their shoulders and their robes hugged tight. "Did you give her a good clout on the nose?" Brother Colin asked hopefully.

Brother Paul looked down at his foot and then at the tough leather snout of Katy. "The kick of my foot would knock down any pig but an elephant," he said.

"You cannot argue with a pig," Brother Colin suggested.

Katy strode ferociously about under the tree. For a long time the Brothers sat in silence, moodily drawing their robes about their ankles. Brother Paul studied the problem with a disfiguring intensity. At last he observed: "You wouldn't say pigs had much the nature of a lion now, would you?"

"More the nature of the devil," Colin said wearily.

Paul sat straight up and scrutinized Katy with new interest. Then he held his crucifix out before him, and, in a terrible voice cried, "APAGE SATANAS!"

Katy shuddered as though a strong wind had struck

her, but still she came on. "APAGE SATANAS!" Paul cried again and Katy was once more buffeted but unbeaten. A third time Brother Paul hurled the exorcism, but Katy had recovered from the first shock now. It had little effect except to singe a few dried leaves on the ground. Brother Paul turned discouraged eyes to Colin. "Nature of the devil," he announced sadly, "but not the Devil's own self, else that pig would have exploded."

Katy ground her teeth together with horrible pleasure.

"Before I got the idea about exorcising," Paul mused, "I was wondering about Daniel in the lion's den, and would the same thing work on a pig?"

Brother Colin regarded him apprehensively. "There may be some flaws in the nature of a lion," he argued. "Maybe lions are not so heretic as pigs. Every time there's a tight place for a pious man to get out of, there's a lion in it. Look at Daniel, look at Sampson, look at any number of martyrs just to stay in the religious list; and I could name many cases like Androcles that aren't religious at all. No, Brother, the lion is a beast especially made for saintliness and orthodoxy to cope with. If there's a lion in all those stories it must be because of all creatures, the lion is the least impervious to the force of religion. I think the lion must have been created as a kind of object lesson. It is a beast built for parables, surely. But the pig now—there is no record in my memory that a pig recognizes any force but a clout on the nose or a knife in the throat. Pigs in general, and this pig in particular, are the most headstrong and heretic of beasts."

"Still," Brother Paul went on, paying little attention to the lesson, "when you've got ammunition like the church in your hand, it would be a dirty shame not to give it a good try, be it on lion or on pig. The exorcism did not work, and that means nothing." He started to unwind the rope which served him for a girdle. Brother Colin regarded him with horror.

"Paul, lad," he cried, "Brother Paul, for the love of God, do not go down to that pig." But Paul paid him no attention. He unwound his girdle, and to the end of it tied the chain of his crucifix; then, leaning back until he was hanging by his knees, and the skirts of his robe about his head, Paul lowered the girdle like a fishing line and dangled the iron crucifix toward Katy.

As for Katy, she came forward stamping and champing, ready to snatch it and tread it under her feet. The face of Katy was a tiger's face. Just as she reached the cross, the sharp shadow of it fell on her face, and the cross itself was reflected in her yellow eyes. Katy stopped—paralyzed. The air, the tree, the earth shuddered in an expectant silence, while goodness fought with sin.

Then, slowly, two great tears squeezed out of the eyes of Katy, and before you could think, she was stretched prostrate on the ground, making the sign of the cross with her right hoof and mooing softly in anguish at the realization of her crimes.

Brother Paul dangled the cross a full minute before he hoisted himself back on the limb.

All this time Roark had been watching from his gate. From that day on, he was no longer a bad man; his whole life was changed in a moment. Indeed, he told the story over and over to anyone who would listen. Roark said he had never seen anything so grand and inspiring in his life.

Brother Paul rose and stood on the limb. He drew himself to his full height. Then, using his free hand for gestures, Brother Paul delivered the Sermon on the Mount in beautiful Latin to the groveling, moaning Katy under the tree. When he finished, there was complete and holy silence except for the sobs and sniffles of the repentant pig.

It is doubtful whether Brother Colin had the fiber of a true priest-militant in his nature. "Do—do you think it is safe to go down now?" he stammered.

For answer, Brother Paul broke a limb from the thorn trees and threw it at the recumbent sow. Katy sobbed aloud and raised a tear-stained countenance to them, a face from which all evil had departed; the yellow eyes were golden with repentance and the resulting anguish of grace. The Brothers scrambled out of the tree, put the cord through Katy's nose-ring again, and down the road they trudged with the redeemed pig trotting docilely behind them.

News that they were bringing home a pig from Roark caused such excitement that, on arriving at the gates of M——, Brothers Paul and Colin found a crowd of monks awaiting them. The Brotherhood squirmed about, feeling the fat sides of Katy and kneading her jowls. Suddenly an opening was broken in the ring, and Father Benedict paced through. His face wore such a smile that Colin was made sure of his sausage and Paul of his praise. Then, to the horror and consternation of everyone present, Katy waddled to a little font beside the chapel door, dipped her right hoof in holy water and crossed herself. It was a moment before anyone spoke. Then Father Benedict's stern voice rang out in anger. "Who was it converted this pig?"

Brother Paul stepped forward. "I did it, Father."

"You are a fool," said the Abbot.

"A fool? I thought you would be pleased, Father."

"You are a fool," Father Benedict repeated. "We can't slaughter this pig. This pig is a Christian."

"There is more rejoicing in heaven—" Brother Paul began to quote.

"Hush!" said the Abbot. "There are plenty of Christians. This year there's a great shortage of pigs."

It would take a whole volume to tell of the thousands of sick beds Katy visited, of the comfort she carried into palaces and cottages. She sat by beds of pain and her dear golden eyes brought relief to the sufferers. For a while it was thought that, because of her sex, she should leave the monastery and enter a nunnery, for the usual ribald tongues caused the usual scandal in the county. But, as the Abbot remarked, one need only look at Katy to be convinced of her purity.

The subsequent life of Katy was one long record of good deeds. It was not until one feast-day morning, however, that the Brothers began to suspect that their community harbored a saint. On the morning in question, while hymns of joy and thanksgiving sounded from a hundred pious mouths, Katy rose from her seat, strode to the altar, and, with a look of seraphic transport on her face, spun like a top on the tip of her tail for one hour and three-quarters. The assembled Brothers looked on with astonishment and admiration. This was a wonderful example of what a saintly life could accomplish.

From that time on M—— became a place of pilgrimage. Long lines of travelers wound into the valley and stopped at the taverns kept by the good Brothers.

Daily at four o'clock, Katy emerged from the gates and blessed the multitudes. If any were afflicted with scrofula or trichina, she touched them and they were healed. Fifty years after her death to a day, she was added to the Calendar of the Elect.

The Proposition was put forward that she should be called Saint Katy the Virgin. However, a minority argued that Katy was not a virgin since she had, in her sinful days, produced a litter. The opposing party retorted that it made no difference at all. Very few virgins, so they said, were virgins.

To keep dissension out of the monastery, a committee presented the problem to a fair-minded and vastly learned barber, agreeing beforehand to be guided by his decision.

"It is a delicate question," said the barber. "You might say there are two kinds of virginity. Some hold that virginity consists in a little bit of tissue. If you have it, you are; if you haven't, you aren't. This definition is a grave danger to the basis of our religion since there is nothing to differentiate between the Grace of God knocking it out from the inside or the wickedness of man from the outside. On the other hand," he continued, "there is virginity by intent, and this definition admits the existence of a great many more virgins than the first does. But here again we get into trouble. When I was a much younger man, I went about in the evenings sometimes with a girl on my arm. Every one of them that ever walked with me was a virgin by intention, and if you take the second definition, you see, they still are."

The committee went away satisfied. Katy had without doubt been a virgin by intent.

In the chapel at M—— there is a gold-bound, jeweled reliquary, and inside, on a bed of crimson satin repose the bones of the Saint. People come great distances to kiss the little box, and such as do, go away leaving their troubles behind them. This holy relic has been found to cure female troubles and ringworm. There is a record left by a woman who visited the chapel to be cured of both. She deposes that she rubbed the reliquary against her cheek, and at the moment her face touched the holy object, a hair mole she had possessed from birth immediately vanished and has never returned.

THE RED PONY

THE RED PONY

I. THE GIFT

At daybreak Billy Buck emerged from the bunkhouse and stood for a moment on the porch looking up at the sky. He was a broad, bandy-legged little man with a walrus moustache, with square hands, puffed and muscled on the palms. His eyes were a contemplative, watery grey and the hair which protruded from under his Stetson hat was spiky and weathered. Billy was still stuffing his shirt into his blue jeans as he stood on the porch. He unbuckled his belt and tightened it again. The belt showed, by the worn shiny places opposite each hole, the gradual increase of Billy's middle over a period of years. When he had seen to the weather, Billy cleared each nostril by holding its mate closed with his forefinger and blowing fiercely. Then he walked down to the barn, rubbing his hands together. He curried and brushed two saddle horses in the stalls, talking quietly to them all the time; and he had hardly finished when the iron triangle started ringing at the ranch house. Billy stuck the brush and currycomb together and laid them on the rail, and went up to breakfast. His action had been so deliberate and yet so wasteless of time that he came to the house while Mrs. Tiflin was still ringing the triangle. She nodded her grey head to him and withdrew into the kitchen. Billy Buck sat down on the steps, because he was a cow-hand, and it wouldn't be fitting that he should go first into the dining-room. He heard Mr. Tiflin in the house, stamping his feet into his boots.

The high jangling note of the triangle put the boy Jody in motion. He was only a little boy, ten years old, with hair like dusty yellow grass and with shy polite grey eyes, and with a mouth that worked when he thought. The triangle picked him up out of sleep. It didn't occur to him to disobey the harsh note. He never had: no one he knew ever had. He brushed the tangled hair out of his eyes and skinned his nightgown off. In a moment he was dressed—blue chambray shirt and overalls. It was late in the summer, so of course there were no shoes to bother with. In the kitchen he waited until his mother got from in front of the sink and went back to the stove. Then he washed himself and brushed back his wet hair with his fingers. His mother turned sharply on him as he left the sink. Jody looked shyly away.

"I've got to cut your hair before long," his mother said. "Breakfast's on the table. Go on in, so Billy can come."

Jody sat at the long table which was covered with white oilcloth washed through to the fabric in some places. The fried eggs lay in rows on their platter.

Jody took three eggs on his plate and followed with three thick slices of crisp bacon. He carefully scraped a spot of blood from one of the egg yolks.

Billy Buck clumped in. "That won't hurt you," Billy explained. "That's only a sign the rooster leaves."

Jody's tall stern father came in then and Jody knew from the noise on the floor that he was wearing boots, but he looked under the table anyway, to make sure. His father turned off the oil lamp over the table, for plenty of morning light now came through the windows.

Jody did not ask where his father and Billy Buck were riding that day, but he wished he might go along. His father was a disciplinarian. Jody obeyed him in everything without questions of any kind. Now, Carl Tiflin sat down and reached for the egg platter.

"Got the cows ready to go, Billy?" he asked.

"In the lower corral," Billy said. "I could just as well take them in alone."

"Sure you could. But a man needs company. Besides your throat gets pretty dry." Carl Tiflin was jovial this morning.

Jody's mother put her head in the door. "What time do you think to be back, Carl?"

"I can't tell. I've got to see some men in Salinas. Might be gone till dark."

The eggs and coffee and big biscuits disappeared rapidly. Jody followed the two men out of the house. He watched them mount their horses and drive six old milk cows out of the corral and start over the hill toward Salinas. They were going to sell the old cows to the butcher.

When they disappeared over the crown of the ridge

Jody walked up the hill in back of the house. The dogs trotted around the house corner hunching their shoulders and grinning horribly with pleasure. Jody patted their heads—Doubletree Mutt with the big thick tail and yellow eyes, and Smasher, the shepherd, who had killed a coyote and lost an ear in doing it. Smasher's one good ear stood up higher than a collie's ear should. Billy Buck said that always happened. After the frenzied greeting the dogs lowered their noses to the ground in a businesslike way and went ahead, looking back now and then to make sure that the boy was coming. They walked up through the chicken yard and saw the quail eating with the chickens. Smasher chased the chickens a little to keep in practice in case there should ever be sheep to herd. Jody continued on through the large vegetable patch where the green corn was higher than his head. The cowpumpkins were green and small yet. He went on to the sagebrush line where the cold spring ran out of its pipe and fell into a round wooden tub. He leaned over and drank close to the green mossy wood where the water tasted best. Then he turned and looked back on the ranch, on the low, whitewashed house girded with red geraniums, and on the long bunkhouse by the cypress tree where Billy Buck lived alone. Jody could see the great black kettle under the cypress tree. That was where the pigs were scalded. The sun was coming over the ridge now, glaring on the whitewash of the houses and barns, making the wet grass blaze softly. Behind him, in the tall sagebrush, the birds were scampering on the ground, making a great noise among the dry leaves; the squirrels piped shrilly on the side-hills. Jody looked along at the farm buildings. He felt an uncertainty in the air, a feeling of change and of loss and of the gain of new and unfamiliar things. Over the hillside two big black buzzards sailed low to the ground and their shadows slipped smoothly and quickly ahead of them. Some animal had died in the vicinity. Jody knew it. It might be a cow or it might be the remains of a rabbit. The buzzards overlooked nothing. Jody hated them as all decent things hate them, but they could not be hurt because they made away with carrion.

After a while the boy sauntered down hill again. The dogs had long ago given him up and gone into the brush to do things in their own way. Back through the vegetable garden he went, and he paused for a moment to smash a green muskmelon with his heel, but he was not happy about it. It was a bad thing to do, he knew perfectly well. He kicked dirt over the ruined melon to conceal it.

Back at the house his mother bent over his rough hands, inspecting his fingers and nails. It did little good to start him clean to school for too many things could happen on the way. She sighed over the black cracks on his fingers, and then gave him his books and his lunch and started him on the mile walk to school. She noticed that his mouth was working a good deal this morning.

Jody started his journey. He filled his pockets with little pieces of white quartz that lay in the road, and every so often he took a shot at a bird or at some rabbit that had stayed sunning itself in the road too long. At the crossroads over the bridge he met two friends and the three of them walked to school together, making ridiculous strides and being rather silly. School had just opened two weeks before. There was still a spirit of revolt among the pupils.

It was four o'clock in the afternoon when Jody topped the hill and looked down on the ranch again. He looked for the saddle horses, but the corral was empty. His father was not back yet. He went slowly, then, toward the afternoon chores. At the ranch house, he found his mother sitting on the porch, mending socks.

"There's two doughnuts in the kitchen for you," she said. Jody slid to the kitchen, and returned with half of one of the doughnuts already eaten and his mouth full. His mother asked him what he had learned in school that day, but she didn't listen to his doughnut-muffled answer. She interrupted, "Jody, tonight see you fill the wood-box clear full. Last night you crossed the sticks and it wasn't only about half full. Lay the sticks flat tonight. And Jody, some of the hens are hiding eggs, or else the dogs are eating them. Look about in the grass and see if you can find any nests."

Jody, still eating, went out and did his chores. He saw the quail come down to eat with the chickens when he threw out the grain. For some reason his father was proud to have them come. He never allowed any shooting near the house for fear the quail might go away.

When the wood-box was full, Jody took his twenty-two rifle up to the cold spring at the brush line. He drank again and then aimed the gun at all manner of things, at rocks, at birds on the wing, at the big black pig kettle under the cypress tree, but he didn't shoot for he had no cartridges and wouldn't have until he was twelve. If his father had seen him aim the rifle in the direction of the house he would have put the cartridges off another year. Jody remembered this and did not point the rifle down the hill again. Two years was enough to wait for cartridges. Nearly all of his father's presents were given with reservations which hampered their value somewhat. It was good discipline.

The supper waited until dark for his father to return. When at last he came in with Billy Buck, Jody could smell the delicious brandy on their breaths. Inwardly he rejoiced, for his father sometimes talked to him when he smelled of brandy, sometimes even told things he had done in the wild days when he was a boy.

After supper, Jody sat by the fireplace and his shy polite eyes sought the room corners, and he waited for his father to tell what it was he contained, for Jody knew he had news of some sort. But he was disappointed. His father pointed a stern finger at him.

"You'd better go to bed, Jody. I'm going to need you in the morning."

That wasn't so bad. Jody liked to do the things he had to do as long as they weren't routine things. He looked at the floor and his mouth worked out a question before he spoke it. "What are we going to do in the morning, kill a pig?" he asked softly.

"Never you mind. You better get to bed."

When the door was closed behind him, Jody heard his father and Billy Buck chuckling and he knew it was a joke of some kind. And later, when he lay in bed, trying to make words out of the murmurs in the other room, he heard his father protest, "But, Ruth, I didn't give much for him."

Jody heard the hoot-owls hunting mice down by the barn, and he heard a fruit tree limb tap-tapping against the house. A cow was lowing when he went to sleep.

When the triangle sounded in the morning, Jody dressed more quickly even than usual. In the kitchen, while he washed his face and combed back his hair, his mother addressed him irritably. "Don't you go out until you get a good breakfast in you."

He went into the dining-room and sat at the long white table. He took a steaming hotcake from the platter, arranged two fried eggs on it, covered them with another hotcake and squashed the whole thing with his fork.

His father and Billy Buck came in. Jody knew from the sound of the floor that both of them were wearing flatheeled shoes, but he peered under the table to make sure. His father turned off the oil lamp, for the day had arrived, and he looked stern and disciplinary, but Billy Buck didn't look at Jody at all. He avoided the shy questioning eyes of the boy and soaked a whole piece of toast in his coffee.

Carl Tiflin said crossly, "You come with us after breakfast!"

Jody had trouble with his food then, for he felt a kind of doom in the air. After Billy had tilted his saucer and drained the coffee which had slopped into it, and had wiped his hands on his jeans, the two men stood up from the table and went out into the morning light together, and Jody respectfully followed a little behind them. He tried to keep his mind from running ahead, tried to keep it absolutely motionless.

His mother called, "Carl! Don't you let it keep him from school."

They marched past the cypress, where a singletree hung from a limb to butcher the pigs on, and past the black iron kettle, so it was not a pig killing. The sun shone over the hill and threw long, dark shadows of the trees and buildings. They crossed a stubble-field to shortcut to the barn. Jody's father unhooked the door and they went in. They had been walking toward the sun on the way down. The barn was black as night in contrast and warm from the hay and from the beasts. Jody's father moved over toward the one box stall. "Come here!" he ordered. Jody could begin to see things now. He looked into the box stall and then stepped back quickly.

A red pony colt was looking at him out of the stall. Its tense ears were forward and a light of disobedience was in its eyes. Its coat was rough and thick as an airedale's fur and its mane was long and tangled. Jody's throat collapsed in on itself and cut his breath short.

"He needs a good currying," his father said, "and if I ever hear of you not feeding him or leaving his stall dirty, I'll sell him off in a minute."

Jody couldn't bear to look at the pony's eyes any more. He gazed down at his hands for a moment, and he asked very shyly, "Mine?" No one answered him. He put his hand out toward the pony. Its grey nose came close, sniffing loudly, and then the lips drew back and the strong teeth closed on Jody's fingers. The pony shook its head up and down and seemed to laugh with amusement. Jody regarded his bruised fingers. "Well," he said with pride—"Well, I guess he can bite all right." The two men laughed, somewhat in relief. Carl Tiflin went out of the barn and walked up a side-hill to be by himself, for he was embarrassed, but Billy Buck stayed. It was easier to talk to Billy Buck. Jody asked again—"Mine?"

Billy became professional in tone. "Sure! That is, if you look out for him and break him right. I'll show you how. He's just a colt. You can't ride him for some time."

Jody put out his bruised hand again, and this time the red pony let his nose be rubbed. "I ought to have a carrot," Jody said. "Where'd we get him, Billy?"

"Bought him at a sheriff's auction," Billy explained. "A show went broke in Salinas and had debts. The sheriff was selling off their stuff."

The pony stretched out his nose and shook the forelock from his wild eyes. Jody stroked the nose a little. He said softly, "There isn't a—saddle?"

Billy Buck laughed. "I'd forgot. Come along."

In the harness room he lifted down a little saddle of red morocco leather. "It's just a show saddle," Billy Buck said disparagingly. "It isn't practical for the brush, but it was cheap at the sale."

Jody couldn't trust himself to look at the saddle either, and he couldn't speak at all. He brushed the shining red leather with his fingertips, and after a long time he said, "It'll look pretty on him though." He thought of the grandest and prettiest things he knew. "If he hasn't a name already, I think I'll call him Gabilan Mountains," he said.

Billy Buck knew how he felt. "It's a pretty long name. Why don't you just call him Gabilan? That means hawk. That would be a fine name for him." Billy felt glad. "If you will collect tail hair, I might be able to make a hair rope for you sometime. You could use it for a hackamore."

Jody wanted to go back to the box stall. "Could I lead him to school, do you think—to show the kids?"

But Billy shook his head. "He's not even halter-broke yet. We had a time getting him here. Had to almost drag him. You better be starting for school though."

"I'll bring the kids to see him here this afternoon," Jody said.

Six boys came over the hill half an hour early that afternoon, running hard, their heads down, their forearms working, their breath whistling. They swept by the house and cut across the stubble-field to the barn. And then they stood self-consciously before the pony, and then they looked at Jody with eyes in which there was a new admiration and a new respect. Before today Jody had been a boy, dressed in overalls and a blue shirt—quieter than most, even suspected of being a little cowardly. And now he was different. Out of a thousand centuries they drew the ancient admiration of the footman for the horseman. They knew instinctively that a man on a horse is spiritually as well as physically bigger than a man on foot. They knew that Jody had been miraculously lifted out of equality with them, and had been placed over them. Gabilan put his head out of the stall and sniffed them.

"Why'n't you ride him?" the boys cried. "Why'n't you braid his tail with ribbons like in the fair?" "When you going to ride him?"

Jody's courage was up. He too felt the superiority of the horseman. "He's not old enough. Nobody can ride him for a long time. I'm going to train him on the long halter. Billy Buck is going to show me how."

"Well, can't we lead him around a little?"

"He isn't even halter broke," Jody said. He wanted to be completely alone when he took the pony out the first time. "Come and see the saddle."

They were speechless at the red morocco saddle, completely shocked out of comment. "It isn't much use in the brush," Jody explained. "It'll look pretty on him though. Maybe I'll ride bareback when I go into the brush."

"How you going to rope a cow without a saddle horn?"

"Maybe I'll get another saddle for every day. My father might want me to help him with the stock." He let them feel the red saddle, and showed them the brass chain throat-latch on the bridle and the big brass buttons at each temple where the headstall and brow band crossed. The whole thing was too wonderful. They had to go away after a little while, and each boy, in his mind, searched among his possessions for a bribe worthy of offering in return for a ride on the red pony when the time should come.

Jody was glad when they had gone. He took brush

and currycomb from the wall, took down the barrier of the box stall and stepped cautiously in. The pony's eyes glittered, and he edged around into kicking position. But Jody touched him on the shoulder and rubbed his high arched neck as he had always seen Billy Buck do, and he crooned, "So-o-o Boy," in a deep voice. The pony gradually relaxed his tenseness. Jody curried and brushed until a pile of dead hair lay in the stall and until the pony's coat had taken on a deep red shine. Each time he finished he thought it might have been done better. He braided the mane into a dozen little pigtails, and he braided the forelock, and then he undid them and brushed the hair out straight again.

Jody did not hear his mother enter the barn. She was angry when she came, but when she looked in at the pony and at Jody working over him, she felt a curious pride rise up in her. "Have you forgot the wood-box?" she asked gently. "It's not far off from dark and there's not a stick of wood in the house, and the chickens aren't fed."

Jody quickly put up his tools. "I forgot, ma'am."

"Well, after this do your chores first. Then you won't forget. I expect you'll forget lots of things now if I don't keep an eye on you."

"Can I have carrots from the garden for him, ma'am?"

She had to think about that. "Oh—I guess so, if you only take the big tough ones."

"Carrots keep the coat good," he said, and again she felt the curious rush of pride.

*

Jody never waited for the triangle to get him out of bed after the coming of the pony. It became his habit to creep out of bed even before his mother was awake, to slip into his clothes and to go quietly down to the barn to see Gabilan. In the grey quiet mornings when the land and the brush and the houses and the trees were silver-grey and black like a photograph negative, he stole toward the barn, past the sleeping stones and the sleeping cypress tree. The turkeys, roosting in the tree out of coyotes' reach, clicked drowsily. The fields glowed with a grey frost-like light and in the dew the tracks of rabbits and of field mice stood out sharply. The good dogs came stiffly out of their little houses, hackles up and deep growls in their throats. Then they caught Jody's scent, and their stiff tails rose up and waved a greeting—Doubletree Mutt with the big thick tail, and Smasher, the incipient shepherd—then went lazily back to their warm beds.

It was a strange time and a mysterious journey, to Jody—an extension of a dream. When he first had the pony he liked to torture himself during the trip by thinking Gabilan would not be in his stall, and worse, would never have been there. And he had other delicious little self-induced pains. He thought how the rats had gnawed ragged holes in the red saddle, and how the mice had nibbled Gabilan's tail until it was stringy and thin. He usually ran the last little way to the barn. He unlatched the rusty hasp of the barn door and stepped in, and no matter how quietly he opened the door, Gabilan was always looking at him over the barrier of the box stall and Gabilan whinnied softly and stamped his front foot, and his eyes had big sparks of red fire in them like oakwood embers.

Sometimes, if the work horses were to be used that day, Jody found Billy Buck in the barn harnessing and currying. Billy stood with him and looked long at Gabilan and he told Jody a great many things about horses. He explained that they were terribly afraid for their feet, so that one must make a practice of lifting the legs and patting the hooves and ankles to remove their terror. He told Jody how horses love conversation. He must talk to the pony all the time, and tell him the reasons for everything. Billy wasn't sure a horse could understand everything that was said to him, but it was impossible to say how much was understood. A horse never kicked up a fuss if some one he liked explained things to him. Billy could give examples, too. He had known, for instance, a horse nearly dead beat with fatigue to perk up when told it was only a little farther to his destination. And he had known a horse paralyzed with fright to come out of it when his rider told him what it was that was frightening him. While he talked in the mornings, Billy Buck cut twenty or thirty straws into neat three-inch lengths and stuck them into his hatband. Then during the whole day, if he wanted to pick his teeth or merely to chew on something, he had only to reach up for one of them.

Jody listened carefully, for he knew and the whole country knew that Billy Buck was a fine hand with horses. Billy's own horse was a stringy cayuse with a hammer head, but he nearly always won the first prizes at the stock trials. Billy could rope a steer, take a double half-hitch about the horn with his riata, and dismount, and his horse would play the steer as an angler plays a fish, keeping a tight rope until the steer was down or beaten.

Every morning, after Jody had curried and brushed the pony, he let down the barrier of the stall, and Gabilan thrust past him and raced down the barn and into the corral. Around and around he galloped, and sometimes he jumped forward and landed on stiff legs. He stood quivering, stiff ears forward, eyes rolling so that the whites showed, pretending to be frightened. At last he walked snorting to the water-trough and buried his nose in the water up to the nostrils. Jody was proud then, for he knew that was the way to judge a horse. Poor horses only touched their lips to the water, but a fine spirited beast put his whole nose and mouth under, and only left room to breathe.

Then Jody stood and watched the pony, and he saw things he had never noticed about any other horse, the sleek, sliding flank muscles and the cords of the buttocks, which flexed like a closing fist, and the shine the sun put on the red coat. Having seen horses all his life, Jody had never looked at them very closely before. But now he noticed the moving ears which gave expression and even inflection of expression to the face. The pony talked with his ears. You could tell exactly how he felt about everything by the way his ears pointed. Sometimes they were stiff and upright and sometimes lax and sagging. They went back when he was angry or fearful, and forward when he was anxious and curious and pleased; and their exact position indicated which emotion he had.

Billy Buck kept his word. In the early fall the training began. First there was the halter-breaking, and that was the hardest because it was the first thing. Jody held a carrot and coaxed and promised and pulled on the rope. The pony set his feet like a burro when he felt the strain. But before long he learned. Jody walked all over the ranch leading him. Gradually he took to dropping the rope until the pony followed him unled wherever he went.

And then came the training on the long halter. That was slower work. Jody stood in the middle of a circle, holding the long halter. He clucked with his tongue and the pony started to walk in a big circle, held in by the long rope. He clucked again to make the pony trot, and again to make him gallop. Around and around Gabilan went thundering and enjoying it immensely. Then he called, "Whoa," and the pony stopped. It was not long until Gabilan was perfect at it. But in many ways he was a bad pony. He bit Jody in the pants and stomped on Jody's feet. Now and then his ears went back and he aimed a tremendous kick at the boy. Every time he did one of these bad things, Gabilan settled back and seemed to laugh to himself.

Billy Buck worked at the hair rope in the evenings before the fireplace. Jody collected tail hair in a bag, and he sat and watched Billy slowly constructing the rope, twisting a few hairs to make a string and rolling two strings together for a cord, and then braiding a number of cords to make the rope. Billy rolled the finished rope on the floor under his foot to make it round and hard.

The long halter work rapidly approached perfection. Jody's father, watching the pony stop and start and trot and gallop, was a little bothered by it.

"He's getting to be almost a trick pony," he complained. "I don't like trick horses. It takes all the—

dignity out of a horse to make him do tricks. Why, a trick horse is kind of like an actor—no dignity, no character of his own." And his father said, "I guess you better be getting him used to the saddle pretty soon."

Jody rushed for the harness-room. For some time he had been riding the saddle on a sawhorse. He changed the stirrup length over and over, and could never get it just right. Sometimes, mounted on the sawhorse in the harness-room, with collars and hames and tugs hung all about him, Jody rode out beyond the room. He carried his rifle across the pommel. He saw the fields go flying by, and he heard the beat of the galloping hoofs.

It was a ticklish job, saddling the pony the first time. Gabilan hunched and reared and threw the saddle off before the cinch could be tightened. It had to be replaced again and again until at last the pony let it stay. And the cinching was difficult, too. Day by day Jody tightened the girth a little more until at last the pony didn't mind the saddle at all.

Then there was the bridle. Billy explained how to use a stick of licorice for a bit until Gabilan was used to having something in his mouth. Billy explained, "Of course we could force-break him to everything, but he wouldn't be as good a horse if we did. He'd always be a little bit afraid, and he wouldn't mind because he wanted to."

The first time the pony wore the bridle he whipped his head about and worked his tongue against the bit until the blood oozed from the corners of his mouth.

He tried to rub the headstall off on the manger. His ears pivoted about and his eyes turned red with fear and with general rambunctiousness. Jody rejoiced, for he knew that only a mean-souled horse does not resent training.

And Jody trembled when he thought of the time when he would first sit in the saddle. The pony would probably throw him off. There was no disgrace in that. The disgrace would come if he did not get right up and mount again. Sometimes he dreamed that he lay in the dirt and cried and couldn't make himself mount again. The shame of the dream lasted until the middle of the day.

Gabilan was growing fast. Already he had lost the longleggedness of the colt; his mane was getting longer and blacker. Under the constant currying and brushing his coat lay as smooth and gleaming as orange-red lacquer. Jody oiled the hoofs and kept them carefully trimmed so they would not crack.

The hair rope was nearly finished. Jody's father gave him an old pair of spurs and bent in the side bars and cut down the strap and took up the chainlets until they fitted. And then one day Carl Tiflin said:

"The pony's growing faster than I thought. I guess you can ride him by Thanksgiving. Think you can stick on?"

"I don't know," Jody said shyly. Thanksgiving was only three weeks off. He hoped it wouldn't rain, for rain would spot the red saddle.

Gabilan knew and liked Jody by now. He nickered when Jody came across the stubble-field, and in the pasture he came running when his master whistled for him. There was always a carrot for him every time.

Billy Buck gave him riding instructions over and over. "Now when you get up there, just grab tight with your knees and keep your hands away from the saddle, and if you get throwed, don't let that stop you. No matter how good a man is, there's always some horse can pitch him. You just climb up again before he gets to feeling smart about it. Pretty soon, he won't throw you no more, and pretty soon he *can't* throw you no more. That's the way to do it."

"I hope it don't rain before," Jody said.

"Why not? Don't want to get throwed in the mud?"

That was partly it, and also he was afraid that in the flurry of bucking Gabilan might slip and fall on him and break his leg or his hip. He had seen that happen to men before, had seen how they writhed on the ground like squashed bugs, and he was afraid of it.

He practiced on the sawhorse how he would hold the reins in his left hand and a hat in his right hand. If he kept his hands thus busy, he couldn't grab the horn if he felt himself going off. He didn't like to think of what would happen if he did grab the horn. Perhaps his father and Billy Buck would never speak to him again, they would be so ashamed. The news would get about and his mother would be ashamed too. And in the school yard—it was too awful to contemplate.

He began putting his weight in a stirrup when Gabilan was saddled, but he didn't throw his leg over the pony's back. That was forbidden until Thanksgiving.

Every afternoon he put the red saddle on the pony and cinched it tight. The pony was learning already to fill his stomach out unnaturally large while the cinching was going on, and then to let it down when the straps were fixed. Sometimes Jody led him up to the brush line and let him drink from the round green tub, and sometimes he led him up through the stubble-field to the hilltop from which it was possible to see the white town of Salinas and the geometric fields of the great valley, and the oak trees clipped by the sheep. Now and then they broke through the brush and came to little cleared circles so hedged in that the world was gone and only the sky and the circle of brush were left from the old life. Gabilan liked these trips and showed it by keeping his head very high and by quivering his nostrils with interest. When the two came back from an expedition they smelled of the sweet sage they had forced through.

Time dragged on toward Thanksgiving, but winter came fast. The clouds swept down and hung all day over the land and brushed the hilltops, and the winds blew shrilly at night. All day the dry oak leaves drifted down from the trees until they covered the ground, and yet the trees were unchanged.

Jody had wished it might not rain before Thanksgiving, but it did. The brown earth turned dark and the trees glistened. The cut ends of the stubble turned black with mildew; the haystacks grayed from exposure to the damp, and on the roofs the moss, which had been all summer as gray as lizards, turned a brilliant yellow-green. During the week of rain, Jody kept the pony in the box stall out of the dampness, except for a little time after school when he took him out for exercise and to drink at the water-trough in the upper corral. Not once did Gabilan get wet.

The wet weather continued until little new grass appeared. Jody walked to school dressed in a slicker and short rubber boots. At length one morning the sun came out brightly. Jody, at his work in the box stall, said to Billy Buck, "Maybe I'll leave Gabilan in the corral when I go to school today."

"Be good for him to be out in the sun," Billy assured him. "No animal likes to be cooped up too long. Your father and me are going back on the hill to clean the leaves out of the spring." Billy nodded and picked his teeth with one of his little straws.

"If the rain comes, though—" Jody suggested.

"Not likely to rain today. She's rained herself out."

Billy pulled up his sleeves and snapped his arm bands. "If it comes on to rain—why a little rain don't hurt a horse."

"Well, if it does come on to rain, you put him in, will you, Billy? I'm scared he might get cold so I couldn't ride him when the time comes."

"Oh sure! I'll watch out for him if we get back in time. But it won't rain today."

And so Jody, when he went to school left Gabilan standing out in the corral.

Billy Buck wasn't wrong about many things. He couldn't be. But he was wrong about the weather that day, for a little after noon the clouds pushed over the hills and the rain began to pour down. Jody heard it start on the schoolhouse roof. He considered holding up one finger for permission to go to the outhouse and, once outside, running for home to put the pony in. Punishment would be prompt both at school and at home. He gave it up and took ease from Billy's assurance that rain couldn't hurt a horse. When school was finally out, he hurried home through the dark rain. The banks at the sides of the road spouted little jets of muddy water. The rain slanted and swirled under a cold and gusty wind. Jody dog-trotted home, slopping through the gravelly mud of the road.

From the top of the ridge he could see Gabilan standing miserably in the corral. The red coat was almost black, and streaked with water. He stood head down with his rump to the rain and wind. Jody arrived running and threw open the barn door and led the wet pony in by his forelock. Then he found a gunny sack and rubbed the soaked hair and rubbed the legs and ankles. Gabilan stood patiently, but he trembled in gusts like the wind.

When he had dried the pony as well as he could, Jody went up to the house and brought hot water down to the barn and soaked the grain in it. Gabilan was not very hungry. He nibbled at the hot mash, but he was not very much interested in it, and he still shivered now and then. A little steam rose from his damp back.

It was almost dark when Billy Buck and Carl Tiflin came home. "When the rain started we put up at Ben Herche's place, and the rain never let up all afternoon," Carl Tiflin explained. Jody looked reproachfully at Billy Buck and Billy felt guilty.

"You said it wouldn't rain," Jody accused him.

Billy looked away. "It's hard to tell, this time of year," he said, but his excuse was lame. He had no right to be fallible, and he knew it.

"The pony got wet, got soaked through."

"Did you dry him off?"

"I rubbed him with a sack and I gave him hot grain."

Billy nodded in agreement.

"Do you think he'll take cold, Billy?"

"A little rain never hurt anything," Billy assured him.

Jody's father joined the conversation then and lectured the boy a little. "A horse," he said, "isn't any lap-dog kind of thing." Carl Tiflin hated weakness and sickness, and he held a violent contempt for helplessness.

Jody's mother put a platter of steaks on the table and boiled potatoes and boiled squash, which clouded the room with their steam. They sat down to eat. Carl Tiflin still grumbled about weakness put into animals and men by too much coddling.

Billy Buck felt bad about his mistake. "Did you blanket him?" he asked.

"No. I couldn't find any blanket. I laid some sacks over his back."

"We'll go down and cover him up after we eat, then." Billy felt better about it then. When Jody's father had gone in to the fire and his mother was washing dishes, Billy found and lighted a lantern. He and Jody walked through the mud to the barn. The barn was dark and warm and sweet. The horses still munched their evening hay. "You hold the lantern!" Billy ordered. And he felt the pony's legs and tested the heat of the flanks. He put his cheek against the pony's grey muzzle and then he rolled up the eyelids to look at the eyeballs and he lifted the lips to see the gums, and he put his fingers inside the ears. "He don't seem so chipper," Billy said. "I'll give him a rub-down."

Then Billy found a sack and rubbed the pony's legs violently and he rubbed the chest and the withers. Gabilan was strangely spiritless. He submitted patiently to the rubbing. At last Billy brought an old cotton comforter from the saddle-room, and threw it over the pony's back and tied it at neck and chest with string.

"Now he'll be all right in the morning," Billy said.

Jody's mother looked up when he got back to the house. "You're late up from bed," she said. She held his chin in her hard hand and brushed the tangled hair out of his eyes and she said, "Don't worry about the pony. He'll be all right. Billy's as good as any horse doctor in the country."

Jody hadn't known she could see his worry. He pulled gently away from her and knelt down in front of the fireplace until it burned his stomach. He scorched himself through and then went in to bed, but it was a hard thing to go to sleep. He awakened after what seemed a long time. The room was dark but there was a greyness in the window like that which precedes the dawn. He got up and found his overalls and searched for the legs, and then the clock in the other room struck two. He laid his clothes down and got back into bed. It was broad daylight when he awakened again. For the first time he had slept through the ringing of the triangle. He leaped up, flung on his clothes and went out of the door still buttoning his shirt. His mother looked after him for a moment and then went quietly back to her work. Her eyes were brooding and kind. Now and then her mouth smiled a little but without changing her eyes at all.

Jody ran on toward the barn. Halfway there he heard the sound he dreaded, the hollow rasping cough of a horse. He broke into a sprint then. In the barn he found Billy Buck with the pony. Billy was rubbing its legs with his strong thick hands. He looked up and smiled gaily. "He just took a little cold," Billy said. "We'll have him out of it in a couple of days."

Jody looked at the pony's face. The eyes were half closed and the lids thick and dry. In the eye corners a crust of hard mucus stuck. Gabilan's ears hung loosely sideways and his head was low. Jody put out his hand, but the pony did not move close to it. He coughed again and his whole body constricted with the effort. A little stream of thin fluid ran from his nostrils.

Jody looked back at Billy Buck. "He's awful sick, Billy."

"Just a little cold, like I said," Billy insisted. "You go get some breakfast and then go back to school. I'll take care of him."

"But you might have to do something else. You might leave him."

"No, I won't. I won't leave him at all. Tomorrow's Saturday. Then you can stay with him all day." Billy had failed again, and he felt badly about it. He had to cure the pony now.

Jody walked up to the house and took his place listlessly at the table. The eggs and bacon were cold and greasy, but he didn't notice it. He ate his usual amount. He didn't even ask to stay home from school. His mother pushed his hair back when she took his plate. "Billy'll take care of the pony," she assured him.

He moped through the whole day at school. He couldn't answer any questions nor read any words. He couldn't even tell anyone the pony was sick, for that might make him sicker. And when school was finally out he started home in dread. He walked slowly and let the other boys leave him. He wished he might continue walking and never arrive at the ranch.

Billy was in the barn, as he had promised, and the pony was worse. His eyes were almost closed now, and his breath whistled shrilly past an obstruction in his nose. A film covered that part of the eyes that was visible at all. It was doubtful whether the pony could see any more. Now and then he snorted, to clear his nose, and by the action seemed to plug it tighter. Jody looked dispiritedly at the pony's coat. The hair lay rough and unkempt and seemed to have lost all of its old luster. Billy stood quietly beside the stall. Jody hated to ask, but he had to know.

"Billy, is he—is he going to get well?"

Billy put his fingers between the bars under the pony's jaw and felt about. "Feel here," he said and he guided Jody's fingers to a large lump under the jaw. "When that gets bigger, I'll open it up and then he'll get better."

Jody looked quickly away, for he had heard about that lump. "What is it the matter with him?"

Billy didn't want to answer, but he had to. He couldn't be wrong three times. "Strangles," he said shortly, "but don't you worry about that. I'll pull him out of it. I've seen them get well when they were worse than Gabilan is. I'm going to steam him now. You can help."

"Yes," Jody said miserably. He followed Billy into the grain room and watched him make the steaming bag ready. It was a long canvas nose bag with straps to go over a horse's ears. Billy filled it one-third full of bran and then he added a couple of handfuls of dried hops. On top of the dry substance he poured a little carbolic acid and a little turpentine. "I'll be mixing it all up while you run to the house for a kettle of boiling water," Billy said.

When Jody came back with the steaming kettle, Billy buckled the straps over Gabilan's head and fitted the bag tightly around his nose. Then through a little hole in the side of the bag he poured the boiling water on the mixture. The pony started away as a cloud of strong steam rose up, but then the soothing fumes crept through his nose and into his lungs, and the sharp steam began to clear out the nasal passages. He breathed loudly. His legs trembled in an ague, and his eyes closed against the biting cloud. Billy poured in more water and kept the steam rising for fifteen minutes. At last he set down the kettle and took the bag from Gabilan's nose. The pony looked better. He breathed freely, and his eyes were open wider than they had been.

"See how good it makes him feel," Billy said. "Now we'll wrap him up in the blanket again. Maybe he'll be nearly well by morning."

"I'll stay with him tonight," Jody suggested.

"No. Don't you do it. I'll bring my blankets down

here and put them in the hay. You can stay tomorrow and steam him if he needs it."

The evening was falling when they went to the house for their supper. Jody didn't even realize that some one else had fed the chickens and filled the wood-box. He walked up past the house to the dark brush line and took a drink of water from the tub. The spring water was so cold that it stung his mouth and drove a shiver through him. The sky above the hills was still light. He saw a hawk flying so high that it caught the sun on its breast and shone like a spark. Two blackbirds were driving him down the sky, glittering as they attacked their enemy. In the west, the clouds were moving in to rain again.

Jody's father didn't speak at all while the family ate supper, but after Billy Buck had taken his blankets and gone to sleep in the barn, Carl Tiflin built a high fire in the fireplace and told stories. He told about the wild man who ran naked through the country and had a tail and ears like a horse and he told about the rabbit-cats of Moro Cojo that hopped into the trees for birds. He revived the famous Maxwell brothers who found a vein of gold and hid the traces of it so carefully that they could never find it again.

Jody sat with his chin in his hands; his mouth worked nervously, and his father gradually became aware that he wasn't listening very carefully. "Isn't that funny?" he asked.

Jody laughed politely and said, "Yes, sir." His father was angry and hurt, then. He didn't tell any more stories. After a while, Jody took a lantern and went down to the barn. Billy Buck was asleep in the hay, and, except that his breath rasped a little in his lungs, the pony seemed to be much better. Jody stayed a little while, running his fingers over the red rough coat, and then he took up the lantern and went back to the house. When he was in bed, his mother came into the room.

"Have you enough covers on? It's getting winter."

"Yes, ma'am."

"Well, get some rest tonight." She hesitated to go out, stood uncertainly. "The pony will be all right," she said.

Jody was tired. He went to sleep quickly and didn't awaken until dawn. The triangle sounded, and Billy Buck came up from the barn before Jody could get out of the house.

"How is he?" Jody demanded.

Billy always wolfed his breakfast. "Pretty good. I'm going to open that lump this morning. Then he'll be better maybe."

After breakfast, Billy got out his best knife, one with a needle point. He whetted the shining blade a long time on a little carborundum stone. He tried the point and the blade again and again on his calloused thumb-ball, and at last he tried it on his upper lip.

On the way to the barn, Jody noticed how the young grass was up and how the stubble was melting day by day into the new green crop of volunteer. It was a cold sunny morning.

As soon as he saw the pony, Jody knew he was

worse. His eyes were closed and sealed shut with dried mucus. His head hung so low that his nose almost touched the straw of his bed. There was a little groan in each breath, a deep-seated, patient groan.

Billy lifted the weak head and made a quick slash with the knife. Jody saw the yellow pus run out. He held up the head while Billy swabbed out the wound with weak carbolic acid salve.

"Now he'll feel better," Billy assured him. "That yellow poison is what makes him sick."

Jody looked unbelieving at Billy Buck. "He's awlful sick."

Billy thought a long time what to say. He nearly tossed off a careless assurance, but he saved himself in time. "Yes, he's pretty sick," he said at last. "I've seen worse ones get well. If he doesn't get pneumonia, we'll pull him through. You stay with him. If he gets worse, you can come and get me."

For a long time after Billy went away, Jody stood beside the pony, stroking him behind the ears. The pony didn't flip his head the way he had done when he was well. The groaning in his breathing was becoming more hollow.

Doubletree Mutt looked into the barn, his big tail waving provocatively, and Jody was so incensed at his health that he found a hard black clod on the floor and deliberately threw it. Doubletree Mutt went yelping away to nurse a bruised paw.

In the middle of the morning, Billy Buck came back and made another steam bag. Jody watched to see whether the pony improved this time as he had before. His breathing eased a little, but he did not raise his head.

The Saturday dragged on. Late in the afternoon Jody went to the house and brought his bedding down and made up a place to sleep in the hay. He didn't ask permission. He knew from the way his mother looked at him that she would let him do almost anything. That night he left a lantern burning on a wire over the box stall. Billy had told him to rub the pony's legs every little while.

At nine o'clock the wind sprang up and howled around the barn. And in spite of his worry, Jody grew sleepy. He got into his blankets and went to sleep, but the breathy groans of the pony sounded in his dreams. And in his sleep he heard a crashing noise which went on and on until it awakened him. The wind was rushing through the barn. He sprang up and looked down the lane of stalls. The barn door had blown open, and the pony was gone.

He caught the lantern and ran outside into the gale, and he saw Gabilan weakly shambling away into the darkness, head down, legs working slowly and mechanically. When Jody ran up and caught him by the forelock, he allowed himself to be led back and put into his stall. His groans were louder, and a fierce whistling came from his nose. Jody didn't sleep any more then. The hissing of the pony's breath grew louder and sharper.

He was glad when Billy Buck came in at dawn. Billy looked for a time at the pony as though he had never seen him before. He felt the ears and flanks. "Jody," he said, "I've got to do something you won't want to see. You run up to the house for a while."

Jody grabbed him fiercely by the forearm. "You're not going to shoot him?"

Billy patted his hand. "No. I'm going to open a little hole in his windpipe so he can breathe. His nose is filled up. When he gets well, we'll put a little brass button in the hole for him to breathe through."

Jody couldn't have gone away if he had wanted to. It was awful to see the red hide cut, but infinitely more terrible to know it was being cut and not to see it. "I'll stay right here," he said bitterly, "You sure you got to?"

"Yes. I'm sure. If you stay, you can hold his head. If it doesn't make you sick, that is."

The fine knife came out again and was whetted again just as carefully as it had been the first time. Jody held the pony's head up and the throat taut, while Billy felt up and down for the right place. Jody sobbed once as the bright knife point disappeared into the throat. The pony plunged weakly away and then stood still, trembling violently. The blood ran thickly out and up the knife and across Billy's hand and into his shirtsleeve. The sure square hand sawed out a round hole in the flesh, and the breath came bursting out of the hole, throwing a fine spray of blood. With the rush of oxygen, the pony took a sudden strength. He lashed out with his hind feet and tried to rear, but Jody held his head down while Billy mopped the new wound with carbolic salve. It was a good job. The blood stopped flowing and the air puffed out the hole and sucked it in regularly with a little bubbling noise.

The rain brought in by the night wind began to fall on the barn roof. Then the triangle rang for breakfast. "You go up and eat while I wait," Billy said. "We've got to keep this hole from plugging up."

Jody walked slowly out of the barn. He was too dispirited to tell Billy how the barn door had blown open and let the pony out. He emerged into the wet grey morning and sloshed up to the house, taking a perverse pleasure in splashing through all the puddles. His mother fed him and put dry clothes on. She didn't question him. She seemed to know he couldn't answer questions. But when he was ready to go back to the barn she brought him a pan of steaming meal. "Give him this," she said.

But Jody did not take the pan. He said, "He won't eat anything," and ran out of the house. At the barn, Billy showed him how to fix a ball of cotton on a stick, with which to swab out the breathing hole when it became clogged with mucus.

Jody's father walked into the barn and stood with them in front of the stall. At length he turned to the boy. "Hadn't you better come with me? I'm going to drive over the hill." Jody shook his head. "You better come on, out of this," his father insisted.

Billy turned on him angrily. "Let him alone. It's his pony, isn't it?

Carl Tiflin walked away without saying another word. His feelings were badly hurt.

All morning Jody kept the wound open and the air passing in and out freely. At noon the pony lay wearily down on his side and stretched his nose out.

Billy came back. "If you're going to stay with him tonight, you better take a little nap," he said. Jody went absently out of the barn. The sky had cleared to a hard thin blue. Everywhere the birds were busy with worms that had come to the damp surface of the ground.

Jody walked to the brush line and sat on the edge of

the mossy tub. He looked down at the house and at the old bunkhouse and at the dark cypress tree. The place was familiar, but curiously changed. It wasn't itself any more, but a frame for things that were happening. A cold wind blew out of the east now, signifying that the rain was over for a little while. At his feet Jody could see the little arms of new weeds spreading out over the ground. In the mud about the spring were thousands of quail tracks.

Doubletree Mutt came sideways and embarrassed up through the vegetable patch, and Jody, remembering how he had thrown the clod, put his arm about the dog's neck and kissed him on his wide black nose. Doubletree Mutt sat still, as though he knew some solemn thing was happening. His big tail slapped the ground gravely. Jody pulled a swollen tick out of Mutt's neck and popped it dead between his thumb-nails. It was a nasty thing. He washed his hands in the cold spring water.

Except for the steady swish of the wind, the farm was very quiet. Jody knew his mother wouldn't mind if he didn't go in to eat his lunch. After a little while he went slowly back to the barn. Mutt crept into his own little house and whined softly to himself for a long time.

Billy Buck stood up from the box and surrendered the cotton swab. The pony still lay on his side and the wound in his throat bellowsed in and out. When Jody saw how dry and dead the hair looked, he knew at last that there was no hope for the pony. He had seen the dead hair before on dogs and on cows, and it was a sure sign. He sat heavily on the box and let down the barrier of the box stall. For a long time he kept his eyes on the moving wound, and at last he dozed, and the afternoon passed quickly. Just before dark his mother brought a deep dish of stew and left it for him and went away. Jody ate a little of it, and, when it was dark, he set the lantern on the floor by the pony's head so he could watch the wound and keep it open. And he dozed again until the night chill awakened him. The wind was blowing fiercely, bringing the north cold with it. Jody brought a blanket from his bed in the hay and wrapped himself in it. Gabilan's breathing was quiet at last; the hole in his throat moved gently. The owls flew through the hayloft, shrieking and looking for mice. Jody put his hand down on his head and slept. In his sleep he was aware that the wind had increased. He heard it slamming about the barn.

It was daylight when he awakened. The barn door had swung open. The pony was gone. He sprang up and ran out into the morning light.

The pony's tracks were plain enough, dragging through the frostlike dew on the young grass, tired tracks with little lines between them where the hoofs had dragged. They headed for the brush line halfway up the ridge. Jody broke into a run and followed them. The sun shone on the sharp white quartz that stuck through the ground here and there. As he followed the plain trail, a shadow cut across in front of him. He looked up and saw a high circle of black buzzards, and the slowly revolving circle dropped lower and lower. The solemn birds soon disappeared over the ridge.

Jody ran faster then, forced on by panic and rage. The trail entered the brush at last and followed a winding route among the tall sage bushes.

At the top of the ridge Jody was winded. He paused, puffing noisily. The blood pounded in his ears. Then he saw what he was looking for. Below, in one of the little clearings in the brush, lay the red pony. In the distance, Jody could see the legs moving slowly and convulsively. And in a circle around him stood the buzzards, waiting for the moment of death they know so well.

Jody leaped forward and plunged down the hill. The wet ground muffled his steps and the brush hid him. When he arrived, it was all over. The first buzzard sat on the pony's head and its beak had just risen dripping with dark eye fluid. Jody plunged into the circle like a cat. The black brotherhood arose in a cloud, but the big one on the pony's head was too late. As it hopped along to take off, Jody caught its wing tip and pulled it down. It was nearly as big as he was. The free wing crashed into his face with the force of a club, but he hung on. The claws fastened on his leg and the wing elbows battered his head on either side. Jody groped blindly with his free hand. His fingers found the neck of the struggling bird. The red eyes looked into his face, calm and fearless and fierce; the naked head turned from side to side. Then the beak opened and vomited a stream of putrefied fluid. Jody brought up his knee and fell on the great bird. He held the neck to the ground with one hand while his other found a piece of sharp white quartz. The first blow broke the beak sideways and black blood spurted from the twisted, leathery mouth corners. He struck again and missed. The red fearless eyes still looked at him, impersonal and unafraid and detached. He struck again and again, until the buzzard lay dead, until its head was a red pulp. He was still beating the dead bird when Billy Buck pulled him off and held him tightly to calm his shaking.

Carl Tiflin wiped the blood from the boy's face with a red bandana. Jody was limp and quiet now. His father moved the buzzard with his toe. "Jody," he explained, "the buzzard didn't kill the pony. Don't you know that?"

"I know it," Jody said wearily.

It was Billy Buck who was angry. He had lifted Jody in his arms, and had turned to carry him home. But he turned back to Carl Tiflin. " 'Course he knows it," Billy said furiously, "Jesus Christ! man, can't you see how he'd feel about it?"

II. THE GREAT MOUNTAINS

In the humming heat of a midsummer afternoon the little boy Jody listlessly looked about the ranch for something to do. He had been to the barn, had thrown rocks at the swallows' nests under the eaves until every one of the little mud houses broke open and dropped its lining of straw and dirty feathers. Then at the ranch house he baited a rat trap with stale cheese and set it where Doubletree Mutt, that good big dog, would get his nose snapped. Jody was not moved by an impulse of cruelty; he was bored with the long hot afternoon. Doubletree Mutt put his stupid nose in the trap and got it smacked, and shrieked with agony and limped away with blood on his nostrils. No matter where he was hurt, Mutt limped. It was just a way he had. Once when he was young, Mutt got caught in a coyote trap, and always after that he limped, even when he was scolded.

When Mutt yelped, Jody's mother called from inside the house, "Jody! Stop torturing that dog and find something to do."

Jody felt mean then, so he threw a rock at Mutt. Then he took his slingshot from the porch and walked up toward the brush line to try to kill a bird. It was a good slingshot, with store-bought rubbers, but while Jody had often shot at birds, he had never hit one. He walked up through the vegetable patch, kicking his bare toes into the dust. And on the way he found the perfect slingshot stone, round and slightly flattened and heavy enough to carry through the air. He fitted it into the leather pouch of his weapon and proceeded to the brush line. His eyes narrowed, his mouth worked strenuously; for the first time that afternoon he was intent. In the shade of the sagebrush the little birds were working, scratching in the leaves, flying restlessly a few feet and scratching again. Jody pulled back the rubbers of the sling and advanced cautiously. One little thrush paused and looked at him and crouched, ready to fly. Jody sidled nearer, moving one foot slowly after the other. When he was twenty feet away, he carefully raised the sling and aimed. The stone whizzed; the thrush started up and flew right into it. And down the little bird went with a broken head. Jody ran to it and picked it up.

"Well, I got you," he said.

The bird looked much smaller dead than it had alive. Jody felt a little mean pain in his stomach, so he took out his pocket-knife and cut off the bird's head. Then he disemboweled it, and took off its wings; and finally he threw all the pieces into the brush. He didn't care about the bird, or its life, but he knew what older people would say if they had seen him kill it; he was ashamed because of their potential opinion. He decided to forget the whole thing as quickly as he could, and never to mention it.

The hills were dry at this season, and the wild grass was golden, but where the spring-pipe filled the round tub and the tub spilled over, there lay a stretch of fine green grass, deep and sweet and moist. Jody drank from the mossy tub and washed the bird's blood from his hands in cold water. Then he lay on his back in the grass and looked up at the dumpling summer clouds. By closing one eye and destroying perspective he brought them down within reach so that he could put up his fingers and stroke them. He helped the gentle wind push them down the sky; it seemed to him that they went faster for his help. One fat white cloud he helped clear to the mountain rims and pressed it firmly over, out of sight. Jody wondered what it was seeing, then. He sat up the better to look at the great mountains where they went piling back, growing darker and more savage until they finished with one jagged ridge, high up against the west. Curious secret mountains; he thought of the little he knew about them.

"What's on the other side?" he asked his father once.

"More mountains, I guess. Why?"

"And on the other side of them?"

"More mountains. Why?"

"More mountains on and on?"

"Well, no. At last you come to the ocean."

"But what's in the mountains?"

"Just cliffs and brush and rocks and dryness."

"Were you ever there?"

"No."

"Has anybody ever been there?"

"A few people, I guess. It's dangerous, with cliffs and things. Why, I've read there's more unexplored country in the mountains of Monterey County than any place in the United States." His father seemed proud that this should be so.

"And at last the ocean?"

"At last the ocean."

"But," the boy insisted, "but in between? No one knows?"

"Oh, a few people do, I guess. But there's nothing there to get. And not much water. Just rocks and cliffs and greasewood. Why?"

"It would be good to go."

"What for? There's nothing there."

Jody knew something was there, something very wonderful because it wasn't known, something secret and mysterious. He could feel within himself that this was so. He said to his mother, "Do you know what's in the big mountains?"

She looked at him and then back at the ferocious range, and she said, "Only the bear, I guess."

"What bear?"

"Why the one that went over the mountain to see what he could see."

Jody questioned Billy Buck, the ranch hand, about the possibility of ancient cities lost in the mountains, but Billy agreed with Jody's father.

"It ain't likely," Billy said. "There'd be nothing to eat unless a kind of people that can eat rocks live there."

That was all the information Jody ever got, and it made the mountains dear to him, and terrible. He thought often of the miles of ridge after ridge until at last there was the sea. When the peaks were pink in the morning they invited him among them: and when the sun had gone over the edge in the evening and the mountains were a purple-like despair, then Jody was afraid of them; then they were so impersonal and aloof that their very imperturbability was a threat.

Now he turned his head toward the mountains of the east, the Gabilans, and they were jolly mountains, with hill ranches in their creases, and with pine trees growing on the crests. People lived there, and battles had been fought against the Mexicans on the slopes. He looked back for an instant at the Great Ones and shivered a little at the contrast. The foothill cup of the home ranch below him was sunny and safe. The house gleamed with white light and the barn was brown and warm. The red cows on the farther hill ate their way slowly toward the north. Even the dark cypress tree by the bunkhouse was usual and safe. The chickens scratched about in the dust of the farmyard with quick waltzing steps.

*

Then a moving figure caught Jody's eye. A man walked slowly over the brow of the hill, on the road from Salinas, and he was headed toward the house. Jody stood up and moved down toward the house too, for if someone was coming, he wanted to be there to see. By the time the boy had got to the house the walking man was only halfway down the road, a lean man, very straight in the shoulders. Jody could tell he was old only because his heels struck the ground with hard jerks. As he approached nearer, Jody saw that he was dressed in blue jeans and in a coat of the same material. He wore clodhopper shoes and an old flat-brimmed Stetson hat. Over his shoulder he carried a gunny sack, lumpy and full. In a few moments he had trudged close enough so that his face could be seen. And his face was as dark as dried beef. A mustache, blue-white against the dark skin, hovered over his mouth, and his hair was white, too, where it showed at his neck. The skin of his face had shrunk back against the skull until it defined bone, not flesh, and made the nose and chin seem sharp and fragile. The eyes were large and deep and dark, with eyelids stretched tightly over them. Irises and pupils were one, and very black, but the eyeballs were brown. There were no wrinkles in the face at all. This old man wore a blue denim coat buttoned to the throat with brass buttons, as all men do who wear no shirts. Out of the sleeves came strong bony wrists and hands gnarled and knotted and hard as peach branches. The nails were flat and blunt and shiny.

The old man drew close to the gate and swung down his sack when he confronted Jody. His lips fluttered a little and a soft impersonal voice came from between them.

"Do you live here?"

Jody was embarrassed. He turned and looked at the house, and he turned back and looked toward the barn where his father and Billy Buck were. "Yes," he said, when no help came from either direction.

"I have come back," the old man said. "I am Gitano, and I have come back."

Jody could not take all this responsibility. He turned abruptly, and ran into the house for help, and the screen door banged after him. His mother was in the kitchen poking out the clogged holes of a colander with a hairpin, and biting her lower lip with concentration.

"It's an old man," Jody cried excitedly. "It's an old *paisano* man, and he says he's come back."

His mother put down the colander and stuck the hairpin behind the sink board. "What's the matter now?" she asked patiently.

"It's an old man outside. Come on out."

"Well, what does he want?" She untied the strings of her apron and smoothed her hair with her fingers.

"I don't know. He came walking."

His mother smoothed down her dress and went out, and Jody followed her. Gitano had not moved.

"Yes?" Mrs. Tiflin asked.

Gitano took off his old black hat and held it with both hands in front of him. He repeated, "I am Gitano, and I have come back."

"Come back? Back where?"

Gitano's whole straight body leaned forward a little. His right hand described the circle of the hills, the sloping fields and the mountains, and ended at his hat again. "Back to the rancho. I was born here, and my father, too."

"Here?" she demanded. "This isn't an old place."

"No, there," he said, pointing to the western ridge. "On the other side there, in a house that is gone."

At last she understood. "The old 'dobe that's washed almost away, you mean?"

"Yes, *señora*. When the rancho broke up they put no more lime on the 'dobe, and the rains washed it down."

Jody's mother was silent for a little, and curious homesick thoughts ran through her mind, but quickly she cleared them out. "And what do you want here now, Gitano?"

"I will stay here," he said quietly, "until I die."

"But we don't need an extra man here."

"I can not work hard any more, *señora*. I can milk a cow, feed chickens, cut a little wood; no more. I will stay here." He indicated the sack on the ground beside him. "Here are my things."

She turned to Jody. "Run down to the barn and call your father."

Jody dashed away, and he returned with Carl Tiflin and Billy Buck behind him. The old man was standing as he had been, but he was resting now. His whole body had sagged into a timeless repose.

"What is it?" Carl Tiflin asked. "What's Jody so excited about?"

Mrs. Tiflin motioned to the old man. "He wants to stay here. He wants to do a little work and stay here."

"Well, we can't have him. We don't need any more men. He's too old. Billy does everything we need."

They had been talking over him as though he did

not exist, and now, suddenly, they both hesitated and looked at Gitano and were embarrassed.

He cleared his throat. "I am too old to work. I come back where I was born."

"You weren't born here," Carl said sharply.

"No. In the 'dobe house over the hill. It was all one rancho before you came."

"In the mud house that's all melted down?"

"Yes. I and my father. I will stay here now on the rancho."

"I tell you you won't stay," Carl said angrily. "I don't need an old man. This isn't a big ranch. I can't afford food and doctor bills for an old man. You must have relatives and friends. Go to them. It is like begging to come to strangers."

"I was born here," Gitano said patiently and inflexibly.

Carl Tiflin didn't like to be cruel, but he felt he must. "You can eat here tonight," he said. "You can sleep in the little room of the old bunkhouse. We'll give you your breakfast in the morning, and then you'll have to go along. Go to your friends. Don't come to die with strangers."

Gitano put on his black hat and stooped for the sack. "Here are my things," he said.

Carl turned away. "Come on, Billy, we'll finish down at the barn. Jody, show him the little room in the bunkhouse."

He and Billy turned back toward the barn. Mrs. Tiflin went into the house, saying over her shoulder, "I'll send some blankets down."

Gitano looked questioningly at Jody. "I'll show you where it is," Jody said.

There was a cot with a shuck mattress, an apple box holding a tin lantern, and a backless rocking-chair in the little room of the bunkhouse. Gitano laid his sack carefully on the floor and sat down on the bed. Jody stood shyly in the room, hesitating to go. At last he said.

"Did you come out of the big mountains?"

Gitano shook his head slowly. "No, I worked down the Salinas Valley."

The afternoon thought would not let Jody go. "Did you ever go into the big mountains back there?"

The old dark eyes grew fixed, and their light turned inward on the years that were living in Gitano's head. "Once—when I was a little boy. I went with my father."

"Way back, clear into the mountains?"

"Yes."

"What was there?" Jody cried. "Did you see any people or any houses?"

"No."

"Well, what was there?"

Gitano's eyes remained inward. A little wrinkled strain came between his brows.

"What did you see in there?" Jody repeated.

"I don't know," Gitano said. "I don't remember."

"Was it terrible and dry?"

"I don't remember."

In his excitement, Jody had lost his shyness. "Don't you remember anything about it?"

Gitano's mouth opened for a word, and remained open while his brain sought the word. "I think it was quiet—I think it was nice."

Gitano's eyes seemed to have found something back

in the years, for they grew soft and a little smile seemed to come and go in them.

"Didn't you ever go back in the mountains again?" Jody insisted.

"No."

Didn't you ever want to?"

But now Gitano's face became impatient. "No," he said in a tone that told Jody he didn't want to talk about it any more. The boy was held by a curious fascination. He didn't want to go away from Gitano. His shyness returned.

"Would you like to come down to the barn and see the stock?" he asked.

Gitano stood up and put on his hat and prepared to follow.

It was almost evening now. They stood near the watering trough while the horses sauntered in from the hillsides for an evening drink. Gitano rested his big twisted hands on the top rail of the fence. Five horses came down and drank, and then stood about, nibbling at the dirt or rubbing their sides against the polished wood of the fence. Long after they had finished drinking an old horse appeared over the brow of the hill and came painfully down. It had long yellow teeth; its hooves were flat and sharp as spades, and its ribs and hip-bones jutted out under its skin. It hobbled up to the trough and drank water with a loud sucking noise.

"That's old Easter," Jody explained. "That's the first horse my father ever had. He's thirty years old." He looked up into Gitano's old eyes for some response.

"No good any more," Gitano said.

Jody's father and Billy Buck came out of the barn and walked over.

"Too old to work," Gitano repeated. "Just eats and pretty soon dies.

Carl Tiflin caught the last words. He hated his brutality toward old Gitano, and so he became brutal again.

"It's a shame not to shoot Easter," he said. "It'd save him a lot of pains and rheumatism." He looked secretly at Gitano, to see whether he noticed the parallel, but the big bony hands did not move, nor did the dark eyes turn from the horse. "Old things ought to be put out of their misery," Jody's father went on. "One shot, a big noise, one big pain in the head maybe, and that's all. That's better than stiffness and sore teeth."

Billy Buck broke in. "They got a right to rest after they worked all of their life. Maybe they like to just walk around."

Carl had been looking steadily at the skinny horse. "You can't imagine now what Easter used to look like," he said softly. "High neck, deep chest, fine barrel. He could jump a five-bar gate in stride. I won a flat race on him when I was fifteen years old. I could of got two hundred dollars for him any time. You wouldn't think how pretty he was." He checked himself, for he hated softness. "But he ought to be shot now," he said.

"He's got a right to rest," Billy Buck insisted.

Jody's father had a humorous thought. He turned to Gitano. "If ham and eggs grew on a side-hill I'd turn you out to pasture too," he said. "But I can't afford to pasture you in my kitchen."

He laughed to Billy Buck about it as they went on toward the house. "Be a good thing for all of us if ham and eggs grew on the side-hills."

Jody knew how his father was probing for a place to hurt Gitano. He had been probed often. Hie father knew every place in the boy where a word would fester.

"He's only talking," Jody said. "He didn't mean it about shooting Easter. He likes Easter. That was the first horse he ever owned."

The sun sank behind the high mountains as they stood there, and the ranch was hushed. Gitano seemed to be more at home in the evening. He made a curious sharp sound with his lips and stretched one of his hands over the fence. Old Easter moved stiffly to him, and Gitano rubbed the lean neck under the mane.

"You like him?" Jody asked softly.

"Yes—but he's no damn good."

The triangle sounded at the ranch house. "That's supper," Jody cried. "Come on up to supper."

As they walked up toward the house Jody noticed again that Gitano's body was as straight as that of a young man. Only by a jerkiness in his movements and by the scuffling of his heels could it be seen that he was old.

The turkeys were flying heavily into the lower branches of the cypress tree by the bunkhouse. A fat sleek ranch cat walked across the road carrying a rat so large that its tail dragged on the ground. The quail on the side-hills were still sounding the clear water call.

Jody and Gitano came to the back steps and Mrs. Tiflin looked out through the screen door at them.

"Come running, Jody. Come in to supper, Gitano."

Carl and Billy Buck had started to eat at the long oilcloth-covered table. Jody slipped into his chair without moving it, but Gitano stood holding his hat until Carl looked up and said, "Sit down, sit down. You might as well get your belly full before you go on." Carl was afraid he might relent and let the old man stay, and so he continued to remind himself that this couldn't be.

Gitano laid his hat on the floor and diffidently sat down. He wouldn't reach for food. Carl had to pass it to him. "Here, fill yourself up." Gitano ate very slowly, cutting tiny pieces of meat and arranging little pats of mashed potato on his plate.

The situation would not stop worrying Carl Tiflin. "Haven't you got any relatives in this part of the country?" he asked.

Gitano answered with some pride, "My brother-in-law is in Monterey. I have cousins there, too."

"Well, you can go and live there, then."

"I was born here," Gitano said in gentle rebuke.

Jody's mother came in from the kitchen, carrying a large bowl of tapioca pudding.

Carl chuckled to her, "Did I tell you what I said to him? I said if ham and eggs grew on the side-hills I'd put him out to pasture, like old Easter."

Gitano stared unmoved at his plate.

"It's too bad he can't stay," said Mrs. Tiflin.

"Now don't you start anything," Carl said crossly.

When they had finished eating, Carl and Billy Buck and Jody went into the living-room to sit for a while, but Gitano, without a word of farewell or thanks, walked through the kitchen and out the back door. Jody sat and secretly watched his father. He knew how mean his father felt.

"This country's full of these old *paisanos,*" Carl said to Billy Buck.

"They're damn good men," Billy defended them. "They can work older than white men. I saw one of them a hundred and five years old, and he could still ride a horse. You don't see any white men as old as Gitano walking twenty or thirty miles."

"Oh, they're tough, all right," Carl agreed. "Say, are you standing up for him too? Listen, Billy," he explained, "I'm having a hard enough time keeping this ranch out of the Bank of Italy without taking on anybody else to feed. You know that, Billy."

"Sure, I know," said Billy. "If you was rich, it'd be different."

"That's right, and it isn't like he didn't have relatives to go to. A brother-in-law and cousins right in Monterey. Why should I worry about him?"

Jody sat quietly listening, and he seemed to hear Gitano's gentle voice and its unanswerable, "But I was born here." Gitano was mysterious like the mountains. There were ranges back as far as you could see, but behind the last range piled up against the sky there was a great unknown country. And Gitano was an old man, until you got to the dull dark eyes. And in behind them was some unknown thing. He didn't ever say enough to let you guess what was inside, under the eyes. Jody felt himself irresistibly drawn toward the bunkhouse. He slipped from his chair while his father was talking and he went out the door without making a sound.

The night was very dark and far-off noises carried in clearly. The hamebells of a wood team sounded from way over the hill on the county road. Jody picked his way across the dark yard. He could see a light through the window of the little room of the bunkhouse. Because the night was secret he walked quietly up to the window and peered in. Gitano sat in the rocking-chair and his back was toward the window. His right arm moved slowly back and forth in front of him. Jody pushed the door open and walked in. Gitano jerked upright and, seizing a piece of deerskin, he tried to throw it over the thing in his lap, but the skin slipped away. Jody stood overwhelmed by the thing in Gitano's hand, a lean and lovely rapier with a golden basket hilt. The blade was like a thin ray of dark light. The hilt was pierced and intricately carved.

"What is it?" Jody demanded.

Gitano only looked at him with resentful eyes, and he picked up the fallen deerskin and firmly wrapped the beautiful blade in it.

Jody put out his hand. "Can't I see it?"

Gitano's eyes smoldered angrily and he shook his head.

"Where'd you get it? Where'd it come from?"

Now Gitano regarded him profoundly, as though he pondered. "I got it from my father."

"Well, where'd he get it?"

Gitano looked down at the long deerskin parcel in his hand. "I don' know?"

"Didn't he ever tell you?"

"No."

"What do you do with it?"

Gitano looked slightly surprised. "Nothing. I just keep it."

"Can't I see it again?"

The old man slowly unwrapped the shining blade and let the lamplight slip along it for a moment. Then he wrapped it up again. "You go now. I want to go to bed." He blew out the lamp almost before Jody had closed the door.

As he went back toward the house, Jody knew one thing more sharply than he had ever known anything. He must never tell anyone about the rapier. It would be a dreadful thing to tell anyone about it, for it would destroy some fragile structure of truth. It was a truth that might be shattered by division.

On the way across the dark yard Jody passed Billy Buck. "They're wondering where you are," Billy said.

Jody slipped into the living-room, and his father turned to him. "Where have you been?"

"I just went out to see if I caught any rats in my new trap."

"It's time you went to bed," his father said.

Jody was first at the breakfast table in the morning. Then his father came in, and last, Billy Buck. Mrs. Tiflin looked in from the kitchen.

"Where's the old man, Billy?" she asked.

"I guess he's out walking," Billy said. "I looked in his room and he wasn't there."

"Maybe he started early to Monterey," said Carl. "It's a long walk."

"No," Billy explained. "His sack is in the little room."

After breakfast Jody walked down to the bunkhouse.

Flies were flashing about in the sunshine. The ranch seemed especially quiet this morning. When he was sure no one was watching him, Jody went into the little room, and looked into Gitano's sack. An extra pair of long cotton underwear was there, an extra pair of jeans and three pairs of worn socks. Nothing else was in the sack. A sharp loneliness fell on Jody. He walked slowly back toward the house. His father stood on the porch talking to Mrs. Tiflin.

"I guess old Easter's dead at last," he said. "I didn't see him come down to water with the other horses."

In the middle of the morning Jess Taylor from the ridge ranch rode down.

"You didn't sell that old gray crowbait of yours, did you, Carl?"

"No, of course not. Why?"

"Well," Jess said. "I was out this morning early, and I saw a funny thing. I saw an old man on an old horse, no saddle, only a piece of rope for a bridle. He wasn't on the road at all. He was cutting right up straight through the brush. I think he had a gun. At least I saw something shine in his hand."

"That's old Gitano," Carl Tiflin said. "I'll see if any of my guns are missing." He stepped into the house for a second. "Nope, all here. Which way was he heading, Jess?"

"Well, that's the funny thing. He was heading straight back into the mountains."

Carl laughed. "They never get too old to steal," he said. "I guess he just stole old Easter."

"Want to go after him, Carl?"

"Hell no, just save me burying that horse. I wonder

where he got the gun. I wonder what he wants back there."

Jody walked up through the vegetable patch, toward the brush line. He looked searchingly at the towering mountains—ridge after ridge after ridge until at last there was the ocean. For a moment he thought he could see a black speck crawling up the farthest ridge. Jody thought of the rapier and of Gitano. And he thought of the great mountains. A longing caressed him, and it was so sharp that he wanted to cry to get it out of his breast. He lay down in the green grass near the round tub at the brush line. He covered his eyes with his crossed arms and lay there a long time, and he was full of a nameless sorrow.

III. THE PROMISE

In a mid-afternoon of spring, the little boy Jody walked martially along the brush-lined road toward his home ranch. Banging his knee against the golden lard bucket he used for school lunch, he contrived a good bass drum, while his tongue fluttered sharply against his teeth to fill in snare drums and occasional trumpets. Some time back the other members of the squad that walked so smartly from the school had turned into the various little canyons and taken the wagon roads to their own home ranches. Now Jody marched seemingly alone, with highlifted knees and pounding feet; but behind him there was a phantom army with great flags and swords, silent but deadly.

The afternoon was green and gold with spring. Underneath the spread branches of the oaks the plants grew pale and tall, and on the hills the feed was smooth and thick. The sagebrushes shone with new silver leaves and the oaks wore hoods of golden green. Over the hills there hung such a green odor that the horses on the flats galloped madly, and then stopped, wondering; lambs, and even old sheep jumped in the air unexpectedly and landed on stiff legs, and went on eating; young clumsy calves butted their heads together and drew back and butted again.

As the gray and silent army marched past, led by Jody, the animals stopped their feeding and their play and watched it go by.

Suddenly Jody stopped. The grey army halted, bewildered and nervous. Jody went down on his knees. The army stood in long uneasy ranks for a moment, and then, with a soft sigh of sorrow, rose up in a faint grey mist and disappeared. Jody had seen the thorny crown of a horny-toad moving under the dust of the road. His grimy hand went out and grasped the spiked halo and held firmly while the little beast struggled. Then Jody turned the horny-toad over, exposing its pale gold stomach. With a gentle forefinger he stroked the throat and chest until the horny-toad relaxed, until its eyes closed and it lay languorous and asleep.

Jody opened his lunch pail and deposited the first game inside. He moved on now, his knees bent slightly, his shoulders crouched; his bare feet were wise and silent. In his right hand there was a long gray rifle. The brush along the road stirred restively under a new and unexpected population of grey tigers and grey bears. The hunting was very good, for by the time

Jody reached the fork of the road where the mail box stood on a post, he had captured two more horny-toads, four little grass lizards, a blue snake, sixteen yellow-winged grasshoppers and a brown damp newt from under a rock. This assortment scrabbled unhappily against the tin of the lunch bucket.

At the road fork the rifle evaporated and the tigers and bears melted from the hillsides. Even the moist and uncomfortable creatures in the lunch pail ceased to exist, for the little red metal flag was up on the mail box, signifying that some postal matter was inside. Jody set his pail on the ground and opened the letter box. There was a Montgomery Ward catalog and a copy of the *Salinas Weekly Journal.* He slammed the box, picked up his lunch pail and trotted over the ridge and down into the cup of the ranch. Past the barn he ran, and past the used-up haystack and the bunkhouse and the cypress tree. He banged through the front screen door of the ranch house calling, "Ma'am, ma'am, there's a catalog."

Mrs. Tiflin was in the kitchen spooning clabbered milk into a cotton bag. She put down her work and rinsed her hands under the tap. "Here in the kitchen, Jody. Here I am."

He ran in and clattered his lunch pail on the sink. "Here it is. Can I open the catalog, ma'am?"

Mrs. Tiflin took up the spoon again and went back to her cottage cheese. "Don't lose it, Jody. Your father will want to see it." She scraped the last of the milk into the bag. "Oh, Jody, your father wants to see you before you go to your chores." She waved a cruising fly from the cheese bag.

Jody closed the new catalog in alarm. "Ma'am?"

"Why don't you ever listen? I say your father wants to see you."

The boy laid the catalog gently on the sink board. "Do you—is it something I did?"

Mrs. Tiflin laughed. "Always a bad conscience. What did you do?"

"Nothing, ma'am," he said lamely. But he couldn't remember, and besides it was impossible to know what action might later be construed as a crime.

His mother hung the full bag on a nail where it could drip into the sink. "He just said he wanted to see you when you got home. He's somewhere down by the barn."

Jody turned and went out the back door. Hearing his mother open the lunch pail and then gasp with rage, a memory stabbed him and he trotted away toward the barn, conscientiously not hearing the angry voice that called him from the house.

Carl Tiflin and Billy Buck, the ranch hand, stood against the lower pasture fence. Each man rested one foot on the lowest bar and both elbows on the top bar. They were talking slowly and aimlessly. In the pasture half a dozen horses nibbled contentedly at the sweet grass. The mare, Nellie, stood backed up against the gate, rubbing her buttocks on the heavy post.

Jody sidled uneasily near. He dragged one foot to give an impression of great innocence and nonchalance. When he arrived beside the men he put one foot on the lowest fence rail, rested his elbows on the second bar and looked into the pasture too. The two men glanced sideways at him.

"I wanted to see you," Carl said in the stern tone he reserved for children and animals.

"Yes, sir," said Jody guiltily.

"Billy, here, says you took good care of the pony before it died."

No punishment was in the air. Jody grew bolder. "Yes, sir, I did."

"Billy says you have a good patient hand with horses."

Jody felt a sudden warm friendliness for the ranch hand.

Billy put in, "He trained that pony as good as anybody I ever seen."

Then Carl Tiflin came gradually to the point. "If you could have another horse would you work for it?"

Jody shivered. "Yes, sir."

"Well, look here, then. Billy says the best way for you to be a good hand with horses is to raise a colt."

"It's the *only* good way," Billy interrupted.

"Now, look here, Jody," continued Carl. "Jess Taylor, up to the ridge ranch, has a fair stallion, but it'll cost five dollars. I'll put up the money, you'll have to work it out all summer. Will you do that?"

Jody felt that his insides were shriveling. "Yes, sir," he said softly.

"And no complaining? And no forgetting when you're told to do something?"

"Yes, sir."

"Well, all right, then. Tomorrow morning you take Nellie up to the ridge ranch and get her bred. You'll have to take care of her, too, till she throws the colt."

"Yes, sir."

"You better get to the chickens and the wood now."

Jody slid away. In passing behind Billy Buck he

very nearly put out his hand to touch the blue-jeaned legs. His shoulders swayed a little with maturity and importance.

He went to his work with unprecedented seriousness. This night he did not dump the can of grain to the chickens so that they had to leap over each other and struggle to get it. No, he spread the wheat so far and so carefully that the hens couldn't find some of it at all. And in the house, after listening to his mother's despair over boys who filled their lunch pails with slimy, suffocated reptiles, and bugs, he promised never to do it again. Indeed, Jody felt that all such foolishness was lost in the past. He was far too grown up ever to put horny-toads in his lunch pail any more. He carried in so much wood and built such a high structure with it that his mother walked in fear of an avalanche of oak. When he was done, when he had gathered eggs that had remained hidden for weeks, Jody walked down again past the cypress tree, and past the bunkhouse toward the pasture. A fat warty toad that looked out at him from under the watering trough had no emotional effect on him at all.

Carl Tiflin and Billy Buck were not in sight, but from a metallic ringing on the other side of the barn Jody knew that Billy Buck was just starting to milk a cow.

The other horses were eating toward the upper end of the pasture, but Nellie continued to rub herself nervously against the post. Jody walked slowly near, saying, "So, girl, so-o, Nellie." The mare's ears went back naughtily and her lips drew away from her yellow teeth. She turned her head around; her eyes were glazed and mad. Jody climbed to the top of the fence and hung his feet over and looked paternally down on the mare.

The evening hovered while he sat there. Bats and nighthawks flicked about. Billy Buck, walking toward the house carrying a full milk bucket, saw Jody and stopped. "It's a long time to wait," he said gently. "You'll get awful tired waiting."

"No I won't, Billy. How long will it be?"

"Nearly a year."

"Well, I won't get tired."

The triangle at the house rang stridently. Jody climbed down from the fence and walked to supper beside Billy Buck. He even put out his hand and took hold of the milk bucket to help carry it.

The next morning after breakfast Carl Tiflin folded a five-dollar bill in a piece of newspaper and pinned the package in the bib pocket of Jody's overalls. Billy Buck haltered the mare Nellie and led her out of the pasture.

"Be careful now," he warned. "Hold her up short here so she can't bite you. She's crazy as a coot."

Jody took hold of the halter itself and started up the hill toward the ridge ranch with Nellie skittering and jerking behind him. In the pasturage along the road the wild oat heads were just clearing their scabbards. The warm morning sun shone on Jody's back so sweetly that he was forced to take a serious stiff-legged hop now and then in spite of his maturity. On the fences the shiny blackbirds with red epaulets clicked their dry call. The meadowlarks sang like water, and the wild doves, concealed among the bursting leaves of the oaks, made a sound of restrained grieving. In the fields the rabbits sat sunning themselves, with only their forked ears showing above the grass heads.

After an hour of steady uphill walking, Jody turned into a narrow road that led up a steeper hill to the ridge ranch. He could see the red roof of the barn sticking up above the oak trees, and he could hear a dog barking unemotionally near the house.

Suddenly Nellie jerked back and nearly freed herself. From the direction of the barn Jody heard a shrill whistling scream and a splintering of wood, and then a man's voice shouting. Nellie reared and whinnied. When Jody held to the halter rope she ran at him with bared teeth. He dropped his hold and scuttled out of the way, into the brush. The high scream came from the oaks again, and Nellie answered it. With hoofs battering the ground the stallion appeared and charged down the hill trailing a broken halter rope. His eyes glittered feverishly. His stiff, erected nostrils were as red as flame. His black, sleek hide shone in the sunlight. The stallion came on so fast that he couldn't stop when he reached the mare. Nellie's ears went back; she whirled and kicked at him as he went by. The stallion spun around and reared. He struck the mare with his front hoof, and while she staggered under the blow, his teeth raked her neck and drew an ooze of blood.

Instantly Nellie's mood changed. She became coquettishly feminine. She nibbled his arched neck with her lips. She edged around and rubbed her shoulder against his shoulder. Jody stood half-hidden in the brush and watched. He heard the step of a horse behind him, but before he could turn, a hand caught him by the overall straps and lifted him off the ground. Jess Taylor sat the boy behind him on the horse.

"You might have got killed," he said. "Sundog's a mean devil sometimes. He busted his rope and went right through a gate."

Jody sat quietly, but in a moment he cried, "He'll hurt her, he'll kill her. Get him away!"

Jess chuckled. "She'll be all right. Maybe you'd better climb off and go up to the house for a little. You could get maybe a piece of pie up there."

But Jody shook his head. "She's mine, and the colt's going to be mine. I'm going to raise it up."

Jess nodded. "Yes, that's a good thing. Carl has good sense sometimes."

In a little while the danger was over. Jess lifted Jody down and then caught the stallion by its broken halter rope. And he rode ahead, while Jody followed, leading Nellie.

It was only after he had unpinned and handed over the five dollars, and after he had eaten two pieces of pie, that Jody started for home again. And Nellie followed docilely after him. She was so quiet that Jody climbed on a stump and rode her most of the way home.

The five dollars his father had advanced reduced Jody to peonage for the whole late spring and summer. When the hay was cut he drove a rake. He led the horse that pulled on the Jackson-fork tackle, and when the baler came he drove the circling horse that put pressure on the bales. In addition, Carl Tiflin taught him to milk and put a cow under his care, so that a new chore was added night and morning.

The bay mare Nellie quickly grew complacent. As she walked about the yellowing hillsides or worked at easy tasks, her lips were curled in a perpetual fatuous smile. She moved slowly, with the calm importance of an empress. When she was put to a team, she pulled steadily and unemotionally. Jody went to see her every day. He studied her with critical eyes and saw no change whatever.

One afternoon Billy Buck leaned the many-tined manure fork against the barn wall. He loosened his belt and tucked in his shirt-tail and tightened the belt again. He picked one of the little straws from his hatband and put it in the corner of his mouth. Jody, who was helping Doubletree Mutt, the big serious dog, to dig out a gopher, straightened up as the ranch hand sauntered out of the barn.

"Let's go up and have a look at Nellie," Billy suggested.

Instantly Jody fell into step with him. Doubletree Mutt watched them over his shoulder; then he dug furiously, growled, sounded little sharp yelps to indicate that the gopher was practically caught. When he looked over his shoulder again, and saw that neither Jody nor Billy was interested, he climbed reluctantly out of the hole and followed them up the hill.

The wild oats were ripening. Every head bent sharply under its load of grain, and the grass was dry enough so that it made a swishing sound as Jody and Billy stepped through it. Halfway up the hill they could see Nellie and the iron-grey gelding, Pete, nibbling the heads from the wild oats. When they approached, Nellie looked at them and backed her ears and bobbed her head up and down rebelliously. Billy walked to her and put his hand under her mane and patted her neck, until her ears came forward again and she nibbled delicately at his shirt.

Jody asked, "Do you think she's really going to have a colt?"

Billy rolled the lids back from the mare's eyes with his thumb and forefinger. He felt the lower lip and fingered the black, leathery teats. "I wouldn't be surprised," he said.

"Well, she isn't changed at all. It's three months gone."

Billy rubbed the mare's flat forehead with his knuckle while she grunted with pleasure. "I told you you'd get tired waiting. It'll be five months more before you can see a sign, and it'll be at least eight months more before she throws the colt, about next January.

Jody sighed deeply. "It's a long time, isn't it?"

"And then it'll be about two years more before you can ride."

Jody cried out in despair, "I'll be grown up."

"Yep, you'll be an old man," said Billy.

"What color do you think the colt'll be?"

"Why, you can't ever tell. The stud is black and the dam is bay. Colt might be black or bay or gray or dappled. You can't tell. Sometimes a black dam might have a white colt."

"Well, I hope it's black, and a stallion."

"If it's a stallion, we'll have to geld it. Your father wouldn't let you have a stallion."

"Maybe he would," Jody said. "I could train him not to be mean."

Billy pursed his lips, and the little straw that had been in the corner of his mouth rolled down to the center. “You can’t ever trust a stallion,” he said critically. “They’re mostly fighting and making trouble. Sometimes when they’re feeling funny they won’t work. They make the mares uneasy and kick hell out of the geldings. Your father wouldn’t let you keep a stallion.”

Nellie sauntered away, nibbling the drying grass. Jody skinned the grain from a grass stem and threw the handful into the air, so that each pointed, feathered seed sailed out like a dart. “Tell me how it’ll be, Billy. Is it like when the cows have calves?”

“Just about. Mares are a little more sensitive. Sometimes you have to be there to help the mare. And sometimes if it’s wrong, you have to——” he paused.

“Have to what, Billy?”

‘Have to tear the colt to pieces to get it out, or the mare’ll die.”

“But it won’t be that way this time, will it, Billy?”

“Oh, no. Nellie’s thrown good colts.”

“Can I be there, Billy? Will you be certain to call me? It’s my colt.”

“Sure, I’ll call you. Of course I will.”

“Tell me how it’ll be.”

“Why, you’ve seen the cows calving. It’s almost the same. The mare starts groaning and stretching, and then, if it’s a good right birth, the head and forefeet come out, and the front hoofs kick a hole just the way the calves do. And the colt starts to breathe. It’s good to be there, ’cause if its feet aren’t right maybe he can’t break the sac, and then he might smother.”

Jody whipped his leg with a bunch of grass. "We'll have to be there, then, won't we?"

"Oh, we'll be there, all right."

They turned and walked slowly down the hill toward the barn. Jody was tortured with a thing he had to say, although he didn't want to. "Billy," he began miserably, "Billy, you won't let anything happen to the colt, will you?"

And Billy knew he was thinking of the red pony, Gabilan, and of how it died of strangles. Billy knew he had been infallible before that, and now he was capable of failure. This knowledge made Billy much less sure of himself than he had been. "I can't tell," he said roughly. "All sorts of things might happen, and they wouldn't be my fault. I can't do everything." He felt badly about his lost prestige, and so he said, meanly, "I'll do everything I know, but I won't promise anything. Nellie's a good mare. She's thrown good colts before. She ought to this time." And he walked away from Jody and went into the saddle-room beside the barn, for his feelings were hurt.

Jody traveled often to the brushline behind the house. A rusty iron pipe ran a thin stream of spring water into an old green tub. Where the water spilled over and sank into the ground there was a patch of perpetually green grass. Even when the hills were brown and baked in the summer that little patch was green. The water whined softly into the trough all the year round. This place had grown to be a center-point for Jody. When he had been punished the cool green grass and the singing water soothed him. When he had been mean the biting acid of meanness left him at the brushline. When he sat in the grass and listened to the purling stream, the barriers set up in his mind by the stern day went down to ruin.

On the other hand, the black cypress tree by the bunkhouse was as repulsive as the water-tub was dear; for to this tree all the pigs came, sooner or later, to be slaughtered. Pig killing was fascinating, with the screaming and the blood, but it made Jody's heart beat so fast that it hurt him. After the pigs were scalded in the big iron tripod kettle and their skins were scraped and white, Jody had to go to the water-tub to sit in the grass until his heart grew quiet. The water-tub and the black cypress were opposites and enemies.

When Billy left him and walked angrily away, Jody turned up toward the house. He thought of Nellie as he walked, and of the little colt. Then suddenly he saw that he was under the black cypress, under the very singletree where the pigs were hung. He brushed his dry-grass hair off his forehead and hurried on. It seemed to him an unlucky thing to be thinking of his colt in the very slaughter place, especially after what Billy had said. To counteract any evil result of that bad conjunction he walked quickly past the ranch house, through the chicken yard, through the vegetable patch, until he came at last to the brushline.

He sat down in the green grass. The trilling water sounded in his ears. He looked over the farm buildings and across at the round hills, rich and yellow with grain. He could see Nellie feeding on the slope. As usual the water place eliminated time and distance. Jody saw a black, long-legged colt, butting against Nellie's flanks, demanding milk. And then he saw himself breaking a large colt to halter. All in a few moments the colt grew to be a magnificent animal, deep of chest, with a neck as high and arched as a sea-horse's neck, with a tail that tongued and rippled like black flame. This horse was terrible to everyone but Jody. In the schoolyard the boys begged rides, and Jody smilingly agreed. But no sooner were they mounted than the black demon pitched them off. Why, that was his name, Black Demon! For a moment the trilling water and the grass and the sunshine came back, and then . . .

Sometimes in the night the ranch people, safe in their beds, heard a roar of hoofs go by. They said, "It's Jody, on Demon. He's helping out the sheriff again." And then . . .

The golden dust filled the air in the arena at the Salinas Rodeo. The announcer called the roping contests. When Jody rode the black horse to the starting chute the other contestants shrugged and gave up first place, for it was well known that Jody and Demon could rope and throw and tie a steer a great deal quicker than any roping team of two men could. Jody was not a boy any more, and Demon was not a horse. The two together were one glorious individual. And then . . .

The President wrote a letter and asked them to help catch a bandit in Washington. Jody settled himself comfortably in the grass. The little stream of water whined into the mossy tub.

The year passed slowly on. Time after time Jody gave up his colt for lost. No change had taken place in Nellie. Carl Tiflin still drove her to a light cart, and she pulled on a hay rake and worked the Jackson-fork tackle when the hay was being put into the barn.

The summer passed, and the warm bright autumn. And then the frantic morning winds began to twist along the ground, and a chill came into the air, and the poison oak turned red. One morning in September, when he had finished his breakfast, Jody's mother called him into the kitchen. She was pouring boiling water into a bucket full of dry midlings and stirring the materials to a steaming paste.

"Yes, ma'am?" Jody asked.

"Watch how I do it. You'll have to do it after this every other morning."

"Well, what is it?"

"Why, it's warm mash for Nellie. It'll keep her in good shape."

Jody rubbed his forehead with a knuckle. "Is she all right?" he asked timidly.

Mrs. Tiflin put down the kettle and stirred the mash with a wooden paddle. "Of course she's all right, only you've got to take better care of her from now on. Here, take this breakfast out to her!"

Jody seized the bucket and ran, down past the bunkhouse, past the barn, with the heavy bucket banging against his knees. He found Nellie playing with the water in the trough, pushing waves and tossing her head so that the water slopped out on the ground.

Jody climbed the fence and set the bucket of steaming mash beside her. Then he stepped back to look at her. And she was changed. Her stomach was swollen. When she moved, her feet touched the ground gently. She buried her nose in the bucket and gobbled the hot breakfast. And when she had finished and had pushed the bucket around the ground with her nose a little, she stepped quietly over to Jody and rubbed her cheek against him.

Billy Buck came out of the saddle-room and walked over. "Starts fast when it starts, doesn't it?"

"Did it come all at once?"

"Oh, no, you just stopped looking for a while." He pulled her head around toward Jody. "She's goin' to be nice, too. See how nice her eyes are! Some mares get mean, but when they turn nice, they just love everything." Nellie slipped her head under Billy's arm and rubbed her neck up and down between his arm and his side. "You better treat her awful nice now," Billy said.

"How long will it be?" Jody demanded breathlessly.

The man counted in whispers on his fingers. "About three months," he said aloud. "You can't tell exactly. Sometimes it's eleven months to the day, but it might be two weeks early, or a month late, without hurting anything."

Jody looked hard at the ground. "Billy," he began nervously, "Billy, you'll call me when it's getting born, won't you? You'll let me be there, won't you?"

Billy bit the tip of Nellie's ear with his front teeth. "Carl says he wants you to start right at the start. That's the only way to learn. Nobody can tell you anything. Like my old man did with me about the saddle blanket. He was a government packer when I was your size, and I helped him some. One day I left a wrinkle in my saddle blanket and made a saddle-sore. My old man didn't give me hell at all. But the next morning he saddled me up with a forty-pound stock saddle. I had to lead my horse and carry that saddle over a whole damn mountain in the sun. It darn near killed me, but I never left no wrinkles in a blanket again. I couldn't. I never in my life since then put on a blanket but I felt that saddle on my back."

Jody reached up a hand and took hold of Nellie's mane. "You'll tell me what to do about everything, won't you? I guess you know everything about horses, don't you?"

Billy laughed. "Why I'm half horse myself, you see," he said. "My ma died when I was born, and being my old man was a government packer in the mountains, and no cows around most of the time, why he just gave me mostly mare's milk." He continued seriously, "And horses know that. Don't you know it, Nellie?"

The mare turned her head and looked full into his eyes for a moment, and this is a thing horses practically never do. Billy was proud and sure of himself now. He boasted a little. "I'll see you get a good colt. I'll start you right. And if you do like I say, you'll have the best horse in the county."

That made Jody feel warm and proud, too; so proud that when he went back to the house he bowed his legs and swayed his shoulders as horsemen do. And he whispered, "Whoa, you Black Demon, you! Steady down there and keep your feet on the ground."

*

The winter fell sharply. A few preliminary gusty showers, and then a strong steady rain. The hills lost their straw color and blackened under the water, and the winter streams scrambled noisily down the canyons. The mushrooms and puffballs popped up and the new grass started before Christmas.

But this year Christmas was not the central day to Jody. Some undetermined time in January had become the axis day around which the months swung. When the rains fell, he put Nellie in a box stall and fed her warm food every morning and curried her and brushed her.

The mare was swelling so greatly that Jody became alarmed. "She'll pop wide open," he said to Billy.

Billy laid his strong square hand against Nellie's swollen abdomen. "Feel here," he said quietly. "You can feel it move. I guess it would surprise you if there were twin colts."

"You don't think so?" Jody cried. "You don't think it will be twins, do you, Billy?"

"No, I don't, but it does happen, sometimes."

During the first two weeks of January it rained steadily, Jody spent most of his time, when he wasn't in school, in the box stall with Nellie. Twenty times a day he put his hand on her stomach to feel the colt move. Nellie became more and more gentle and friendly to him. She rubbed her nose on him. She whinnied softly when he walked into the barn.

Carl Tiflin came to the barn with Jody one day. He looked admiringly at the groomed bay coat, and he felt the firm flesh over ribs and shoulders. "You've done a good job," he said to Jody. And this was the greatest praise he knew how to give. Jody was tight with pride for hours afterward.

The fifteenth of January came, and the colt was not born. And the twentieth came; a lump of fear began to form in Jody's stomach. "Is it all right?" he demanded of Billy.

"Oh, sure."

And again, "Are you sure it's going to be all right?"

Billy stroked the mare's neck. She swayed her head uneasily. "I told you it wasn't always the same time, Jody. You just have to wait."

When the end of the month arrived with no birth, Jody grew frantic. Nellie was so big that her breath came heavily, and her ears were close together and straight up, as though her head ached. Jody's sleep grew restless, and his dreams confused.

On the night of the second of February he awakened crying. His mother called to him, "Jody, you're dreaming. Wake up and start over again."

But Jody was filled with terror and desolation. He lay quietly a few moments, waiting for his mother to go back to sleep, and then he slipped his clothes on, and crept out in his bare feet.

The night was black and thick. A little misting rain fell. The cypress tree and the bunkhouse loomed and then dropped back into the mist. The barn door screeched as he opened it, a thing it never did in the daytime. Jody went to the rack and found a lantern and a tin box of matches. He lighted the wick and walked down the long straw-covered aisle to Nellie's stall. She was standing up. Her whole body weaved from side to side. Jody called to her, "So, Nellie, so-o,

Nellie," but she did not stop her swaying nor look around. When he stepped into the stall and touched her on the shoulder she shivered under his hand. Then Billy Buck's voice came from the hayloft right above the stall.

"Jody, what are you doing?"

Jody started back and turned miserable eyes up toward the nest where Billy was lying in the hay. "Is she all right, do you think?"

"Why sure, I think so."

"You won't let anything happen, Billy, you're sure you won't?"

Billy growled down at him, "I told you I'd call you, and I will. Now you get back to bed and stop worrying that mare. She's got enough to do without you worrying her."

Jody cringed, for he had never heard Billy speak in such a tone. "I only thought I'd come and see," he said. "I woke up."

Billy softened a little then. "Well, you get to bed. I don't want you bothering her. I told you I'd get you a good colt. Get along now."

Jody walked slowly out of the barn. He blew out the lantern and set it in the rack. The blackness of the night and the chilled mist struck him and enfolded him. He wished he believed everything Billy said as he had before the pony died. It was a moment before his eyes, blinded by the feeble lantern-flame, could make any form of the darkness. The damp ground chilled his bare feet. At the cypress tree the roosting turkeys chattered a little in alarm, and the two good dogs responded to their duty and came charging out, barking to frighten away the coyotes they thought were prowling under the tree.

As he crept through the kitchen, Jody stumbled over a chair. Carl called from his bedroom, "Who's there? What's the matter there?"

And Mrs. Tiflin said sleepily, "What's the matter, Carl?"

The next second Carl came out of the bedroom carrying a candle, and found Jody before he could get into bed. "What are you doing out?"

Jody turned shyly away. "I was down to see the mare."

For a moment anger at being awakened fought with approval in Jody's father. "Listen," he said, finally, "there's not a man in this country that knows more about colts than Billy. You leave it to him."

Words burst out of Jody's mouth. "But the pony died——"

"Don't you go blaming that on him," Carl said sternly. "If Billy can't save a horse, it can't be saved."

Mrs. Tiflin called, "Make him clean his feet and go to bed, Carl. He'll be sleepy all day tomorrow."

It seemed to Jody that he had just closed his eyes to try to go to sleep when he was shaken violently by the shoulder. Billy Buck stood beside him, holding a lantern in his hand. "Get up," he said. "Hurry up." He turned and walked quickly out of the room.

Mrs. Tiflin called, "What's the matter? Is that you, Billy?"

"Yes, ma'am."

"Is Nellie ready?"

"Yes, ma'am."

"All right, I'll get up and heat some water in case you need it."

Jody jumped into his clothes so quickly that he was out the back door before Billy's swinging lantern was halfway to the barn. There was a rim of dawn on the mountain-tops, but no light had penetrated into the cup of the ranch yet. Jody ran frantically after the lantern and caught up to Billy just as he reached the barn. Billy hung the lantern to a nail on the stall-side and took off his blue denim coat. Jody saw that he wore only a sleeveless shirt under it.

Nellie was standing rigid and stiff. While they watched, she crouched. Her whole body was wrung with a spasm. The spasm passed. But in a few moments it started over again, and passed.

Billy muttered nervously, "There's something wrong." His bare hand disappeared. "Oh, Jesus," he said. "It's wrong."

The spasm came again, and this time Billy strained, and the muscles stood out on his arm and shoulder. He heaved strongly, his forehead beaded with perspiration. Nellie cried with pain. Billy was muttering, "It's wrong. I can't turn it. It's way wrong. It's turned all around wrong."

He glared wildly toward Jody. And then his fingers made a careful, careful diagnosis. His cheeks were growing tight and grey. He looked for a long questioning minute at Jody standing back of the stall. Then Billy stepped to the rack under the manure window and picked up a horseshoe hammer with his wet right hand.

"Go outside, Jody," he said.

The boy stood still and stared dully at him.

"Go outside, I tell you. It'll be too late."

Jody didn't move.

Then Billy walked quickly to Nellie's head. He cried, "Turn your face away, damn you, turn your face."

This time Jody obeyed. His head turned sideways. He heard Billy whispering hoarsely in the stall. And then he head a hollow crunch of bone. Nellie chuckled shrilly. Jody looked back in time to see the hammer rise and fall again on the flat forehead. Then Nellie fell heavily to her side and quivered for a moment.

Billy jumped to the swollen stomach; his big pocket-knife was in his hand. He lifted the skin and drove the knife in. He sawed and ripped at the tough belly. The air filled with the sick odor of warm living entrails. The other horses reared back against their halter chains and squealed and kicked.

Billy dropped the knife. Both of his arms plunged into the terrible ragged hole and dragged out a big, white, dripping bundle. His teeth tore a hole in the covering. A little black head appeared through the tear, and little slick, wet ears. A gurgling breath was drawn, and then another. Billy shucked off the sac and found his knife and cut the string. For a moment he held the little black colt in his arms and looked at it. And then he walked slowly over and laid it in the straw at Jody's feet.

Billy's face and arms and chest were dripping red. His body shivered and his teeth chattered. His voice was gone; he spoke in a throaty whisper. "There's your colt. I promised. And there it is. I had to do it—had to." He stopped and looked over his shoulder into the box stall. "Go get hot water and a sponge, he whispered. "Wash him and dry him the way his mother would. You'll have to feed him by hand. But there's your colt, the way I promised."

Jody stared stupidly at the wet, panting foal. It stretched on its chin and tried to raise its head. Its blank eyes were navy blue.

"God damn you," Billy shouted, "will you go now for the water? *Will you go?*"

Then Jody turned and trotted out of the barn into the dawn. He ached from his throat to his stomach. His legs were stiff and heavy. He tried to be glad because of the colt, but the bloody face, and the haunted, tired eyes of Billy Buck hung in the air ahead of him.

THE LEADER OF THE PEOPLE

Note: This story, which first appeared in book form as printed here, is in fact Part IV of *The Red Pony* and was included as such when *The Red Pony* was published as a separate volume in 1945.

THE LEADER OF THE PEOPLE

On Saturday afternoon Billy Buck, the ranch-hand, raked together the last of the old year's haystack and pitched small forkfuls over the wire fence to a few mildly interested cattle. High in the air small clouds like puffs of cannon smoke were driven eastward by the March wind. The wind could be heard whishing in the brush on the ridge crests, but no breath of it penetrated down into the ranch-cup.

The little boy, Jody, emerged from the house eating a thick piece of buttered bread. He saw Billy working on the last of the haystack. Jody tramped down scuffing his shoes in a way he had been told was destructive to good shoe-leather. A flock of white pigeons flew out of the black cypress tree as Jody passed, and circled the tree and landed again. A half-grown tortoise-shell cat leaped from the bunkhouse porch, galloped on stiff legs across the road, whirled and galloped back again. Jody picked up a stone to help the game along, but he was too late, for the cat was under the porch before the stone could be discharged. He threw the stone into the cypress tree and started the white pigeons on another whirling flight.

Arriving at the used-up haystack, the boy leaned against the barbed wire fence. "Will that be all of it, do you think?" he asked.

The middle-aged ranch-hand stopped his careful raking and stuck his fork into the ground. He took off his black hat and smoothed down his hair. "Nothing left of it that isn't soggy from ground moisture," he said. He replaced his hat and rubbed his dry leathery hands together.

"Ought to be plenty mice," Jody suggested.

"Lousy with them," said Billy. "Just crawling with mice."

"Well, maybe, when you get all through, I could call the dogs and hunt the mice."

"Sure, I guess you could," said Billy Buck. He lifted a forkful of the damp ground-hay and threw it into the air. Instantly three mice leaped out and burrowed frantically under the hay again.

Jody sighed with satisfaction. Those plump, sleek, arrogant mice were doomed. For eight months they had lived and multiplied in the haystack. They had been immune from cats, from traps, from poison and from Jody. They had grown smug in their security, overbearing and fat. Now the time of disaster had come; they would not survive another day.

Billy looked up at the top of the hills that surrounded the ranch. "Maybe you better ask your father before you do it," he suggested.

"Well, where is he? I'll ask him now."

"He rode up to the ridge ranch after dinner. He'll be back pretty soon."

Jody slumped against the fence post. "I don't think he'd care."

As Billy went back to his work he said ominously, "You'd better ask him anyway. You know how he is."

Jody did know. His father, Carl Tiflin, insisted upon giving permission for anything that was done on the ranch, whether it was important or not. Jody sagged farther against the post until he was sitting on the ground. He looked up at the little puffs of wind-driven cloud. "Is it like to rain, Billy?"

"It might. The wind's good for it, but not strong enough."

"Well, I hope it don't rain until after I kill those damn mice." He looked over his shoulder to see whether Billy had noticed the mature profanity. Billy worked on without comment.

Jody turned back and looked at the side-hill where the road from the outside world came down. The hill was washed with lean March sunshine. Silver thistles, blue lupins and a few poppies bloomed among the sage bushes. Halfway up the hill Jody could see Doubletree Mutt, the black dog, digging in a squirrel hole. He paddled for a while and then paused to kick bursts of dirt out between his hind legs, and he dug with an earnestness which belied the knowledge he must have had that no dog had ever caught a squirrel by digging in a hole.

Suddenly, while Jody watched, the black dog stiffened, and backed out of the hole and looked up the hill toward the cleft in the ridge where the road came through. Jody looked up too. For a moment Carl Tiflin on horseback stood out against the pale sky and then he moved down the road toward the house. He carried something white in his hand.

The boy started to his feet. "He's got a letter," Jody cried. He trotted away toward the ranch house, for the letter would probably be read aloud and he wanted to be there. He reached the house before his father did, and ran in. He heard Carl dismount from his creaking saddle and slap the horse on the side to send it to the barn where Billy would unsaddle it and turn it out.

Jody ran into the kitchen. "We got a letter!" he cried.

His mother looked up from a pan of beans. "Who has?"

"Father has. I saw it in his hand."

Carl strode into the kitchen then, and Jody's mother asked, "Who's the letter from, Carl?"

He frowned quickly. "How did you know there was a letter?"

She nodded her head in the boy's direction. "Big Britches Jody told me."

Jody was embarrassed.

His father looked down at him contemptuously. "He *is* getting to be a Big-Britches," Carl said. "He's minding everybody's business but his own. Got his big nose into everything."

Mrs. Tiflin relented a little. "Well, he hasn't enough to keep him busy. Who's the letter from?"

Carl still frowned on Jody. "I'll keep him busy if he isn't careful." He held out a sealed letter. "I guess it's from your father."

Mrs. Tiflin took a hairpin from her head and slit open the flap. Her lips pursed judiciously. Jody saw her eyes snap back and forth over the lines. "He says," she translated, "he says he's going to drive out Saturday to stay for a little while. Why, this is Saturday. The letter must have been delayed." She looked at the postmark. "This was mailed day before yesterday. It should have been here yesterday." She looked up questioningly at her husband, and then her face darkened angrily. "Now what have you got that look on you for? He doesn't come often."

Carl turned his eyes away from her anger. He could be stern with her most of the time, but when occasionally her temper arose, he could not combat it.

"What's the matter with you?" she demanded again.

In his explanation there was a tone of apology Jody himself might have used. "It's just that he talks," Carl said lamely. "Just talks."

"Well, what of it? You talk yourself."

"Sure I do. But your father only talks about one thing."

"Indians!" Jody broke in excitedly. "Indians and crossing the plains!"

Carl turned fiercely on him. "You get out, Mr. Big-Britches! Go on, now! Get out!"

Jody went miserably out the back door and closed the screen with elaborate quietness. Under the kitchen window his shamed, downcast eyes fell upon a curiously shaped stone, a stone of such fascination that he squatted down and picked it up and turned it over in his hands.

The voices came clearly to him through the open

kitchen window. "Jody's damn well right," he heard his father say. "Just Indians and crossing the plains. I've heard that story about how the horses got driven off about a thousand times. He just goes on and on, and he never changes a word in the things he tells."

When Mrs. Tiflin answered her tone was so changed that Jody, outside the window, looked up from his study of the stone. Her voice had become soft and explanatory. Jody knew how her face would have changed to match the tone. She said quietly, "Look at it this way, Carl. That was the big thing in my father's life. He led a wagon train clear across the plains to the coast, and when it was finished, his life was done. It was a big thing to do, but it didn't last long enough. Look!" she continued, "it's as though he was born to do that, and after he finished it, there wasn't anything more for him to do but think about it and talk about it. If there'd been any farther west to go, he'd have gone. He's told me so himself. But at last there was the ocean. He lives right by the ocean where he had to stop."

She had caught Carl, caught him and entangled him in her soft tone.

"I've seen him," he agreed quietly. "He goes down and stares off west over the ocean." His voice sharpened a little. "And then he goes up to the Horseshoe Club in Pacific Grove, and he tells people how the Indians drove off the horses."

She tried to catch him again. "Well, it's everything to him. You might be patient with him and pretend to listen."

Carl turned impatiently away. "Well, if it gets too bad, I can always go down to the bunkhouse and sit with Billy," he said irritably. He walked through the house and slammed the front door after him.

Jody ran to his chores. He dumped the grain to the chickens without chasing any of them. He gathered the eggs from the nests. He trotted into the house with the wood and interlaced it so carefully in the wood-box that two armloads seemed to fill it to overflowing.

His mother had finished the beans by now. She stirred up the fire and brushed off the stove-top with turkey wing. Jody peered cautiously at her to see whether any rancor toward him remained. "Is he coming today?" Jody asked.

"That's what his letter said."

"Maybe I better walk up the road to meet him."

Mrs. Tiflin clanged the stove-lid shut. "That would be nice," she said. "He'd probably like to be met."

"I guess I'll just do it then."

Outside, Jody whistled shrilly to the dogs. "Come on up the hill," he commanded. The two dogs waved their tails and ran ahead. Along the roadside the sage had tender new tips. Jody tore off some pieces and rubbed them on his hands until the air was filled with the sharp wild smell. With a rush the dogs leaped from the road and yapped into the brush after a rabbit. That was the last Jody saw of them, for when they failed to catch the rabbit, they went back home.

Jody plodded on up the hill toward the ridge top. When he reached the little cleft where the road came through, the afternoon wind struck him and blew up his hair and ruffled his shirt. He looked down on the little hills and ridges below and then out at the huge green Salinas Valley. He could see the white town of

Salinas far out in the flat and the flash of its windows under the waning sun. Directly below him, in an oak tree, a crow congress had convened. The tree was black with crows all cawing at once.

Then Jody's eyes followed the wagon road down from the ridge where he stood, and lost it behind a hill, and picked it up again on the other side. On that distant stretch he saw a cart slowly pulled by a bay horse. It disappeared behind the hill. Jody sat down on the ground and watched the place where the cart would reappear again. The wind sang on the hilltops and the puff-ball clouds hurried eastward.

Then the cart came into sight and stopped. A man dressed in black dismounted from the seat and walked to the horse's head. Although it was so far away, Jody knew he had unhooked the check-rein, for the horse's head dropped forward. The horse moved on, and the man walked slowly up the hill beside it. Jody gave a glad cry and ran down the road toward them. The squirrels bumped along off the road, and a road-runner flirted its tail and raced over the edge of the hill and sailed out like a glider.

Jody tried to leap into the middle of his shadow at every step. A stone rolled under his foot and he went down. Around a little bend he raced, and there, a short distance ahead, were his grandfather and the cart. The boy dropped from his unseemly running and approached at a dignified walk.

The horse plodded stumble-footedly up the hill and the old man walked beside it. In the lowering sun their giant shadows flickered darkly behind them. The grandfather was dressed in a black broadcloth suit and he wore kid congress gaiters and a black tie on a short, hard collar. He carried his black slouch hat in his hand. His white beard was cropped close and his white eyebrows overhung his eyes like moustaches. The blue eyes were sternly merry. About the whole face and figure there was a granite dignity, so that every motion seemed an impossible thing. Once at rest, it seemed the old man would be stone, would never move again. His steps were slow and certain. Once made, no step could ever be retraced; once headed in a direction, the path would never bend nor the pace increase nor slow.

When Jody appeared around the bend, Grandfather waved his hat slowly in welcome, and he called, "Why, Jody! Come down to meet me, have you?"

Jody sidled near and turned and matched his step to the old man's step and stiffened his body and dragged his heels a little. "Yes, sir," he said. "We got your letter only today."

"Should have been here yesterday," said Grandfather. "It certainly should. How are all the folks?"

"They're fine, sir." He hesitated and then suggested shyly, "Would you like to come on a mouse hunt tomorrow, sir?"

"Mouse hunt, Jody?" Grandfather chuckled. "Have the people of this generation come down to hunting mice? They aren't very strong, the new people, but I hardly thought mice would be game for them."

"No, sir. It's just play. The haystack's gone. I'm going to drive out the mice to the dogs. And you can watch, or even beat the hay a little."

The stern, merry eyes turned down on him. "I see.

You don't eat them, then. You haven't come to that yet."

Jody explained, "The dogs eat them, sir. It wouldn't be much like hunting Indians, I guess."

"No, not much—but then later, when the troops were hunting Indians and shooting children and burning teepees, it wasn't much different from your mouse hunt."

They topped the rise and started down into the ranch cup, and they lost the sun from their shoulders. "You've grown," Grandfather said. "Nearly an inch, I should say."

"More," Jody boasted. "Where they mark me on the door, I'm up more than an inch since Thanksgiving even."

Grandfather's rich throaty voice said, "Maybe you're getting too much water and turning to pith and stalk. Wait until you head out, and then we'll see."

Jody looked quickly into the man's face to see whether his feelings should be hurt, but there was no will to injure, no punishing nor putting-in-your-place light in the keen blue eyes. "We might kill a pig," Jody suggested.

"Oh, no! I couldn't let you do that. You're just humoring me. It isn't the time and you know it."

"You know Riley, the big boar, sir?"

"Yes. I remember Riley well."

"Well, Riley ate a hole into that same haystack, and it fell down on him and smothered him."

"Pigs do that when they can," said Grandfather.

"Riley was a nice pig, for a boar, sir. I rode him sometimes, and he didn't mind."

A door slammed at the house below them, and they saw Jody's mother standing on the porch waving her apron in welcome. And they saw Carl Tiflin walking up from the barn to be at the house for the arrival.

The sun had disappeared from the hills by now. The blue smoke from the house chimney hung in flat layers in the purpling ranch-cup. The puff-ball clouds, dropped by the falling wind, hung listlessly in the sky.

Billy Buck came out of the bunkhouse and flung a wash basin of soapy water on the ground. He had been shaving in mid-week, for Billy held Grandfather in reverence, and Grandfather said that Billy was one of the few men of the new generation who had not gone soft. Although Billy was in middle age, Grandfather considered him a boy. Now Billy was hurrying toward the house too.

When Jody and Grandfather arrived, the three were waiting for them in front of the yard gate.

Carl said, "Hello, sir. We've been looking for you."

Mrs. Tiflin kissed Grandfather on the side of his beard, and stood still while his big hand patted her shoulder. Billy shook hands solemnly, grinning under his straw moustache. "I'll put up your horse," said Billy, and he led the rig away.

Grandfather watched him go, and then, turning back to the group, he said as he had said a hundred times before, "There's a good boy. I knew his father, old Mule-tail Buck. I never knew why they called him Mule-tail except he packed mules."

Mrs. Tiflin turned and led the way into the house. "How long are you going to stay, Father? Your letter didn't say."

"Well, I don't know. I thought I'd stay about two weeks. But I never stay as long as I think I'm going to."

In a short while they were sitting at the white oilcloth table eating their supper. The lamp with the tin reflector hung over the table. Outside the dining-room windows the big moths battered softly against the glass.

Grandfather cut his steak into tiny pieces and chewed slowly. "I'm hungry," he said. "Driving out here got my appetite up. It's like when we were crossing. We all got so hungry every night we could hardly wait to let the meat get done. I could eat about five pounds of buffalo meat every night."

"It's moving around does it," said Billy. "My father was a government packer. I helped him when I was a kid. Just the two of us could about clean up a deer's ham."

"I knew your father, Billy," said Grandfather. "A fine man he was. They called him Mule-tail Buck. I don't know why except he packed mules."

"That was it," Billy agreed. "He packed mules."

Grandfather put down his knife and fork and looked around the table. "I remember one time we ran out of meat—" His voice dropped to a curious low singsong, dropped into a tonal groove the story had worn for itself. "There was no buffalo, no antelope, not even rabbits. The hunters couldn't even shoot a coyote. That was the time for the leader to be on the watch. I was the leader, and I kept my eyes open. Know why? Well, just the minute the people began to get hungry they'd start slaughtering the team oxen. Do you believe that? I've heard of parties that just ate up their draft cattle. Started from the middle and worked toward the ends. Finally they'd eat the lead pair, and then the wheelers. The leader of a party had to keep them from doing that."

In some manner a big moth got into the room and circled the hanging kerosene lamp. Billy got up and tried to clap it between his hands. Carl struck with a cupped palm and caught the moth and broke it. He walked to the window and dropped it out.

"As I was saying," Grandfather began again, but Carl interrupted him. "You'd better eat some more meat. All the rest of us are ready for our pudding."

Jody saw a flash of anger in his mother's eyes. Grandfather picked up his knife and fork. "I'm pretty hungry, all right," he said. "I'll tell you about that later."

When supper was over, when the family and Billy Buck sat in front of the fireplace in the other room, Jody anxiously watched Grandfather. He saw the signs he knew. The bearded head leaned forward; the eyes lost their sternness and looked wonderingly into the fire; the big lean fingers laced themselves on the black knees. "I wonder," he began, "I just wonder whether I ever told you how those thieving Piutes drove off thirty-five of our horses."

"I think you did," Carl interrupted. "Wasn't it just before you went up into the Tahoe country?"

Grandfather turned quickly toward his son-in-law. "That's right. I guess I must have told you that story."

"Lots of times," Carl said cruelly, and he avoided his wife's eyes. But he felt the angry eyes on him, and he said, " 'Course I'd like to hear it again."

Grandfather looked back at the fire. His fingers unlaced and laced again. Jody knew how he felt, how his insides were collapsed and empty. Hadn't Jody been called a Big-Britches that very afternoon? He arose to heroism and opened himself to the term Big-Britches again. "Tell about Indians," he said softly.

Grandfather's eyes grew stern again. "Boys always want to hear about Indians. It was a job for men, but boys want to hear about it. Well, let's see. Did I ever tell you how I wanted each wagon to carry a long iron plate?"

Everyone but Jody remained silent. Jody said, "No. You didn't."

"Well, when the Indians attacked, we always put the wagons in a circle and fought from between the wheels. I thought that if every wagon carried a long plate with rifle holes, the men could stand the plates on the outside of the wheels when the wagons were in the circle and they would be protected. It would save lives and that would make up for the extra weight of the iron. But of course the party wouldn't do it. No party had done it before and they couldn't see why they should go to the expense. They lived to regret it, too."

Jody looked at his mother, and knew from her expression that she was not listening at all. Carl picked at a callus on his thumb and Billy Buck watched a spider crawling up the wall.

Grandfather's tone dropped into its narrative groove again. Jody knew in advance exactly what words would fall. The story droned on, speeded up for the attack, grew sad over the wounds, struck a dirge at the burials on the great plains. Jody sat quietly watching Grandfather. The stern blue eyes were detached. He looked as though he were not very interested in the story himself.

When it was finished, when the pause had been politely respected as the frontier of the story, Billy Buck stood up and stretched and hitched his trousers. "I guess I'll turn in," he said. Then he faced Grandfather. "I've got an old powder horn and a cap and ball pistol down to the bunkhouse. Did I ever show them to you?"

Grandfather nodded slowly. "Yes, I think you did, Billy. Reminds me of a pistol I had when I was leading the people across." Billy stood politely until the little story was done, and then he said, "Good night," and went out of the house.

Carl Tiflin tried to turn the conversation then. "How's the country between here and Monterey? I've heard it's pretty dry."

"It is dry," said Grandfather. "There's not a drop of water in the Laguna Seca. But it's a long pull from '87. The whole country was powder then, and in '61 I believe all the coyotes starved to death. We had fifteen inches of rain this year."

"Yes, but it all came too early. We could do with some now." Carl's eye fell on Jody. "Hadn't you better be getting to bed?"

Jody stood up obediently. "Can I kill the mice in the old haystack, sir?"

"Mice? Oh! Sure, kill them all off. Billy said there isn't any good hay left."

Jody exchanged a secret and satisfying look with Grandfather. "I'll kill every one tomorrow," he promised.

Jody lay in his bed and thought of the impossible world of Indians and buffaloes, a world that had ceased to be forever. He wished he could have been living in the heroic time, but he knew he was not of heroic timber. No one living now, save possibly Billy Buck, was worthy to do the things that had been done. A race of giants had lived then, fearless men, men of a staunchness unknown in this day. Jody thought of the wide plains and of the wagons moving across like centipedes. He thought of Grandfather on a huge white horse, marshaling the people. Across his mind marched the great phantoms, and they marched off the earth and they were gone.

He came back to the ranch for a moment, then. He heard the dull rushing sound that space and silence make. He heard one of the dogs, out in the doghouse, scratching a flea and bumping his elbow against the floor with every stroke. Then the wind arose again and the black cypress groaned and Jody went to sleep.

He was up half an hour before the triangle sounded for breakfast. His mother was rattling the stove to make the flames roar when Jody went through the kitchen. "You're up early," she said. "Where are you going?"

"Out to get a good stick. We're going to kill the mice today."

"Who is 'we'?"

"Why, Grandfather and I."

"So you've got him in it. You always like to have someone in with you in case there's blame to share."

"I'll be right back," said Jody. "I just want to have a good stick ready for after breakfast."

He closed the screen door after him and went out into the cool blue morning. The birds were noisy in the dawn and the ranch cats came down from the hill like blunt snakes. They had been hunting gophers in the dark, and although the four cats were full of gopher meat, they sat in a semi-circle at the back door and mewed piteously for milk. Doubletree Mutt and Smasher moved sniffing along the edge of the brush, performing the duty with rigid ceremony, but when Jody whistled, their heads jerked up and their tails waved. They plunged down to him, wriggling their skins and yawning. Jody patted their heads seriously, and moved on to the weathered scrap pile. He selected an old broom handle and a short piece of inch-square scrap wood. From his pocket he took a shoelace and tied the ends of the sticks loosely together to make a flail. He whistled his new weapon through the air and struck the ground experimentally, while the dogs leaped aside and whined with apprehension.

Jody turned and started down past the house toward the old haystack ground to look over the field of slaughter, but Billy Buck, sitting patiently on the back steps, called to him, "You better come back. It's only a couple of minutes till breakfast."

Jody changed his course and moved toward the house. He leaned his flail against the steps. "That's to drive the mice out," he said. "I'll bet they're fat. I'll bet they don't know what's going to happen to them today."

"No, nor you either," Billy remarked philosophically, "nor me, nor anyone."

Jody was staggered by this thought. He knew it was

true. His imagination twitched away from the mouse hunt. Then his mother came out on the back porch and struck the triangle, and all thoughts fell in a heap.

Grandfather hadn't appeared at the table when they sat down. Billy nodded at his empty chair. "He's all right? He isn't sick?"

"He takes a long time to dress," said Mrs. Tiflin. "He combs his whiskers and rubs up his shoes and brushes his clothes."

Carl scattered sugar on his mush. "A man that's led a wagon train across the plains has got to be pretty careful how he dresses."

Mrs. Tiflin turned on him. "Don't do that, Carl! Please don't!" There was more of threat than of request in her tone. And the threat irritated Carl.

"Well, how many times do I have to listen to the story of the iron plates, and the thirty-five horses? That time's done. Why can't he forget it, now it's done?" He grew angrier while he talked, and his voice rose. "Why does he have to tell them over and over? He came across the plains. All right! Now it's finished. Nobody wants to hear about it over and over."

The door into the kitchen closed softly. The four at the table sat frozen. Carl laid his mush spoon on the table and touched his chin with his fingers.

Then the kitchen door opened and Grandfather walked in. His mouth smiled tightly and his eyes were squinted.

"Good morning," he said, and he sat down and looked at his mush dish.

Carl could not leave it there. "Did—did you hear what I said?"

Grandfather jerked a little nod.

"I don't know what got into me, sir. I didn't mean it. I was just being funny."

Jody glanced in shame at his mother, and he saw that she was looking at Carl, and that she wasn't breathing. It was an awful thing that he was doing. He was tearing himself to pieces to talk like that. It was a terrible thing to him to retract a word, but to retract it in shame was infinitely worse.

Grandfather looked sidewise. "I'm trying to get right side up," he said gently. "I'm not being mad. I don't mind what you said, but it might be true, and I would mind that."

"It isn't true," said Carl. "I'm not feeling well this morning. I'm sorry I said it."

"Don't be sorry, Carl. An old man doesn't see things sometimes. Maybe you're right. The crossing is finished. Maybe it should be forgotten, now it's done."

Carl got up from the table. "I've had enough to eat. I'm going to work. Take your time, Billy!" He walked quickly out of the dining-room. Billy gulped the rest of his food and followed soon after. But Jody could not leave his chair.

"Won't you tell any more stories?" Jody asked.

"Why, sure I'll tell them, but only when—I'm sure people want to hear them."

"I like to hear them, sir."

"Oh! Of course you do, but you're a little boy. It was a job for men, but only little boys like to hear about it."

Jody got up from his place. "I'll wait outside for you, sir. I've got a good stick for those mice."

He waited by the gate until the old man came out on the porch. "Let's go down and kill the mice now," Jody called.

"I think I'll just sit in the sun, Jody. You go kill the mice."

"You can use my stick if you like."

"No, I'll just sit her a while."

Jody turned disconsolately away, and walked down toward the old haystack. He tried to whip up his enthusiasm with thoughts of the fat juicy mice. He beat the ground with his flail. The dogs coaxed and whined about him, but he could not go. Back at the house he could see Grandfather sitting on the porch, looking small and thin and black.

Jody gave up and went to sit on the steps at the old man's feet.

"Back already? Did you kill the mice?"

"No, sir. I'll kill them some other day."

The morning flies buzzed close to the ground and the ants dashed about in front of the steps. The heavy smell of sage slipped down the hill. The porch boards grew warm in the sunshine.

Jody hardly knew when Grandfather started to talk. "I shouldn't stay here, feeling the way I do." He examined his strong old hands. "I feel as though the crossing wasn't worth doing." His eyes moved up the side-hill and stopped on a motionless hawk perched on a dead limb. "I tell those old stories, but they're not what I want to tell. I only know how I want people to feel when I tell them.

"It wasn't Indians that were important, nor adventures, nor even getting out here. It was a whole bunch of people made into one big crawling beast. And I was the head. It was westering and westering. Every man wanted something for himself, but the big beast that was all of them wanted only westering. I was the leader, but if I hadn't been there, someone else would have been the head. The thing had to have a head.

"Under the little bushes the shadows were black at white noonday. When we saw the mountains at last, we cried—all of us. But it wasn't getting here that mattered, it was movement and westering.

"We carried life out here and set it down the way those ants carry eggs. And I was the leader. The westering was as big as God, and the slow steps that made the movement piled up and piled up until the continent was crossed.

"Then we came down to the sea, and it was done." He stopped and wiped his eyes until the rims were red. "That's what I should be telling instead of stories."

When Jody spoke, Grandfather started and looked down at him. "Maybe I could lead the people some day," Jody said.

The old man smiled. "There's no place to go. There's the ocean to stop you. There's a line of old men along the shore hating the ocean because it stopped them."

"In boats I might, sir."

"No place to go, Jody. Every place is taken. But that's not the worst—no, not the worst. Westering has died out of the people. Westering isn't a hunger any more. It's all done. Your father is right. It is finished." He laced his fingers on his knee and looked at them.

Jody felt very sad. "If you'd like a glass of lemonade I could make it for you."

Grandfather was about to refuse, and then he saw

Jody's face. "That would be nice," he said. "Yes, it would be nice to drink a lemonade."

Jody ran into the kitchen where his mother was wiping the last of the breakfast dishes. "Can I have a lemon to make a lemonade for Grandfather?"

His mother mimicked— "And another lemon to make a lemonade for you."

"No, ma'am. I don't want one."

"Jody! You're sick!" Then she stopped suddenly. "Take a lemon out of the cooler," she said softly. "Here, I'll reach the squeezer down to you."